'A rich and elegant piece of work, full of learning and insight. Quite apart from the author's erudition and the book's increasing pace, much of the enjoyment in this cleverly wrought novel is to be found in the odd sense of shifting ground one experiences as the threads of these stories unwind and the lines begin to blur, between fact and fiction, truth and lies, modern day reality and ancient fantasy. A powerful romance, on many levels - part political thriller, part esoteric journey, and part moving love story. I couldn't put it down and came away both informed and satisfied.'
William Ayot, author Re-enchanting the Forest

'Masterfully combines elements of the transcendent with historical fact and throws in a romance for good measure… A hauntingly beautiful story...'
Rated Five Stars *****
San Francisco Book Review

'A powerful story of love, betrayal, occult mysteries and human intrigue. A vividly true portrayal of war, friendship and our deepest desires. Compelling writing and research. Superb.'
Dr Brian Bates, author The Way of Wyrd

'A brave book. Iconaclastic, disturbing and vivid. An eloquent journey beyond the boundaries that hold us all.'
Peter Owen-Jones, priest and author

'For someone who rarely reads novels, this was an amazing experience. The material is fascinating. Poised between fact and fiction, reality and imagination, *The Prophecies* explores complex morality beside what it means to step beyond our illusions, and what it means to face an order of truth that is inescapable for all of us.'
Jay Ramsay, author Crucible of Love

D0924532

'The author deftly weaves fact, fiction, and the gray area in between into a compelling tale of love and betrayal in occupied France.' Rated Five Stars *****
Manhattan Book Review

'An incredible story. Mysterious, magical, erotic. Utterly enchanting.'
Mark Townsend, author The Gospel of Falling Down

'A fascinating and original story - a powerful insight into the madness of the Nazi obsession with the occult and its devastating effect on the characters in a small community in occupied France.'
Richard Waring, playwright, author Golem

'The book is engaging and lucidly written throughout, and its intriguing story is very well told, but I was particularly impressed by the honesty with which it confronts the issue of how, even among well-intentioned people, the mythological vision gets corrupted, and even becomes toxic, when it is suborned by the will to power.
The Prophecies is extraordinary because it dares to map a terrain which Europe ignores at its peril.'
Lindsay Clarke, author The Chymical Wedding

'What a fascinating and unusual book - brilliantly handled. I enjoyed it enormously.'
Barbara Erskine, Sunday Times Bestselling Author

THE

PROPHECIES

PHILIP CARR-GOMM

Published by The Oak Tree Press 2016

PO Box 1333, Lewes, East Sussex, BN7 1DX England

Tel/Fax +44 (0)1273 470888 Email office@druidry.org

ISBN: 1903232031
ISBN-13: 978-1-903232-03-3

Le Bonheur! On court après lui, il s'évanouit comme une ombre…

Happiness! One runs after it, it vanishes like a shadow…

Geneviève Zaepffel, The Dictionary of Happiness

CHAPTER ONE

Just over five years ago I came across a story that was so haunting I couldn't stop thinking about it until I had set it down in writing. I was about to tell you that I stumbled upon it quite by chance, but perhaps there is no such thing.

It all began in Paris, one afternoon in September. I was staying there because I needed a break. I had been working on one book after another for years until, just when I had achieved some success as a writer, I found myself without an idea to fire my imagination. I needed to slow down and wait for the inspiration to arrive, and what better place to do this than Paris, the 'City of Light' that gave birth to the idea of the *boulevardier,* someone who would stroll the avenues and boulevards without any particular aim, just absorbing the atmosphere, pausing every now and then in a café or restaurant to observe the unfolding of other lives.

After four or five days of trying to do this myself, I abandoned the attempt. It was an activity no longer suited to the pace of living in twenty-first century Paris. Too many cars, too much tension in the air. And there are only so many times a coffee on the Champs Elysée can be sensed as romantic, only so many Parisians or tourists one can observe with fascination.

And so instead I went to browse amongst the collections of books and prints that the  *bouquinistes* offer from their metal boxes fixed to the walls that line both sides the Seine. I looked through perhaps a dozen boxes, and was about to abandon my search, when - almost hidden behind various books on philosophy - I came across a small volume entitled *The Dictionary of Happiness*. Its author, whose name was Geneviève Zaepffel, had written on the title page: 'To Marcel, I prophesy December 1937: he will know an immense success.'

In this dusty little book, the letters of the alphabet had been given varying amounts of entries. 'A' had eleven, with titles ranging from *Abandon* to *Avenir* (the Future), via entries such as *Amour* (Love) and *Arbres* (Trees). 'B' had just three: *Baiser* (Kiss), *Banque* (the Bank), and *Blessure* (the Wound). I read the first entry:

ABANDON - You who are despairing and believe yourself to be abandoned by God, know that God never abandons the beings He creates. An enrichment of the soul, a new power, a deeper journey, can be born out of this solitude that you believe grips you. That which you call an abandonment is actually a gift.

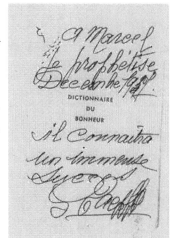

At that moment in my life I found this particular thought reassuring, but above all it was the title of the book that I found appealing. Perhaps, if this woman has created a dictionary of happiness, I could try to write an alphabet of happiness. I turned over in my mind the thought of a book that explored the building blocks of a joyful life, in twenty-six chapters each inspired by a word beginning with successive letters of the alphabet. But then I looked down at the book I held in my hands, and realized that it was not its title that was calling to me, but the person who had written it.

I bought the book, and walked across the road to a café where I could sit in the sun. Who was this Geneviève Zaepffel? Her first name was French, but her surname sounded Jewish. What was her life like? Did she find happiness? I wondered if she survived the war, or whether - if she was really Jewish - she was deported, like so many thousands of French Jews, to the concentration camps in the East. I opened a page at random and read the first line: *Le Bonheur! On court après lui, il s'évanouit comme une ombre...* Happiness! One runs after it, it vanishes like a shadow... Perhaps, as she wrote, she could sense the horror that was already stirring in the darkness of those years.

I decided, there and then, that I would find out all I could about this woman, and that if she was interesting enough, I would write about her life. I walked back over the road to the *bouquiniste* and asked him if he knew anything about her. He took the book from me and glanced through it for a few moments. "Geneviève Zaepffel was a famous clairvoyant. She predicted world events and was uncannily accurate, or so they say. They called her the Druidess of Brocéliande. Beyond that I'm afraid I cannot help you. The Dictionary of Happiness is the only work of hers I've ever seen, and I've been here a long time."

Why had I not heard of her before? "Perhaps the Bibliothèque Nationale will have other books of hers?"

A shrug of resignation from the *bouquiniste*. "You can try them, of course, but they are a useless bunch in my opinion. But try them, try them!"

The Bibliothèque Nationale was a short walk away, and soon I was climbing an endless succession of steps to approach a glass and concrete building that could easily have been mistaken for the headquarters of some global corporation. There I was told that although their records showed a number of books by Geneviève Zaepffel, these were now held in storage and it would take weeks for them to be retrieved. The young librarian, looking for all the world as if she wished I would go away, informed me that books considered obscure or of little merit, that had not been consulted for decades, were consigned to depots in the provinces and were removed from their tombs only for serious scholars. Was I entitled to see their collections? Had I completed their application forms?

I followed her advice and filled in the forms, inventing for myself a Phd in case this was necessary to be considered 'serious'. I then requested the five books their records showed were held in storage. From looking at their entries, I could see that Geneviève Zaepffel must have survived the war. Her first book was published in 1937, her last in 1967. It was possible they were issued posthumously, of course, so I could not entirely dismiss the thought that she had died tragically during the war. Even so, a part of me was disappointed that this was unlikely. It would have been awful if she had been seized in the mass round-up of the *Rafle*, for example, and taken to the Vélodrôme d'Hiver in Paris, when in 1942 over 13,000 Jewish men, women and children were arrested by the French Police, and kept for days without food or water, before being shipped off to their deaths. But it would have made a moving story: of a woman who predicted the future but never saw her own fate bearing down on her like the hot wind of summer. I shuddered as I stood there, not only at the images that appeared in my mind of the trains bearing their human cargo out of Paris, but at the recognition of my disappointment that I did not have such a tragic story in my sights.

An internet search as soon as I reached my hotel yielded little information except one promising detail: her home, in an area called Brocéliande in Brittany, was now being run as a guest house. It would be weeks before I heard from the Bibliothèque Nationale. The obvious course of action was to go to Brittany at once, to stay in her home and research her life. They would probably have a collection of her books there, and if not, I could return to Paris when they became available.

The easiest way to explain what Brittany is like to anyone familiar with the British Isles is to say simply this: Brittany is the Wales of France. It is different from the main body of the country - wilder, wetter, and with a brooding elemental power that comes out of the ground and whips in the wind through the trees. It can grind you down or make you fall in love with its lakes and forests, its waterfalls and rocky coastlines. Like the Welsh, the Bretons have their own language, and their own nationalist movement that at times has been radicalised, with bombs being set off in the homes of 'outsiders' and with angry demands for independence. Most of the Founding Saints of Brittany came from Wales in the sixth century. Both countries share a preoccupation with Druidism too, with lovers of their language and culture gathering under the banner of the Druid Revival movements of the nineteenth century. Most mysteriously of all, perhaps, amongst the connections that exist between these parts of the world, the old myths which cling to the landscape of Wales, and much of Britain, have also made their way into the heart of Lesser Britain, as Brittany was once called to distinguish it from Greater Britain. Brocéliande, a remnant of ancient forest a little west of the country's capital, Rennes, is home to megalithic remains - old dolmens and standing stones - that became known as the haunts of King Arthur and his Knights of the Round Table. According to Breton folklore, Arthur's magician Merlin died, not in the greenwoods of Wales or Scotland, but in the darkness of Brocéliande.

Like the Welsh, the Bretons have had to put up with the arrogance and brutality of a ruling elite who tried to suppress their language and culture. The English repressed the speaking of Welsh until the nineteenth century, Breton was banned in the French school system until 1951. No wonder the country leans out into the Atlantic as if it wants to distance itself from the rest of France.

Times have changed, though, and now you will find little difference in allegiances as you travel from Paris to Rennes and further west. The young, for the most part, are no longer interested in separating themselves from the rest of the country. But speak to the old people, research the history of the place, and you discover old wounds that run deep - a bitterness that has occasionally erupted into violence even as late as the 1960s. It is in Brittany where the only successful terrorist attack on a nuclear facility has been carried out. The French government decided to build one of its first nuclear power stations, despite the protests of local residents and Breton nationalists, at Brenilis, a place fittingly known as the 'Gates of Hell', the entrance to the realm of the dead according to local legend. They started building the reactor in 1962 but it was shut down for a while in 1979 by an attack on the site by the Liberation Front of Brittany, then shut down forever six years later.

Until the 1960s many of the roads in Brittany were dirt tracks. Poverty was rife. It had always seemed to many Bretons that they were second-class citizens, ignored by the central administration in Paris. No wonder, perhaps, that when Germany invaded France in 1940 and promised it would soon declare Brittany a separate country, their occupation encountered little resistance, and Breton nationalists were attracted to National Socialism. In many towns and villages not much changed during those dark years.

I read my history of Brittany as the train made its way towards Rennes. I had already telephoned the guest house, the Manoir du Tertre, to reserve a room. "I have no-one else staying at the moment," the proprietor told me. "And so you shall have the best room - *La Chambre des Druides.*"

I rented a car at the station and drove straight to the Manoir, passing through Brocéliande. Although I had read that the forest was much reduced in size from its former glory when it stretched for miles across the land, it seemed to me, as I entered it, that it was as wide as the Earth herself. I drove through winding roads beneath canopies of chestnut and oak, along great avenues lined with beech, and then up on to heathlands which rapidly led me back down into valleys, which were at times alluring, with sparkling streams running under bridges, and at times almost sinister in the way the sunlight was obscured by the density of the woodland and its shadows.

I arrived finally in Paimpont, a small town that lies beside a lake in the heart of the forest, and continued for just a few kilometres until I reached the hamlet of Le Bout de Haut. A turn to the right and then I could see it. The Manoir stood alone on high ground, a large house, with

a small barn to one side, the forest standing guard behind, and in front, a garden and fields stretching down to the road.

I parked the car beneath great boughs of oak, but I could find no obvious entrance. There was a door that seemed to lead to the kitchen, but it was clearly a back door. I explored both sides of the house and then entered into the garden to find a pair of old patio doors facing the lawn. A curtain was drawn behind them and there was no bell to ring. I returned to the kitchen door and knocked. Soon I could see through the glass pane an elderly man, stooped, with white hair and a small beard and moustache, walking towards me. He opened the door, and as he did so he seemed to force himself to stand erect before breaking into a warm smile, and looking directly into my eyes. He took my hand.

"Good afternoon and welcome to the Manoir du Tertre. You must be the Englishman who telephoned yesterday?"

"I am indeed. I am delighted to be here. Tell me," I said, looking back towards my car, "Is this the correct place to park?"

"You may park wherever you wish. We are hardly busy, even though it is still the summer."

"And is this the correct door to use? I tried to find another."

"It is peculiar, I grant you, but yes, this is the door for you to use, though you are welcome to enter by the garden should the patio doors ever be open. Come, let me show you to your room. As I said, I have given you the best - you are my only guest."

We crossed the kitchen floor and entered a large room that seemed to occupy at least half the ground floor of the house. Tall windows looked out across the lawn. Bookcases lined the walls nearest to us. My host shuffled forwards and we came to the patio doors that I had seen from outside. He drew aside the curtains.

"Even in the summer, the draughts can be terrible. And for those of us who are getting old, draughts are our bitter enemies."

Opposite the doors was a broad oak staircase that was situated almost in the centre of the room. "Seventeenth century," said my host as I stopped to admire it. Three hundred years of use and of beeswax repeatedly rubbed into its surface had created a staircase that was alive. No tread was even, the banisters were riddled with the tiny holes of woodworm. It reminded me

of the old yew that lives in Wilmington, near my home in Sussex, which itself has become a kind of living stairway. Being sixteen hundred years old, it has leaned over to such a degree that its flowing dark red trunk has turned into a great river that invites you to climb into its branches, to look down on the nine hundred year-old church it grows beside.

"Your bedroom is upstairs, but first perhaps you would like to meet Madame Zaepffel?" My heart missed a beat. For a moment I thought the great clairvoyant would emerge from the shadows - that I would find that she was still alive, a hundred years old perhaps. After all, one of the world's oldest women had just died in France at the age of 122 - a woman who gave up smoking at 117 and when asked about her favourite food, replied that it was bread and beef dripping with plenty of salt.

Instead I found my host was leading me towards a full length portrait that hung behind the staircase. And there was Geneviève Zaepffel, as if alive. Her penetrating eyes looked directly into mine, and seemed to follow me as I moved from side to side. I had the uncanny sensation that I was indeed meeting the mistress

of the Manoir, that through her portrait, the clairvoyant was in reality standing there in front of me. "It is astonishing," I managed to say after some time.

"I am glad you like the picture," said the old man, whose name I had forgotten to ask. "Some people are frightened by this portrait, and they say the house is haunted. Perhaps this is why we receive so few bookings." He added this last remark as if he was speaking to himself - as if the idea had never occurred to him before. I continued to stare at the image. I could see why it could be sensed as frightening. There was something challenging, something so direct about her gaze, that I imagined it could upset some people, perhaps those with deep-seated fears or a secret they dared not face.

"Come upstairs now," said my host. "I will show you your room. It was Madame Zaepffel's bedroom. We call it the Room of the Druids, because, as I'm sure you know, Madame was extremely fond of those old priests of the Celts, and was herself called the Druidess of Brocéliande."

I longed to ask my host question after question. How on earth did she become a Druid? What were her prophecies? What was her life like? Did she find happiness and fulfilment? But I refrained from asking anything. It was not the moment.

We climbed the staircase which moved and creaked as we mounted. I held the banister and imagined I was the seer retiring to her bedroom. What a surprise to be sleeping in her room! And then to the right, at the top of the staircase, my host opened a door and I was ushered into the Chambre des Druides. A bathroom was directly in front of me - a new addition I was told - and to my right a fourposter bed stood majestically beside a small desk and chair.

We returned downstairs, and I collected my suitcases from the car, while my host prepared tea. We were soon sitting at the small table beside the staircase. Here was my opportunity to find out more about the woman whose bed I would be lying in that night. As I stirred my tea, I began by asking my host how he came to be at the Manoir. It turned out that he

had arrived quite by chance. His brother had bought the building from his friend, Geneviève's husband René, just before he died in 1983, having outlived his wife by twelve years. My host, who by now I had learnt was Antoine, explained to me that his brother had then died himself, a few years later, leaving him the property. Coming from the south of Brittany, Antoine had at first found living in the forest oppressive, but over the years he had grown fond of the place. A born naturalist drawn to a study of birds and wildlife, in hot summers, when he had the time, he would walk for hours in the shade of the forest. In the long dark winters he would roast chestnuts on the open fire and drink brandy with his guests. Regulars, who came year after year at the same time, would sometimes invite him to dine with them in Paimpont, in the hotel beside the lake. Because of the reputation of the forest and the legends attached to it, he explained, the area attracted interesting, if eccentric, people - folk interested in mythology, in esoteric studies and sacred geometry, people who were intrigued by the house and by the stories that had gathered around its mistress whose portrait hung behind us as we took our tea.

I asked Antoine about Geneviève. It turned out he had never met her, nor read any of her books, and he had found none of them in the house when he inherited it. But he did know something of her prophecies.

"She predicted much that came to pass. She warned everyone about the atom bomb - she saw it being dropped years before Hiroshima and Nagasaki. She foresaw the Japanese attack on Pearl Harbour, and she described the gas chambers of the Nazis and the awful Holocaust." He sighed and glanced the portrait. "But not all her prophecies were of disaster. She predicted the creation of the European union and even described its flag with its circle of stars." He looked proudly at me, as if he had made the predictions himself. "And now, as every day we struggle to hold back the tide of immigration from Africa, I can tell you that her clairvoyance foresaw even this."

"That's extraordinary. Where can I read these prophecies? Has anyone written a book about this?"

"I'm afraid I can't help you. I have never seen any account of her prophecies, and I know of no book about her. All that I have told you comes from my brother and from conversations with friends and acquaintances of hers."

I was dismayed and yet pleased at the same time. Dismayed, because it seemed outrageous that a woman whose ability to predict the future with such accuracy had been forgotten, and pleased because there is nothing more disheartening than getting excited about a subject, sketching out the details for a book, only to find that it has already been written by someone else.

That night, as I lay in the four-poster bed, without thinking of the consequences and almost involuntarily, I imagined Geneviève Zaepffel was lying beside me. At first the thought was troubling, however much I told myself this fantasy was logical since she would of course have lain there in the past. After a while I became used to the idea, and the sense of her became ever more real, until I started to wonder whether I had somehow summoned her ghost to lie beside me. In the end I sat up, and looking down into those clear dark eyes, I spoke aloud: "I want to restore your memory. I want the world to know of your gifts and your powers. Speak to me if you will. Talk to me in my dreams. Guide me on this path that I am taking now to discover more about your life, more about your work in the world of prophecy and mystery." And then I allowed myself to imagine that I kissed her - just briefly - before lying down beside her and going to sleep.

CHAPTER TWO

I wish I could tell you I had received messages from Geneviève as I slept, or that my dreams had been filled with strange images from the Otherworld which I then had to decipher. But, in truth, I slept without even the memory of my dreams and woke in the morning filled with excitement for the day ahead. My host was nowhere to be seen. I looked outside and saw that his car was no longer there. I was alone in the house. For a moment I was concerned, but then I realised that - of course - he had gone to fetch breakfast.

He returned soon, and as he laid the table, I invited him to join me, and once he had poured our coffee, he began to talk about Geneviève, picking up our conversation of the previous night as if it had ended only minutes ago. "When she was a young woman, a child really, I have been told she used to meet American soldiers on their way to the trenches from the military base of Coëtquidan, just over the hill there. She offered them oak leaves that she told them would act as talismans to keep them alive. Imagine the confidence, the conviction, of that child!"

Over the years, I have found the simplest trick for obtaining information, and I have been astonished at how few people use this approach. The trick is simply to say nothing. I learnt it when training in psychotherapy. Often people will pause for a moment, and in normal conversation we politely respond to what they have just said. But if one simply waits, paying attention respectfully, leaning forwards perhaps and nodding or smiling, the other person will often offer more information, or the conversation will go deeper.

"I suppose I should have written all that I have heard down," Antoine continued. "I am starting to forget things now. But I remember another story that she was so convinced greater bloodshed could be averted, she travelled behind the lines after the German invasion of 1940, sleeping in her car in the forest at night to get to Bordeaux, where the remnants of the French government had fled. She was a pacifist - she wanted to persuade them to sue for peace, which is I suppose what happened when the Vichy government was allowed to run half the country."

"And her husband René?"

"They say she adored him, and was devoted to him from the moment they met. His family was from Alsace in the east of the country, but he grew up in Paris. He managed her career, put her on stage, arranged contracts with publishers, and edited the bulletin of the Spiritualist society they ran." Antoine stood up slowly, and carefully straightened his back. He then began to search through a folder tucked beside books on a shelf nearby. "Here they are. I'm not sure when this was taken." He handed me a faded photograph.

"He looks quite a bright fellow, doesn't he? He adored her too, or so they say. Of course, he got a house out of her, as well as sharing an income from her books and séances, but I mustn't be cynical. They had a good life - the king and queen in their castle. He used to call the Manoir his Camelot."

He dug around in the folder and produced another. "Here she is sometime in the 1930s - before the war. Quite a beauty don't you think? But she was also, they say, quite frail. She nearly died when she was a child. And the war must have taken it out of her, I suppose."

Again those eyes! Perhaps it is easier to fall in love with people we will never meet, who can never disappoint us with a discovery of their failings. Here was a woman who had apparently predicted some of the most significant events of the twentieth century, and yet she was completely unknown. Why had no-one studied what she had to say about the future, about our world which is now faced with so many problems? Dozens of books can be found on prophets like Nostrodamus and Edgar Cayce - why were there none about Geneviève Zaepffel? It was the usual business, of course - she was a woman in a world that has been dominated by men for centuries. If a man had made such predictions we would all know about him. She clearly needed a champion - someone who would bring her the recognition she deserved. Her story needed to be told.

Suddenly my host clapped his hands together. "Of course! Why didn't I think of this before? If you would really like to know more about Madame Zaepffel, the Comte de Mevilliac is the man to talk to." He started walking towards the telephone. "Would you like to meet him? I can call him now if you wish."

The Château de Vosque was just fifteen minutes away. Surrounded by the forest, like the Manoir it seemed lost in another world. A pot-holed drive led to a courtyard of stables and outbuildings in various states of disrepair. I was greeted at the door by the Comte and his wife. In their eighties, both wearing tweed with scarves, they showed me into their home. It was eleven o'clock in the morning, but the Comte insisted I join him in a malt whisky. We stood in the drawing room, making small talk about the weather, and the start of the hunting season, and then, almost abruptly, he began: "I understand you are interested in Madame Zaepffel. But first let me show you our home. It has an important history, you know." He then led me through the château. As we entered each room, he told me a little of the story of his family and the estate, as if he had done this many times before. There was an elegance, a grandeur here, but an air of melancholy too. It was cold, even though we were at the height of summer, and in many of the rooms damp had forced the paper to peel away from the walls. The weight of the past lay heavily wherever I looked - every painting and piece of furniture redolent with history. When we reached the library, the Comte began to speak of the war.

"The Germans liked it here. They felt safe. There was little fighting, which left them free to put all their efforts into building the U-boat pens at St.Nazaire, and great concrete forts by the sea, building up their Atlantic defences. They took over the airfield just down the road from here at Point-Clos. In fact they had so much time on their hands, in addition to building extra runways, they built seven swimming pools there. Can you imagine? We lived in strange times then. The war raged around us, but those of us living in the country had plenty to eat and life carried on much the same. Of course there were always stories. At Guilliers some fool shot a German who was making a play for his girlfriend, and as a result all the young men in the village were shipped off to the east. Violence breeds violence - we see the same thing all over the world."

The Comte showed me their first editions of Balzac and Flaubert, their collection of porcelain in a glass cabinet, and then we made our way back to the sitting room via a hallway of dust-coated hunting trophies that hung above our heads as we passed. Pausing by the family's coat of arms, displayed between the stuffed heads of wild boar shot in the forest behind the château, the Comte explained the heraldry. We then rejoined his wife, who had remained in the sitting-room while we made our tour. As he refilled my glass, smiling at my insistence I needed no more, and clearly delighting in ignoring my wishes, I decided it was time to remind him to talk about his experiences with Geneviève. He paused for a moment, as if debating whether to speak frankly. "Well, she was fond of the Germans, you know. Her husband was from Alsace, and in that part of the country they can never decide whether they are French or German. Their loyalties change with the passing of the seasons. She was an idealist, she wanted world peace. Towards the end of the war she led a peace march in Paris from Avenue Wagram to the Rue du Bac. Hundreds followed her. She held up a banner saying 'Peace to all Mankind' and they finished at the chapel of the Virgin Mary, where she gave some rousing address calling on the authorities to stop fighting. I suppose she was quite mad, but courageous nonetheless. At her séances in Paris she drew crowds of thousands. It was really quite remarkable. I'm afraid to say I never attended. One always regrets not having paid more attention." The Comte gazed out of the window. "But I am not a mystic. I am too wedded to the world to interest myself in these things. I have never even bothered to visit that church of the Holy Grail that our local priest started building during the war - Abbé Gillard - he was a friend of Geneviève." He then turned to look directly at me. "And you know, I suppose, that she took a German officer as a lover during the war?"

CHAPTER THREE

March 1933

Climbing in wide arcs through the clouds, Hermann reached at last the blue and the gold, the sunlight blinding him for a moment. The sound of the wind against the fuselage fell away. High above the mountain he was floating in silence as his wings rested on a thermal - some great god or angel holding his plane up to heaven.

It must feel like this when you die, he thought, as he looked at the crested hills of cloud beneath him, brilliant white in the morning sun. He glanced at his watch. He had been in the air for over an hour. Now he could claim his licence as a glider pilot - he would be able to make cross-country flights, exhibit at air shows, and - best of all - start training with an airline. He laughed out loud for joy. He wanted to stay up in the sky forever, but knew it was time to return. Dipping his left wing, he began the slow descent around the Borkenberge, until - dropping out of the clouds - he could see his friends from the Gelsenkirchen aero club standing on the hillside waving.

His father was the first to shake his hand. "I am so proud of you, Hermann. You've done it!"

Back at the house his mother had baked a cake. She hugged him tight as soon as he walked through the door. Then his sister Milly threw herself at him. "You'll take me up soon won't you?"

"If you promise not to scream."

She kissed him. "I'll scream if you fly the way you drive your motorbike!"

They all sat down while his father filled their glasses with Schnapps. "To Hermann who is now a true Wandervögel."

"To my very clever brother."

"To my darling son."

His mother began cutting the cake. "Does this mean you'll be leaving us soon?"

"I'm afraid so. I told you, remember? Luft Hansa said I can start as soon as I have my certificate."

"You know why you want to fly so much?" Milly spoke as if she had just received a revelation. Her blue eyes grew wider as she pushed back her hair and leaned forward with excitement. She still looked like a little girl to Hermann, even though she was only two years younger than him. "I've seen it. I closed my eyes and I saw you running down the lawn with your friends at Freilichtpark going 'Eeow' with your arms out wide, running straight into the sea. You did that every day, every summer, for years and years and years."

"And you never joined in the game."

"I'm a girl. I don't shout 'Eeow' and I don't run straight into ice cold water - with or without any clothes."

"Actually I will soon be dashing towards ice cold water a lot."

For a moment she looked alarmed. "What on earth do you mean?"

"I'll be learning how to fly seaplanes - great big Albatrosses. We have to go up to Warnemuende for three months for that."

"Where is Warnemuende? I've never heard of it."

"It's on the Baltic coast. Maybe you should go back to school."

Milly stood up and hit him. "Ow!" She had hurt her hand.

"Serves you right, you vicious child who just pretends to be an adult." Hermann turned to his parents. "Don't worry - I'll be having the time of my life and I'll come back as often as I can. Luft Hansa say it will take two or three weeks to receive notice of my posting from the time I send in my certificate, so in the meanwhile I will take off with the Wandervögel for a few days, maybe a week."

His father sighed. They all looked at him. "You're not going to be able to do that, I'm sorry to say. I don't want to spoil your day, Hermann, but something has happened which you should know about. It was announced on the radio this morning."

"What's that?"

"Our new Chancellor…"

Milly interrupted: "That horrible little man with the silly moustache?"

"Yes that vulgar man, or rather his minister Göring, has announced that all nudist resorts must immediately close. Apparently the movement is one of the greatest dangers to German morality. All police measures, he said, would be taken to destroy - what an idiot he is - the so-called nude culture. And all Wandervögel groups must be disbanded too."

"Are they mad? Why?"

"Because there are communists and Jews and freethinkers in these groups, that's why. The National Socialism of Herr Hitler and his friends is so weak it will never survive in the open air of free debate. And they know that."

"But what will happen to Freilichtpark and the Zimmermans?"

"I have no idea. They have only just released this edict. No discussion. Just 'bang' there you are - take it or leave it."

His mother looked at Hermann and then at Milly. "We've had our holidays there ever since you were born."

It happened at the same time every year. As soon as the university term was over, his father took a few days clearing his desk, and his mother packed for the family. They took a train to Lübeck and Paul Zimmerman, the owner of the park, was always there for them at the station. He drove them in his old Opel for an hour or so through the countryside, his father sitting at the front, the two of them catching up with each other after a year apart.

They would drive up to the stone barn Zimmerman had converted into his 'Forest Tavern' and unload the suitcases. Hermann, like his father and Zimmerman, stripped off his clothes as soon as they were out of the car, but Milly and his mother were always more reticent. They waited until they were in one of the wooden chalets built amongst the pines that bordered the main lawn. After unpacking, and provided it was warm enough, they would come out of their chalet carrying towels like shields over their arms.

Hermann used to love his first race, with whatever boys were there, running down the main lawn that led to the beach on the Grosser Ponitzer See. Whatever the weather, the water was always freezing and part of the point of running was to force themselves into the lake, which would act as an unbearable brake bringing them all to a halt with a scream. Maybe Milly was right - he often stretched out his arms as he ran, pretending he was a plane or a bird. Maybe he came out of the womb that way.

"What are you thinking about, Hermann?" Milly was making a funny face, peering into his eyes.

"About the park. I can't believe they'll just shut the place down." He stood up and went to look out of the window. "Why do people enjoy controlling other people so much? What's wrong with the Wandervögel? It's just a few people hiking together at the weekends."

Hermann had recently become conscious of the way his entire outlook had been shaped by his parents and their friends – at home, but also most vividly during their holidays at the park, when for night after night they had sat around the tables of the Forest Tavern. On those evenings Hermann said little, but he listened intently, drinking in the conversation that flowed between the adults. As they sipped malt beer and watched the setting sun, or someone stoked the flames in the brick fire-place Zimmerman had built outdoors, conversations turned to the benefits and dangers of industrialization, to the latest developments in food or health reform, social housing or education. Teachers debated the relative merits of Froebel, Montessori and Steiner, doctors discussed eugenics and birth control.

His father had also introduced him to the Wandervögel, the 'Wandering Birds', a youth movement that organised hikes in the countryside. Their aim was to break free from the grip of the city, to get back to Nature through learning campcraft, walking in the fresh air and swimming and sunbathing naked. In his fifteenth year he had joined the local Wandervögel group, and it was on their hikes that he formed attractions and began his first romances - most often tentative and clumsy affairs, clouded with the confusions of adolescence. But with each experience he grew a little more confident, until in his seventeenth year he fell in love with Rosamunde, Rosie as he called her. On one excursion, after they had tiptoed away from their friends camped beside the Königsee, they lay down in the high grass of a meadow and, having first flattened an area by rolling about in laughter and peering above the grass to make sure they were invisible, they made love, both for the first time. As two young people whose parents had ensured they received a complete education in matters of birth control and what was known as 'sexual hygiene', they were still helpless before their own desires. Even so, at the last minute, Hermann found he was able to pull himself quickly away from Rosie, just as he was overwhelmed with waves of pleasure that for the rest of his life would determine his fate in equal measure to his pursuit of the spiritual quest.

It was in his father's library, a few years earlier, that he had awoken to the power of that quest. It was there that he found a short lyrical work - a life of the Buddha. Even though he was still young, he found it thrilling to read about this sage who had gained enlightenment seated calmly beneath the boughs of a sacred fig tree. Throughout his childhood he had watched as his grandmother had grown older with the passing years. He had seen her suffer with an illness the doctors were unable to cure, and he had seen her die in his mother's arms one cold October night as the first of the autumn winds rattled against the windowpanes. The story of the young prince Siddharta witnessing the reality of old age, suffering and death, and his subsequent spiritual search became the catalyst for Hermann's own quest to find meaning in life. Since his father was a professor of religious studies at the University of Berlin he was surrounded by every opportunity to pursue this interest. Most of the other books in the library seemed desperately dull, but every now and then a phrase or an image would catch his attention, and occasionally he would read an entire work. His father would talk to him about mythology and religion, and his mother told him stories of the visits she had made when she was a young woman to the Mountain of Truth in Switzerland, to dance with Rudolf Laban and listen to the ideas of freethinkers and intellectuals from every corner of Europe.

His love of flying was born even before he began exploring the library. When he was five, his parents had taken him to the Berlin air show, and he could still remember being captivated by the aerobatic displays - biplanes that looked like giant dragonflies, swooping and diving, almost touching the ground then turning upwards in great arcs towards the sun. And every summer, lying on the lawns at Freilichtpark, he used to watch the gliders drifting silently overhead, and it always seemed to him that it must be the most wonderful thing to be up in a plane - as free as a bird on the wing.

At the age of eighteen he received his first lessons in meditation from an Indian teacher who was visiting the university, and it was then that he knew these two interests, flying and spiritual seeking, would remain his lifelong companions. As he settled into the routine that he was taught, of focussing on his breath and simply returning his mind to this awareness whenever it wandered, he began to see the parallels with flying. There were days when weather conditions made it impossible, just as there were days when meditation seemed out of the question - thoughts or feelings, surges of desire or simply tiredness, made any attempt to lift the lumbering aircraft of his soul into the air doomed to failure. Careful attention to the take-off procedure was vital. A lack of patience, too much ambition to succeed, the call of other matters that should have been attended to, all interfered with his ability to gain peace of mind or clarity as he sat in his bedroom before leaving for university, or before going to bed. Landing with care was important too. Milly had sometimes crashed into his room while he was seated, eyes closed before a candle, and at first she had made the mistake of teasing him - tickling him or pretending to leave the room and then hiding until she began to make rude noises or pretended to snore. But she soon learnt not to disturb her brother, whose spiritual ambitions she secretly admired, and he agreed to hang a sign over his door whenever he meditated, so that she would know he should not be disturbed. It was a card his grandmother had given him of an eagle flying towards the sun.

His efforts were repaid only now and again, but when they were, it made the whole enterprise worthwhile. After a carefully controlled take-off in perfect weather conditions, there came a moment when he could throw some switch within his mind. From focussing his attention on his breath with an effort of will, he would surrender all effort only to find himself soaring in consciousness, his sense of possessing a body dropping away as he bathed in feelings of intense joy, and a freedom of the soul hard to describe even to himself when he had landed.

He felt those same feelings of freedom in his soul, though anchored within the experience of his body and its sensations, when he and his friends joined Wandervögel groups hiking in the mountains. A few clothes, some bread and a block of cheese in a pack on their backs, the green valleys spread out below them, the stars spread out above them when they walked at night or sat around the camp fire - that was true freedom.

"And the Wandervögel are to be outlawed? Are you sure?" His father must have misunderstood the announcement.

CHAPTER FOUR

Before Hermann began his new life as a trainee pilot, and to fill the two or three weeks of waiting he knew he would have to endure before he received notice of his posting from Luft Hansa, he decided that if he couldn't go hiking with the Wandervögel, he would take off on his own. He would make a pilgrimage in the footsteps of one of his heroes - the author Hermann Hesse.

In 1906 Hesse had seen four long-haired and bearded young men wearing sandals walking through his village on their way to Switzerland - to Monte Verita in Ascona. He had heard stories about this place, where a group of radicals and artists had gathered around a sanatorium, built above the town on a hill called Manescia

that they had renamed Monte Verita, the Mountain of Truth. Over the years it had become a Mecca for Life Reform enthusiasts. Struggling with alcohol and depression, and in search of a cure, Hesse decided to follow the young men.

At the sanatorium he rented one of the 'air and light' huts on the hillside and stayed for a month. There he found a community of like minds. He followed a vegetarian diet, took cold water baths and an 'earth bath' buried up to his neck in soil to let the energies of the earth seep into him; he sunbathed in the 'Parsifal' meadow.

Now, almost thirty years later, Hermann began his own journey by taking a train to Radolfzell and walking to Hesse's starting point of Gaienhofen. He then walked and hitchhiked to Ascona along the same road his namesake had taken all those years before.

Hermann arrived in the town after five days of travelling. He took his breakfast in one of the cafés that lined the lake-side. As he waited for his food, he watched the sailing boats setting out for their morning trips, the reflection of the sun on the water forcing him to shield his eyes. A purple heron stood as still as a statue on a rock not far from him, then darted into the water, emerging seconds later with a fish in its beak and flying slowly towards the farther shore. In stark contrast to the gentle beauty of this lakeland scene, alpine peaks stood as distant guardians beyond the forested foothills.

He finished his breakfast and then walked up to the old church with its tall spire. From there he took the winding road that left the town and climbed steeply upward. The archway that led to the sanatorium was long gone, but Hermann could recognize the house from the old

photographs he had seen. It was now clearly in private ownership, but there was the Parsifal Meadow he had read about, fringed with its exotic collection of trees that flourished in the warmth of Ascona's micro-climate. Palms and olive trees mingled happily with camellias, oaks and weeping magnolia trees covered in pink flowers. He paused to take photographs to show his mother. What a pity they would be in black-and white! He could see her now - dancing with

Rudolf Laban on the lawn, Kropotkin standing by the camellias, holding forth on the virtues of anarchy, the

inspired madman Gusto Gräser spouting his philosophy to all who would listen.

There was nothing more he needed to do, he simply had to have been there once in his life. He touched the ground as a symbolic gesture, and then began to make his way back down the hill, to find a hostel by the lake shore. There he spent his days hiking in the surrounding countryside, reading Hesse, sometimes stopping to look up at the hill he could see from the hostel to think about his hero staying there - shaking off his demons, sunbathing on the lawn, finding the inspiration for his novels.

By the time he returned home, the new regime had already started to change its mind about nudism, which they now believed could further the aims of fostering a healthy race. A state-sponsored nudist organization, purged of dissident elements, would soon be created, and the ideals of the Wandervögel co-opted too, to create the only permitted organization - the Hitler Youth. But holidays in nudist resorts or hiking with friends were no longer an option for Hermann. Confirmation of his posting had arrived from Luft Hansa, and in what seemed like a moment when time all of a sudden speeded up, Hermann was waving goodbye to his family, and making his way to Warnemuende, to begin the first stage of his training as a pilot.

In between learning how to fly sea-planes and studying for theoretical exams, he still found time to write to his parents and to Milly, telling them as much as he could about his training and about how he looked forward to the moment he would became the captain of his first commercial flight.

After ten weeks by the grey Baltic sea, he was ready for his next posting - to the aerobatic flying school at Schleissheim, near Munich. Learning how to roll and loop was so exciting, he wrote few letters and hardly missed his family or his Wandervögel friends. At the school he was being taught how to make sudden drops out of the sky - how to dive steeply and then swing up into the clouds again without losing his nerve. He liked the way the training was testing his mettle - forcing him to develop his powers of concentration, his ability to control his fears.

Back on the ground after one of these training sessions, a fellow pilot asked his opinion. "Do you think they're really training us for something else?"

"What do you mean?"

"You don't have to roll and dive in a passenger plane, Hermann."

"They're just making sure we know the ins and outs of every kind of aircraft - they're making us into the most proficient pilots we can possibly be..."

"Isn't it obvious? We're being trained for the air force."

"We don't have an air force, Hans."

"I know that. But what if the Chancellor tells the rest of the world to go to hell? What if he tells them they can stuff the Treaty of Versailles - that we'll break it, and build an air force to make Germany proud again."

"So they're really teaching us to fly fighters?"

"Exactly."

His friend was right. A little over a year later he was ready for his next posting. In February 1935 he was sent to the Central Airline Pilot School in Berlin. Almost as soon as he arrived, he was told that within a few days Chancellor Hitler would defy the treaty and announce the creation of a military air force. Hermann was twenty-eight years old. Physically fit, reasonably handsome, or so his friends and family insisted, and driven by an insatiable curiosity, he accepted the offer of a post in this new air force without a second thought.

CHAPTER FIVE

The best part about flying, thought Hermann, was the aerobatics - soaring through the air, looping and rolling, plunging up and down through the sky as if gravity was not a force he had to fight against, but a playmate he could sometimes defy and at other times willingly surrender to as he went into free-fall. And though he hated to admit it, once he was taught how to fire the guns on his plane, he liked pressing the trigger. All he had to do was squeeze his right hand over the control stick, and press hard, and he could feel and hear the thud thud thud of the bullets as they shot out, one by one, between the blades of his propellers on certain aircraft, or from guns mounted on the wings, or either side of the fuselage on others. He was a boy spitting apple pips at his enemies in the playground. He shouldn't enjoy it, he knew that, but he did. He suspected there was some deep connection between the pleasure he took in firing his guns and his sexual urges. The writings of Freud had alerted the world to the hidden power of instinctive drives, and Hermann could recognize in his own psyche the peculiar link that existed between aggression and sexual expression. He had noticed when he made love, at first to Rosie, and then from time to time with young women he had known during his time at university and during his training, that mixed up amongst his desire to tenderly caress a woman's body was the urge, not to hurt it, but to vigorously, aggressively, take possession of it. He reasoned that, since he was a man, his biology required him to penetrate and inseminate, and one couldn't fulfill this role passively. Understanding the power of symbolism, and of the way gestures and postures of the body, as used in the eastern disciplines of yoga and meditation, conveyed meaning and created different effects in the heart and mind, he noticed that the reverse also applied, and that the activity he was pursuing during the day seemed to determine the position he preferred to adopt when making love. When he was younger, reading the poetry of the Romantics and walking the countryside with friends, he would face his lovers, looking into their eyes. Now, as he trained to be a fighter pilot, he found himself wanting to turn them on their stomachs or have them stand, leaning against a windowsill or the side of the bed, to enter them from behind like an animal, to push hard against them. He noticed too that as he trained - in effect - to kill people, his erotic desires were amplified, as if his body was attempting to redress the deaths he would cause by trying to engender new life.

For the next seven years, Hermann was obliged to fulfill the destiny he had set in motion the day he joined the Luftwaffe. Although he agreed in principle with the viewpoint of pacifists like Hermann Hesse, and held no sympathies for the politics of the new regime, he found it quite possible to separate the beliefs he favoured from his everyday activities, and - like thousands of other young German men - had joined the armed forces out of a sense of duty and patriotism that owed nothing to the doctrines of the new Chancellor.

While he turned his back on the world of politics, his fascination for the spiritual quest remained as ardent as ever. He read the works of Indian sages and Theosophists, and found reassurance in the thought, expressed in the Bhagavad Gita, that Krishna had encouraged Arjuna to fight in battle - since, after all, death is an illusion. He had also discovered the works of the New England Transcendentalists Emerson and Thoreau, and loved the way in which they revered nature. He read them in fits and starts as time allowed, but once the war began, he abandoned all attempts at such study. Meditation felt almost impossible in the circumstances, although he tried, at least for a few moments in every day, to consciously recognize the existence of the divine flame within him. There were two writers, though, he did manage to consistently turn to throughout this period - one was his favourite Hermann Hesse, whose novels he read, sometimes two or three times over, and the other was Rainer Maria Rilke, whose poetry spoke directly to his soul.

While his intellectual and spiritual life was reduced to a few sources of nourishment during those years of increasing conflict, his romantic life gradually withered to the occasional fleeting liaison as he was moved from base to base, first as a fighter pilot and then as a trainer of glider pilots. Central command believed that gliders would play a significant role in any airborne invasion, and plans were already under way to use substantial numbers of them both for cargo and for troops to invade Crete, and later Britain. Hermann's skill as a glider pilot had been recognized, and he was told he would soon be posted to a base in Brittany, to train pilots and coordinate the fleet that was already on its way there.

Occultists often write of seven year cycles, and so it was not surprising to Hermann when he found, early in 1942, that his life was about to change. On a bright and cold February morning, he was summoned to his commander's office.

"Captain, allow me introduce you to SS-Obersturmbannführer Krause. He would like to ask you a few questions." A short man with dark hair and grey deep-set eyes, was standing utterly still in the corner of the office gazing intently at Hermann. He was wearing civilian clothing.

"Please sit down Captain," said Krause quietly. Hermann's Commander, Colonel Frenzel, swiveled his chair, turning his back on them both, and gazed out of the window. Krause continued to stand. "Let me explain the purpose of my requesting a meeting with you today. I am responsible for a department of the SS division of the Ahnenerbe, which - as I am sure you know - conducts research into our ancestral heritage. We are researchers, not soldiers. Hence we have no need for uniform, although we are entitled to wear one, if we choose." Hermann wished that he was also wearing civilian clothing. His uniform was uncomfortable. "Your colonel tells us," Krause went on, "that you are particularly well-versed in matters that we could term esoteric or occult, is that not correct?

"I would prefer the term spiritual or paranormal, sir."

"Tell us why you have this interest."

"My father was a professor of religious studies until he retired. It must have rubbed off on me. We spent our holidays at Freilichtpark and I joined the Wandervögel. The talk in those circles was often - how can I put it? - romantic and idealistic."

"There is nothing paranormal about idealism, Captain. Every man in this country, from the Führer to the farm worker, has dreams of greatness. And why should a youth spent in healthy pursuits lead you to be so interested in the occult, or the paranormal, as you prefer to call it?" Krause paused. "Look, no one is suspicious of you, I can assure you. Quite the contrary. We simply need to know more about you."

"I understand. Everyone in my parents' circle is interested in something unusual - something connected with other ways of seeing the world. Some are mainly concerned with unconventional methods of healing, but most have some fascination for the paranormal, the Otherworldly."

"Who are these people? Give me a few names."

A moment's hesitation. Should he tell the truth? He could hardly be held to account for the company his parents kept.

"Well I remember Gusto Gräser - who was interested in oriental philosophy. Then there was Rudolf Laban - my mother used to dance with him in Ascona. My father knew two professors, Hermann Jacobi and Heinrich Lüders, I think they have both died now, who often visited our house. They were specialists in the religions of the Far East."

"Religion and dance, Captain, this isn't particularly out of the ordinary. Do you speak any foreign languages?"

"Only French."

"Colonel Frenzel told us you could almost be mistaken for a Frenchman. What books have you read that fired your imagination? Before you answer, let me stress again: we are not interrogating you to catch you out. We want someone who has a knowledge of this sort of thing, and Colonel Frenzel informed us that you and he have often discussed such matters. He was impressed with what he heard. He thinks you might be our man. So tell us what books have made an impression on you."

" 'Mein Kampf', of course."

"Yes, of course," said Krause irritably, waving his hand. "What else?"

"When I was young I was inspired by 'The Splendour of Asia' - a book by an English woman about the life of the Buddha. Later I discovered Hermann Hesse and have read all of his novels."

"The Russian Madame Blavatsky? Have you read any of her work?"

"Yes."

"Good!" said Krause, a broad grin on his face. He now began to fire questions at Hermann. "Do you know something of astrology?"

"Yes."

"A lot or a little? Can you cast a horoscope?"

"I suppose I know a good deal. I can cast a horoscope, yes."

"That Jewish system, the Kabbalah. Do you understand it?"

"Yes sir."

"The Tarot. You have used it?"

"Yes sir."

"Have you been to Externsteine?

"Yes sir."

"Do you know of the theories of Wilhelm Teudt?"

"Yes sir."

"You clearly know a good deal, Captain. Are you a Christian, by the way?"

Hermann knew what a strained relationship the Nazis had with the Church, sometimes quite openly attacking it, sometimes treating it as a close ally - a bastion of traditional values. He wasn't sure what they had in mind for him, but he trusted the situation. "I find some aspects of the religion touch me deeply. Others I find disturbing, even repugnant. But I believe all religions have, at their core, a universal truth."

"So you are a Theosophist then? Or perhaps a follower of that fellow Steiner?"

"No sir. My father likes the works of Steiner, but I prefer being a free spirit - a Wandervögel."

"Thank you, Captain."

Within days Hermann was summoned for a further interview, this time at the headquarters of the SS Ahnenerbe in Berlin. After hours on the train, he needed to exercise, and decided to walk to his interview through Grunewald Park. A light dusting of snow lay on the ground, and the lakes used for bathing in the summer were frozen over. Occasionally someone rode by on a horse, greeting Hermann with a wave. It was hard to believe that Germany was at war on such a day.

The headquarters of the Ahnenerbe were in the centre of the Dahlem district, with its spacious mansions and broad avenues lined with linden trees. Hermann arrived at the wrought iron gates of 19 Pücklerstrasse and rang the bell. A guard appeared from a nearby hut, asked for his papers, and then directed him towards the largest of the three buildings in the compound.

A young woman at the reception desk, with short blonde hair and a brisk, confident manner, told him the Obersturmbannführer would meet him shortly, and suggested that while he waited he might like to view a display of photographs of some of the Ahnenerbe's many foreign expeditions on show in the foyer.

"Ah, Captain Kaestner, there you are!" called out Krause from the staircase a few minutes later.

Saluting and then shaking him vigorously by the hand, he offered to show Hermann the facilities. "As we look around, I can explain the work that we do, and then we can discuss how you might be able to assist us." He led Hermann outside. "We purchased this estate in 1937. We have three buildings here, all built in 1910. One of them," he said, pointing to a house that stood across the courtyard, "is the private residence of our director, Standartenführer Sievers. Over there, in that other building, we have our workshops. Let's take a brief look at these first."

They crossed the gravel courtyard and entered a large single-storied structure. Walking along a wide corridor, Krause opened one door after another, allowing Hermann a glimpse inside each room as he talked. In one, a sculptor was chiseling at a statue, in another two men were bent over a table covered with bones, in a third a pool of typists were hard at work over their machines.

"Our people are preparing exhibits that illustrate the bodily and facial distinctions between the different races. We have measured, in living examples, the physical characteristics of almost every race and now we are refining these measurements with our collection of skeletons and bones from across the world, obtained during our many expeditions. I imagine you know about these?" Krause smiled at Hermann with a look of pride and satisfaction.

"I do indeed. I have read the articles that have appeared in the newspapers about them. And I have seen the photographs in the entrance hall. I understand you have sent expeditions to the Himalayas, Tibet, and South America - and wasn't an expedition mounted to the Canary Islands recently?"

"It was - and we have visited other places too. My colleagues have examined rock art in the Pyrenees, the archaeological and ethnographic collections in the major museums of Paris and London - before the war of course. And we must not forget our first major expedition: to examine the rock carvings in Sweden that show evidence of the nobility of our Aryan forebears. Come - I'll show you what we discovered there!"

They strode back into the main building and Krause walked Hermann briskly along the corridors on both floors. "Here we have more than two dozen individual offices for our staff, a photographic studio, a darkroom, a laboratory, a microscopy room, a conservatory and dining room, and also…" reaching a pair of highly polished oak doors, Krause triumphantly pushed them open: "a library."

Elegantly furnished with Persian rugs, leather armchairs and wide oak desks, each wall of the library was lined with books from floor to ceiling. "We have over 40,000 volumes here," said Krause, inviting Hermann into the room. "We are interested, you see, in revealing the glory of our Aryan past that has been forgotten with time and with deceit. Look - here is an example of our work on the expedition to Sweden that I mentioned." A large book lay open on a desk, displaying drawings of symbols that had been carved into rocks in Upsälla. "Some of the earliest ideographs known to humanity, and clear evidence of the genius of our forebears."

Hermann had no interest in theories of racial origins, and had long ago decided to focus his attentions on the world of esoteric knowledge and hidden wisdom, as well as on that other love of his - flying. Even so, he believed it was important to keep an open mind, and now he wanted to learn as much as he could about this strange institution. A part of him was attracted by the sheer eccentricity of the place. And how much more interesting to be surrounded by scholars and researchers, mounting expeditions to exotic places, than being holed up in a barracks, unable to fly freely, just waiting to kill or be killed.

Krause continued: "The Ahnenerbe's task lies at the heart of our Führer's vision for the Third Reich. Its work will provide the historical and scientific basis for our belief that the Aryans are the most superior race on Earth - a race destined to rule all of humanity and to advance the cause of civilization and of evolution."

Hermann glanced at the book on the desk. It seemed odd to him that Krause believed examining Swedish rock art would advance their cause. "And how do you plan to fulfil your objectives?"

"Through research, my dear Captain! Research and more research, and gradually - like washing a diamond that has been soiled by centuries of filth piled upon it - the world will be able to understand the importance of racial purity, of the necessity for rebuilding the Aryan civilization. Here in this library we have gathered the findings of Darwin and the evolutionary scientists, the findings of paleontologists, archaeologists, linguists, historians. The weight of evidence is building, Captain, and our job is to increase the momentum until only a fool - or a Jew - will ever dream of denying the validity of our theories. But come to my study now, I want to discuss with you another dimension to our work."

Krause ushered Hermann into his office and closed the door quietly behind him. Hermann looked around the book-lined study. On the walls hung photographs of

Tibetan lamas, their wrinkled faces gazing with bemusement into this room that smelled of old books and pipe tobacco. In glass display cases stood figurines of animals and gods, samples of bone and clusters of feathers. There were clearly insufficient shelves - four large bookcases were already filled, and stacks of books lay on the floor. "There is so much to know! So much to learn!" said Krause quietly from behind him, as if he had read Hermann's thoughts. "Sit down please."

Taking his place behind the desk, Krause leaned forward. "I am delighted that you are here. You are clearly well-versed in precisely those subjects that interest me, and many of my colleagues here. And of course our Reichsführer himself. Those of us who understand the occult know that scientific research must go hand in hand with the more arcane disciplines with which you and I are acquainted. The physical is, after all, the result of forces that exist on subtler levels, as any astrologer or magician knows."

Hermann nodded. This idea was fundamental to every occult theory from astrology to the Kabbalah. Krause continued: "The Ahnenerbe that you have seen on our brief tour is, in reality, merely the outer, exoteric manifestation of its true nature. There is an inner heart, an inner core to our organization, which drives that outer vehicle." Krause paused for dramatic effect, or so it seemed to Hermann.

"There is an inner fire and an outer shell to everything, is there not? Popular religion is the exoteric shell fuelled by the flames of the esoteric orders that are in contact with the divine powers - with the gods, if you like that language. Our research and our expeditions look for material evidence of Aryan supremacy and for the tragic results of racial mixing, but there are those amongst us who have a higher aim - who seek the spiritual and magical secrets of those inner orders of beings who are in touch with the sources of real power in this world: sources which lie beyond the physical in the worlds of the astral and causal planes. And so we travel to Tibet, and try to find out what wisdom and lore these sages hold." Krause pointed to the portrait of the lama behind him. "People like the old Rinpoche here, the shamans we have interviewed in Lapland, the mystics and sadhus we have found in the Himalayas, they all hold scraps of the old knowledge of Atlantis. And it is our goal to piece together these scraps until they form one glorious picture that depicts the world in which our ancestors lived. A picture that will also show us the way forward!"

Krause had leant so far forward over his desk, it looked as if he was about to stand up, but instead he sank back into his chair. Hermann felt obliged to say something. "This is an extraordinary vision you have presented. Thank you."

Krause beamed with satisfaction, and taking a handkerchief from his pocket, wiped his forehead. "Now let me explain why we have asked you here, Captain. There is some work to be done, closer to home and admittedly in a less exotic region of the world, but with its charms nonetheless. We understand you are due to be posted to France."

"Yes, to the new base at Point-Clos in Brittany."

"We have an interest in this region, Captain, and we would like you to work for us."

Hermann was intrigued. "I feel honoured, but what exactly would you require of me?"

"We have become aware of a woman who calls herself a prophet, and who believes she can see into the destiny of people and nations. She has attracted thousands of followers." Krause opened a drawer of his desk, and took out a file. "Her name is Geneviève Zaepffel. She is the director of a group that calls itself the Spiritualist Centre, and she currently lives just twenty minutes or so from where you will be stationed. From there she runs her centre and issues pamphlets on her prophecies." Krause handed a press cutting to Hermann. "She has made one visit to the United States - in 1937. That caused quite a stir. The cutting is from 'The New York Times'. It reports on her prophecy that Roosevelt will remain President until his death."

Krause took out a small, creased photograph from the file and handed it across his desk. Geneviève Zaepffel looked out at Hermann with a clear, confident expression that seemed both innocent and knowing at the same time.  "All the predictions we have seen so far have been remarkably accurate. She foretold the abdication of

Britain's King Edward because of his infatuation with that American woman. She predicted the war between China and Japan that is still raging. These are just some examples - she has made dozens of prophecies over the years. And so far, these have been innocuous regarding our campaigns, but clearly this woman needs to be kept under surveillance, Captain, wouldn't you agree?"

"Of course, I understand entirely."

"In the event that she ever began to issue unfavourable prophecies, either publicly in séances or bulletins, or in private to close friends, we would have to ensure she never spoke again."

There was uneasy silence. Hermann nodded in agreement.

"But we also have another aim in our desire to know more about Madame Zaepffel. Here in the Ahnenerbe we understand that certain human beings are gifted with supernatural abilities, powers of Extra-Sensory Perception, that allow them to see into the future. We are currently conducting a research project examining the work of prophets throughout history. You will be familiar of course with the writings of Nostradamus, and the uncanny accuracy of some of his quatrains, but there have been hundreds, perhaps thousands of prophets in the course of history, and we have taken it upon ourselves to initiate a comprehensive survey. From what we have studied of Zaepffel's work, we believe she may well possess genuine prophetic powers, and therefore the information she supplies could be of significant use in our strategic planning. For this reason I can tell you that this project is the subject of the closest attention at the highest level."

Krause rubbed his hands together and continued, "Since the paranormal is one of your special interests, Captain, and you are about to be transferred to within a few kilometres of this unusual woman, we believe you are our man. You will be ideally placed to keep a close eye on her."

Hermann was excited. Krause's proposition was perfectly logical and the woman looked attractive. "How exactly would you like to proceed?"

"I understand you are needed in the Luftwaffe and we have been warned about draining the forces of manpower, so we must be cautious. But you will need a cover, and you will be perfectly suited for this work. Madame Zaepffel entertains officers at her Manoir and offers them private consultations, or so we hear. We would like you to continue in your position in the Luftwaffe, but in addition we would like to second you to the Ahnenerbe, with one sole objective: that you provide us with as much information as you can about this 'Druidess' as she is called. We are familiar with her published material of course, which is readily available. We also have our source in the French administration, and we are aware of their opinion of her. Having no esoteric understanding, they simply believe she is deluded. We know better, naturally, and we want you to get close to her, gain her confidence, visit her as frequently as possible, and inform us of anything she might say that you think may be of strategic interest. What do you say, Captain?"

Hermann looked down at the photograph in his hands, and then across the desk to Krause. He had already made up his mind. He could feel the direction of his life changing effortlessly. It reminded him of that sublime moment when, with just one slight movement of the hand, an aircraft responds by changing course, to fly over new landscapes, through new skies.

"I will be very pleased to take on this challenge."

"I am delighted you have agreed, Captain. From now on, you are both a pilot in the Luftwaffe and an intelligence officer in the SS-Ahnenerbe. Congratulations!" Krause stood up to shake Hermann's hand. "I will inform Colonel Frenzel. There will be paperwork of course. I assume you are a party member?"

"I have never been interested in politics, sir. I do not belong to any party." Hermann's elation began to slip away. His liberal education had led him to dislike National Socialist doctrines, but he had deliberately avoided thinking about them. He had lied about reading 'Mein Kampf' - he had simply skimmed it and concluded it was of no interest.

Krause sat down behind his desk once again and looked directly at him as he leaned back in his chair. "To join the SS, Captain, you must join the party. It is a simple procedure, I will give you the forms. You must, of course, be of pure blood. Proof is required. I assume you have records?" Hermann looked at him blankly. "You will need to provide birth certificates, or other evidence, not only for yourself, but for your parents and grandparents. Perhaps further back, I can't remember." Herman nodded. "I will get the forms sent up to me. Meanwhile, I have here the report on Madame Zaepffel sent to us from our contact in the French police, together with other documents. Take this file to the library. Study it closely and then return it to me here."

Hermann found himself alone in the library. All he could hear was the distant sound of typing. Footsteps in the corridor. A door closing. He sat at a desk and opened the file.

THE ZAEPFFEL DOSSIER

Madame Zaepffel, né Lefeuvre Geneviève Marie Josephine, is married to René Alexis Theodore Zaepffel, and has no children. From January 1939, she has lived at 17, rue Legendre where she pays an annual rent of 10,000 francs. Prior to that she lived for many years at No.54 in the same street. Since June 1939 she has been staying in her country home 'Le Manoir du Tertre' outside Paimpont.

Mme Zaepffel is on earth, according to her, to accomplish a 'mission', namely to 'revive the energy of France with the help of faith.'

As a writer and lecturer, Mme Zaepffel makes a considerable amount of money in Paris in her practice of the occult sciences. Every day she receives numerous visitors in her home, between 20 to 40 persons, for whom, for a substantial fee, she predicts the future.

To advertise, each year she organizes under the auspices of 'The Spiritualist Centre in Paris', a number of 'prophetic' talks at the Salle Pleyel, 252 rue du Faubourg Saint Honoré, which draw audiences estimated at 3,000 people. At these talks we have noticed the presence of influential politicians and foreign ambassadors. She also holds smaller weekly meetings in the Mustel Room at 16, avenue de Wagram.

Mme Zaepffel has published a monthly newspaper called 'The Spiritualist Centre in Paris Bulletin'. She has also published two books, 'My Psychic Battle' and 'The Book of Prophecies' edited by Baudinière, 27 rue du Moulin Vert in Paris. She has also travelled to England and America to lecture on spiritualism.

Mme Zaepffel is considered by some of those around her as eccentric, arrogant, and wanting above all else, to be noticed.

Her husband, from Alsace, is an engineer, initially employed by the Westinghouse company in Sevran. Before the Occupation he was mobilized as a captain in the radiography division of the 8th Engineering Company of the French army in postal sector 110. He is the editor of 'The Spiritualist Centre in Paris Bulletin', and it is he who presents his wife on stage.

Of the Catholic faith, Mme Zaepffel does not appear on any lists in the recent census of Jews.

This brief introduction was followed by reports from a series of informers who recounted statements made by the seer during her public séances, or in private sittings. In the file there was also a selection of the bulletins issued by the Spiritualist Centre in Paris. Gradually, as Hermann turned the pages, he began to feel as if Geneviève was standing there beside him, speaking the words he was reading. Sometimes she stressed certain phrases, moved quickly over others, explaining to him that she had not been seeing clearly in those instances. He closed his eyes and breathed in deeply. He could smell her perfume and feel the warmth of her body close to him. He knew what was happening. Their destinies were being drawn together. One of the most universal doctrines in esoteric teachings is the idea that everything is connected - a hidden web of subtle energies linking every sentient creature. When fate or affinity bring two people together, their souls have already been connected - even before they have physically met.

"I suggest you travel to your new posting via Paris," said Krause, when Hermann returned the file. "Madame Zaepffel is currently holding court with her séances there. You will be able to observe our prophet in full flood, as it were - and enjoy the city of course."

Hermann couldn't help smiling. He had never been to Paris.

"There are advantages to a post in the SS, Captain. I have already cabled Colonel Frenzel to advise him of your secondment. He has replied, telling me you can leave Schleissheim tomorrow for Paris. He envies you, of course, and is a little cross with me, but he is pleased you have not been totally stolen from him." Krause gestured to Hermann to be seated. "I was in Paris myself recently," he continued, with a clear sense of excitement in his voice. "As our Führer has said: 'Jeder einmal nach Paris'. We should all visit the City of Light at least once in our lives. I have asked my secretary to reserve a room for you at the Hotel Lotti. I think you will find it satisfactory." He turned to glance at the photograph of the lama behind him. "We are all tribal, you know. The SS tribe is staying at the Lotti, Military Intelligence are holed up in the Hotel Lutetia, and your friends in the Luftwaffe have managed to commandeer the Ritz, but only for the top brass, of course." Krause shot Hermann a mischievous glance. "Fieldmarshal Göring is ensconced in the Imperial Suite and spends most of his time there, I understand. The Lotti is only a short walk away from the Salle Pleyel, and I suggest you refrain from wearing your uniform while you are there. This will allow you anonymity when you attend our seer's performance."

"I understand."

"The city is remarkably civilized, I have to say, even in these difficult times. We have heard that the Russian occultist Gurdjieff gives classes in the Rue des Colonels, but I advise you not to give in to curiosity. He is a canny operator and will see through any attempt to deceive him. I suggest a simpler and more pleasurable activity. You can avail yourself of one of the several dozen bordellos we now control. The women are superb." Krause opened a drawer of his desk, taking out a book. "An essential for you, Captain: 'The German Guide: What to Do in Paris' - it gives all their addresses. Another essential of course will be condoms. These are available from the Medical Officer in each establishment. Disease is rife."

Hermann had never visited a brothel and had no desire to do so. He leafed through the guide book. "I see it recommends using the Metro."

"Yes," said Krause. "It is the most effective way to travel around the city. As a German, you are entitled to use the first-class car, easily recognized - it is the middle car, painted red. The final car is for Jews." There was a knock at the door, and Krause's secretary entered. She placed a handful of papers on his desk. "Ah good. Here are the party application forms."

CHAPTER SIX

Paris was suffering its worst winter in living memory. Only weeks before, the city had lain under a blanket of snow for over a fortnight, until that was washed away by freezing rain. As he stood outside the Gare de Lyon, Hermann's coat seemed to offer no protection from the cold, but he didn't care. He was here at last. Outside the station the streets seemed unnaturally quiet, with hardly a vehicle in sight. People hurried by, lowering their heads against the wind. Seeing no taxis, Hermann decided to make his way to the hotel in one of the covered rickshaws drawn by two cyclists that were waiting for passengers outside the station. Although he still felt bitterly cold, at least the carriage he climbed into afforded protection from the wind. A pale sun began to emerge from behind the clouds as they moved along the almost empty roads.

Wherever he looked, he could see the proud displays of the occupation - long swastika banners of black and red, draped from flag poles and balconies, fluttered in the wind. The golden angel on his column still presided over the Place de la Bastille, but he had lost the battle to keep his city free.

As they turned into the Rue Castiglione, they entered the zone reserved only for German vehicles or business. Soldiers standing beside a concrete blockhouse, built at the cross-roads with the Rue Saint Honoré, asked for his papers and then waved him on. The Hotel Lotti was a grand affair, a short distance from the blockhouse, and Hermann realized the incongruity of arriving at this luxurious building in such a humble vehicle. A porter helped him with his bags, and he soon found himself alone in a large bedroom decorated in the Louis XIV style. Tall windows allowed him a view towards the Place Vendôme, where - for all he knew - Field marshal Göring was just beginning to wake up in his Imperial Suite at the Ritz.

Krause had given him the names of officers he could contact, but Hermann wanted to experience the city on his own. He had most of the day ahead of him - he simply had to make sure he was at the Salle Pleyel by the evening. He decided he would assume his French identity at once, starting with a coffee, not somewhere grand, like the Champs Elysée, but in a side street wherever serendipity would lead him.

He found a small café on the Rue Gaillon and ordered a coffee, only to discover he would have to make do with a chicory and barley substitute. "They're still keeping the real thing for themselves," the barman explained with a dismissive grimace. Hermann settled down to study his copy of the guide book. As the waitress served him, he noticed the smile rapidly disappearing from her face when she glanced at what he was reading. He was pleased his accent had fooled the barman, but realized he should be more cautious in future. He decided to plan his route. From here he would cross the Seine to the Île de la Cité to visit the cathedral of Notre-Dame. The Louvre was not worth visiting, according to the guide book - most of its contents had been spirited away. Many of the museums and galleries were apparently closed, and so he decided that after perhaps exploring the Latin Quarter he would make his way on the Metro to the northern part of Paris, to wander through the streets of Montmartre and climb up to the Basilica of Sacré-Coeur, to take in its famous view of the city.

As he was planning his itinerary, he became aware of something happening around him. Gradually, one by one, the occupants of the adjacent tables were leaving. Some took their drinks and papers to the bar, others simply left the café. By the time he rose to leave, he was surrounded by a 'cordon sanitaire' of empty tables and chairs. Krause had told him about this kind of passive resistance. No wonder uniformed officers clustered together in the more well-known cafés on the boulevards.

Outside, the city was starting to wake up. Buses swept past, carrying soldiers on leave being shown the sites, their windows filled with eager young faces, cameras pointing in every direction. Hermann walked across the Place de la Concorde, remembering the story of the three Messerschmitt reconnaissance planes that had landed there in a display of bravado during the early days of the occupation.

By the time he reached Notre-Dame, a military band had begun its morning concert on a bandstand in front of the cathedral. Groups of tourist soldiers posed for photographs. Hermann entered the darkness of the church and tried to sense its atmosphere. The smell of incense from morning Mass hung in the air. Strains of Bavarian marching music competed with the sounds of visitors' footsteps. Beams of colour from the South Rose Window failed to illuminate the cathedral, and surrendered instead to the all-encompassing gloom. Hermann felt he was trapped in a mausoleum, and after making one circuit to admire the stained glass, he left the building in search of daylight.

He walked through a few streets of the Latin Quarter, but he was cold, and so decided to head straight for the Metro. Although the station smelled of the trains and too many people - a peculiar mixture of cigarette smoke, burnt rubber from the brakes of the trains, and body odour - at least it was warm down there. When the train arrived, he chose not to ride in the central carriage, opting instead for the last but one. He looked at the impassive faces of the French who surrounded him. Craning his neck, he could see the passengers standing in the pariahs' car behind.

The white domes of Sacré Coeur rose above the street ahead of him as he emerged out of the station into the light and cold. By now he was hungry. He found a small bistro, and walked in - determined to defy any attempt to discover he was German. He kept his guide book in his pocket, spoke in the best accent he could muster, and smiled warmly at the patron and his staff. This seemed to work. He ate chicken and drank wine, and listened intently to the conversations around him. The talk was of rationing, of local gossip, and above all, of the weather - why it was that for the second year in a row they had experienced such a harsh winter.

He left the bistro and climbed up to Sacré Coeur, walking at first onto the terrace to admire the panorama of the city below. There he could see the city stretched out before him, the Eiffel tower in the distance.

Inside the basilica, he sat for a while to admire the mosaic of the Risen Christ in the apse. There was the gold and the blue - the two colours he loved above all others: the blue of the open sky, the gold of the noon-day sun, and of the alchemists and Pharaohs. Instead of a tortured and dying man, here was the resurrected Christ bringing light to the Earth. The perfect image of Tiphareth, he thought, as he remembered the Kabalistic Tree of Life, with its ten spheres depicting different aspects of the Cosmos. Tiphareth was the central sphere of the sun, symbolized in gold and related to the heart. And there was Christ's heart laid out in gold mosaic.

Outside the afternoon sun was starting towards the horizon. Hermann decided to walk back to his hotel, to take a brief rest and perhaps change, before continuing on to the Salle Pleyel. The walk was longer than he expected, and the sky began to darken. As he crossed the Boulevard des Italiens, he saw ahead of him an enormous poster that covered the entire façade of a corner building. 'The Jew and France' was written in great letters above a drawing of a haggard old man with long hair clutching at a globe. Hermann stood still. It was an exhibition Krause had told him he should visit - an idea Hermann had dismissed without a thought. Just as he would dip the wing of his aircraft to turn away from danger or a less attractive view, he looked away from the poster and continued walking.

At the Salle Pleyel, the young woman who sold him one of the last tickets managed a smile. "You are lucky. I only have two left now."

Hermann took his ticket. "A full house for you. How many...?"

"Three thousand."

"Quite remarkable. What a success."

As he worked his way through the crowd in the foyer, it seemed as if all of Paris had become curious about its future. Every class of person had been drawn here. There were no children, but there were young men and women, and the elderly too, tottering on their canes, or clutching at the arms of companions, staring into the distance, ignoring those around them, as if by doing so they could plough through the crowd more easily.

In the softly lit auditorium Hermann found his seat a dozen rows from the front and to one side. The lights were dimmed. A respectful silence descended. The 'Evening of Prophecies' was about to begin. The dark red curtain at the back of the stage rippled, and out stepped a slim man in his forties, a bright yellow handkerchief in the top pocket of his double-breasted suit. He appeared confident and, without a trace of hesitation, strode to the front of the stage.

"Good evening ladies and gentlemen. My name is René Zaepffel. It is with great pleasure that I welcome you here this evening. Tonight you will know your future. Tonight you will bathe in the atmosphere of a prophet - the atmosphere of Geneviève Zaepffel - the Druidess of Brocéliande." A wave of applause ran through the auditorium.

Zaepffel's husband was clearly a master of holding the crowd's attention, even though he was almost comical in his fairground manner. He paused just long enough to allow the tension to build before speaking once again. "When Madame Zaepffel utters her prophecies, she becomes light itself. She speaks to captivate every soul in the room, to envelop each one of us in a single powerful thought and raise us up to the marvellous summit of prophecy."

Another pause as he paced the stage, looking into the faces of the audience.

"Remember, the Druidess holds nothing from you. The truth pours from her lips as if from a well of hidden knowledge. Who was it who said, in the midst of a period of abundance, that we would go hungry? Who was it who announced, at a time of complete calm, the Spanish revolution and the French Popular Front? Who was it who prophesied, at a time of stability in the Franco-British alliance, that Britain would leave us in the midst of chaos? She holds nothing back. She does not soften her words to calm you, to lead you into a false sense of security. She tells you the truth, however painful or difficult it might be to hear or heed her message."

A pause again, to let his words land.

"Who was it who talked of the conflict between Germany and Russia when these two powers were working amicably together? Who was it who revealed, in the midst of international euphoria, the impending world conflict between Germany, France, England, Poland and

Russia? It was, ladies and gentlemen, Geneviève Zaepffel... and here she is!"

The crowd began clapping enthusiastically. There was another ripple of the curtains, and out stepped a short woman with blonde untamed hair and piercing dark eyes. She was wearing a white robe, tied by a golden cord decorated with acorns. She stood still for a moment - again perfect timing - before walking to the front of the stage. As the applause died down, with just the hint of a smile, she solemnly bowed towards the audience. René moved behind her and placed a cape on her shoulders. "This cape," he announced as he stepped back, "is embroidered with images of mistletoe and a sickle. These are the sacred emblems of a seer of the ancient forest! These are the symbols of the Druidess of Brocéliande!"

He bowed, and left the stage. The lone figure of the prophetess looked slowly around the hall, and it seemed for a moment as if she gazed directly into Hermann's eyes. And then she began to speak:

"My friends, I am so pleased to see you all here. We are living through dark, difficult times, and yet God and his angels have not abandoned us. The choice, as always, is between the Light and the Dark, between the way of Good and the way of Evil. These are testing times for every soul, but my mission, my sole aim in life, is to help bring light to the world, to alleviate suffering, to bring peace to mankind.

I come, as you know, from the forest of Brocéliande, from the land of the Druids, which even today continues to radiate its magnetism, its power to initiate. It is a land protected by the magic spells of Viviane, that fairy spirit who announced the coming of Joan of Arc centuries before her birth. Perhaps, indeed, Joan of Arc was the reincarnation of the spirit Viviane."

Geneviève stopped speaking and again looked around the hall. Like René, she seemed a master of holding an audience in the palm of her hand. Her leap from the usual claim of spiritual teachers that they are bringing light to the world to talking about a fairy spirit and Joan of Arc, was surprising to Hermann and almost ridiculous, but he admired her assurance. She clearly knew that if you have style and confidence, you can say almost anything and get away with it. And who was he to say whether she was right or wrong?

Now the prophetess changed tack. Her face broke into a warm smile.

"This evening, my dear friends, I have good news for you. I have asked the occupation authorities to set up canteens in stations for children and the needy, and I have been given permission to take care of this, and I can tell you that soon we will be distributing cups of chocolate for fifty centimes. I urge you to help me in this task. You will find a desk in the foyer with helpers who will note down your name and address and offers of assistance."

Cheers rose from the crowd. Geneviève bowed slightly, then gestured for silence. She took in a deep breath and closed her eyes. "I can feel the Spirit is upon me. I am entering the trance." René appeared from behind the curtain and, taking a chair that had been standing to one side, carried it towards her and gently guided her to sit down.

For a few moments, utter silence reigned in the auditorium, until a single cough from far back in the stalls broke the spell. Geneviève began to speak: "France, the hour has come for you to understand - so the hymn of your resurrection can be sung! I shall interpret these voices I hear from far away, that their echoes may reverberate as far as the summits of Tibet, where the lama initiates even now are writing on humanity's stone of destiny." Geneviève moved in her chair, and Hermann could see that she was going deeper, her facial muscles relaxing. She started to take on the same appearance as mediums he had observed at séances.

"I see images falling like fire in front of me. The world is being purified. The conflict is between two forces - good and evil. I see the Garden of Olives, Gethsemane. Each nation now moves towards its Golgotha.

For France, I see our prisoners returning soon. They return on a luminous path - a magnificent symbol. France seems calm, but everything men plan is mistaken. By next May, we will be fighting in all our colonies. Everything will be so fast, so overwhelming, that nothing we do will prepare ourselves for this. But within two years we will live well. The money we use will have a different shape and real value.

I see England now. England, listen to me, the time of territorial conquests is over. Your face will change. Your colonies will detach themselves from you, but despite this, agreement will reign between you because a power, which I do not understand, links each colony to your capital."

Hermann was watching Geneviève closely. She seemed to be genuinely speaking from some other plane of awareness, unless, of course, she was an accomplished actress.

"Some years ago I predicted the assassination attempt on England's King Edward VIII. As I foresaw, the king was saved and I now predict he will help guide England towards a united Europe."

As Hermann looked around, he could see the faces of the crowd - both men and women - drinking in every word that was uttered, as if all that Geneviève said was undoubtedly true, as if God Himself was speaking. Some, he saw, were taking notes. He knew this was unnecessary for his work. Krause had explained that in Paris a stenographer recorded every utterance of the Druidess, and within days a bulletin of the Spiritualist Centre would be issued and mailed to all subscribers. Little subterfuge was necessary - Krause had used a pseudonym and received regular copies of the bulletin in Berlin. Hermann's mission was not to relay the prophecies Geneviève had already pronounced or published - it was to get close enough to her to hear any predictions she might make in private, before she broadcast them, and -

as Krause had explained - to discover whether she was a charlatan or whether she was truly gifted with clairvoyance.

Geneviève had been sitting in silence for a while, and Hermann wondered if she was coming out of her trance, but then she began speaking again: "Now I am in Germany. It is strange - one half seems in the light, the other in the dark, as if it wants to divide into two. Hitler is standing there - he reaches out his hand. A French soldier stretches his hand out too, but hesitates. The world almost seems to stop. And for Russia, oh immense Russia... it is terrifying. Only a few houses are left standing."

Slowly, the prophetess raised her hands to her brow, stroking it with her finger-tips as if washing her forehead, or perhaps, thought Hermann, freeing herself of her visions to help her return to everyday consciousness. She opened her eyes, and looked at her audience. "My dear friends, let me finish by telling you this. The trees will shed their leaves two more times before this war is over. But then there will be a rebirth. A youthfulness will begin to flow throughout Europe. It will feel as if we have come out of our tombs, rejoicing, understanding that our sacrifice was not in vain." The audience began clapping, but she silenced the crowd with a wave of her hand. "Try to understand what I am going to say now. There are two engines, two motors, that exist in the world. Both produce millions of volts of force. One creates misery and suffering, the other creates joy and happiness. In becoming happy you create a wave, an energy field of happiness all around you that connects you with the positive motor. Bad thoughts or feelings create bitterness and connect you to the negative one. It is up to each of us to radiate goodness, love and light - to radiate the positive and not the negative!"

A moment's silence reigned, and then a roar of applause broke out. Geneviève smiled, opened her arms out wide as if wanting to embrace the entire audience, then bowed, turned and left the stage. René emerged as the clapping died down. "The words of the Druidess of Brocéliande fall like seeds of thought," he called out. "A supernatural power flows through her, and all of us are conquered. Thank you all for coming tonight. You will find literature on sale in the foyer."

As Hermann left the Salle Pleyel that evening, he was filled with excitement. The Druidess had given an impressive performance. As a teenage boy he had once made a pact with himself that, whatever happened, he would make sure his life was filled with adventure, and here he was in Paris, being paid to clandestinely observe a woman who commanded the fascination of thousands. Soon he would be close to her, and he would discover whether she was genuinely psychic or simply fraudulent or deluded. And now that he was here in this romantic city for just one night, perhaps, he thought, he should make himself experience something new, something adventurous that would require some courage. Perhaps he should visit one of those establishments Krause had recommended, if only to learn more about human nature.

'One Two Two', the city's most famous bordello located at 122 Rue de Provence, was only a few streets away, in the direction of his hotel, and the description of it in the German guide book made it sound extraordinary, not at all vulgar. It was apparently a meeting place for the city's cultural elite. On the first floor there was an elegant café, and on the floors above, rooms were designed as jungles, Roman baths and harems. It accepted both a French and German clientele, and officers were asked to visit in civilian clothing. He noticed his heart racing as he imagined being led upstairs, after drinking champagne with a beautiful French woman whose sole intention was to give him pleasure.

He braced himself against the cold night air, and started walking towards the Rue de Provence. Occasionally a car would pass, its headlights reduced to two sinister slithers of light to comply with the black-out regulations. Windows were shuttered, the street lamps unlit. The crowd that had spilled out of the Salle Pleyel had dispersed, and the city now seemed eerily quiet.

Silence reigned only until he pushed open the door of 'One Two Two'. Inside, a three piece band was playing jazz in one corner of the room. The air was filled with smoke. Everything was designed to make him feel relaxed, and to make him spend money. A hostess brought him wine and introduced him to a woman seated alone at a table who must have been in her mid-thirties, about Hermann's age. With dark hair cut in page-boy style, and wide brown eyes framed with artificial lashes, she was charming with him, and he enjoyed pretending he was French. But he could sense the wall she had built around herself to protect her feelings. The thought of engaging in any intimacy with her, with any total stranger, felt alien to him, but as the evening wore on and one glass of wine followed another, he found himself considering her proposition to go upstairs. He explained that he had never done such a thing before, that he found the idea exciting, but he was still not convinced it was sensible. She moved closer to him, and he felt her hand sliding gently over his thigh. Her fingers then moved to his flies, and after unbuttoning them, as she stared at him intently, she plunged her hand inside, and made her way towards her goal that was by now easy to find. He laughed with astonishment and moved closer to the table, so no-one could observe their game. But all of a sudden she withdrew her hand. "If you want more, you'll have to come upstairs and you'll have to pay."

At that moment, above the music of the band, came a more sinister sound - the wail of air raid sirens spreading across the city. People started running out of the building. He turned and saw his companion had already gone. Buttoning his trousers and then grabbing his coat at the cloakroom, he ran outside. The sky was alive with the beams of searchlights. He had been told there was an air raid shelter in the basement of the hotel, and he decided to make his way there as fast as he could. As he crossed the Rue de Provence, he broke into a run.

He could hear the sound of the anti-aircraft guns in the distance now, and he imagined his English counterparts, RAF men in Lancaster bombers, looking down on the city, trying to identify their targets. And then there were great crashes of sound as the bombs hit the ground. They were some way off - out in the suburbs, where the city's factories and warehouses were located. That made sense, Hermann figured, no one would want to bomb the heart of this glorious place.

CHAPTER SEVEN

"They hit the Renault factory." The man sitting opposite him leant forward as they moved slowly out of the city. "We should see it in a minute, when we get to Boulogne-Bilancourt."

Hermann, still dressed in civilian clothing, had spent a restless night in the hotel. His train had been delayed by an hour but he was pleased they were now on the move. "I heard the noise last night. Has there been much damage?"

Clearly taking him for a Frenchman, his fellow passenger offered him a cigarette. "I don't know, but I expect so." After ten minutes the train came to a halt. "Look - now we can see for ourselves." The devastation was clearly visible: warehouses with half their walls reduced to rubble, their metal roofs ripped open to the sky. Piles of brick and twisted girders lay near the track.

After a long wait, the train started to move again, inching forward, as if picking its way through the debris.

Once past the suburb, it gathered speed. Hermann took out of his suitcase one of the bulletins of the Zaepffel's Spiritualist Centre, that he had picked up at the Salle Pleyel, and began reading. He would be in Rennes in a few hours, where a car was due to meet him at the station.

"I was informed by Berlin of your secondment to the SS-Ahnenerbe, Captain." Alfred Ernst, the Commandant of Point-Clos, was an impressive man. Heavily built, with a square, open face, Hermann had already been told of his liking for fast cars and attractive women. "I have to say your timing is impeccable. You ask me to engineer a meeting with the Zaepffels, and here on my desk is an invitation to dine with this most unusual of couples on Saturday. And look, Madame Zaepffel has written: 'Do bring several of your fellow officers, my dear Commandant. We have just returned from Paris, bringing with us various delicacies, and as you know, we love to entertain.' You are in luck, Captain." Ernst turned to peer out of the window as two Dornier bombers heaved themselves into the grey sky. "It is true they are sociable," he continued, turning back to Hermann, "but they are no fools. Our officers are Madame Zaepffel's best clients, and of course we always bring them gifts - wine, meat, tobacco. You can come with lieutenant Koch, the base photographer. You've met him haven't you? I think he'll appreciate a visit to the Manoir - it has great charm. He will probably want to photograph it."

They approached the Manoir in the evening light. The Commandant was right. There was a sense of mystery in the way the tall oaks of the forest grew so close to the western side of the house that they seemed to be claiming the building for their own. And yet, once the officers had walked along the path that led to the eastern entrance, they were all at once in an open landscape - facing a wide lawn with fields beyond. It was as if the house lay partly in one world and partly in another. Through its tall windows Hermann could see Geneviève and her husband talking beside the fire-place.

"Madame Zaepffel, allow me to introduce you to Captain Hermann Kaestner, a new arrival at Point-Clos." Hermann took Geneviève's hand and bowed.

"Enchantée," replied Geneviève, just as René approached to greet the new arrivals. Peter Koch was carrying sausages and candied fruit in a small box, together with a bottle of Gewürztraminer. "Ah, you haven't forgotten my home country!" exclaimed René as he read the label.

The conversation flowed easily over dinner. At a certain moment Hermann found himself surprised at how comfortable he felt. He looked across at Geneviève and they exchanged smiles.

"Madame Zaepffel," said Peter, from across the table, "I have read that there are legends which state that Christ himself once stayed in the forest that surrounds your Manoir. Do you believe this could have happened?"

Geneviève nodded, placing her glass on the table. "I am certain this is true. The grail has been here. Christ has been here. My spirit guides have told me that our house stands upon the very spot where our Lord was sheltered." Hermann admired the way she spoke with such assurance. "Having feigned death at the crucifixion," Geneviève continued, "our Lord fled to Avalon in the west of Britain, with his uncle Joseph of Arimathea and Mary Magdalene, passing through this forest on their way to safety."

"So they were not safe here?" asked Peter.

"Brittany has always been a lawless land, Captain. There were bears and wolves in the forest, brigands too. But there were also the druids - and they welcomed Christ, took care of the party and led them onwards, to a safe harbour on the coast."

"You must feel a great affinity for the druids, Madame Zaepffel, since you are known yourself as a druidess," said Ernst.

"I do indeed, Commandant. The forest of Brocéliande belongs to their great magician Merlin, who lives still amongst its shadows."

Ernst smiled at Geneviève. "You speak with such poetry, Madame. And, if I may say so, your cooking is as exquisite as your language."

Hermann and Peter added their praises, and Ernst suggested a toast to the chef. Then Hermann spoke: "Madame Zaepffel, I have been told of your remarkable powers of prophecy. Are you able to tell us how events will unfold for us all here in this region?"

Geneviève shook her head from side to side with a sigh: "We will escape the worst of the conflagration here in Brittany. It will be those in Paris and the big cities who will suffer."

"The bombing of Rennes was most unfortunate," said Ernst.

"Thank Heavens it has been an isolated instance," said René, as he stood to refill their glasses. "And the suffering has been much alleviated by the support your administration has offered to the nationalist movement. When Berlin announced that Brittany will become a separate state after the war, there was much rejoicing."

"As a native of Alsace you must sympathize with Breton sensibilities, Captain Zaepffel," replied Ernst.

"I do indeed. There is a good deal of pro-German sentiment in this region. After four centuries of domination by France, many people here feel your appearance offers hope that one day their country will be free."

This was why he could feel so relaxed with his hosts, realized Hermann. They bore the German occupation forces no ill will. In fact they saw them as saviours. Alsace had been reunited with Germany just two years ago, and in Berlin he had been told that Propaganda-Staffel's funding of the Breton nationalist Radio station had been well received, and that key figures in the Breton Nationalist movement saw Germany as their ally. Hermann turned to Geneviève. "I do not wish to put you on the spot, Madame Zaepffel, but I know you are a particular expert on this subject and that you regularly address packed halls in Paris. So if I may return to my question, how do you see the future of our countries over the coming years?"

Geneviève closed her eyes for a moment, and then addressed the assembled company as if they were her audience at the Salle Pleyel: "There will be much bloodshed, I regret to say. There will be moments when it seems as if everything will be destroyed, but in the end, once peace is restored, our two countries will lead a United States of Europe. The borders will be dissolved, and just one currency will be used throughout this union."

Geneviève looked around the table. No-one was eating. Everyone was looking at her - waiting for her next prediction. René stood and began removing their plates to make way for the next course, moving around the table almost silently. She continued: "Several years ago I predicted that Japan would attack the United States, but recently I have seen the Japanese people paralyzed by a frightening cataclysm: I have seen the heavens opening and a rain of fire pouring forth, destroying everything in its path." Geneviève sat back, a distant look in her eyes. Hermann was impressed - this woman was capable of casting a spell on her audience whether there were just a few people present or whether she was faced with a gathering of thousands.

Silence reigned at the table for a moment, until she spoke again. "Despite all I have said, we have nothing to fear, gentlemen, I can assure you." The officers smiled politely, and the conversation turned to lighter matters. Once the meal was finished, René invited them all to sit beside the fire. How civilized, thought Hermann, here they were, away from the brutality of war, seated in comfortable chairs around a blazing hearth, an excellent meal in their stomachs. An old hunting map of Brocéliande hung above the fireplace, the pendulum of the Comtoise grandfather clock standing in the corner of the room swung gently back and forth. Nothing had really changed here for centuries. God willing, nothing would change.

Geneviève left the room and returned with a bottle of cognac. "We have only a few bottles left. But the tides will turn and together our countries will lead the world to peace, and we will all be able to replenish our cellars. René, my darling, will you offer our friends a toast?"

"To peace!" they all said loudly, standing up, warmed by the fire, then warmed by the cognac itself. Peter turned to Geneviève: "I understand from my fellow officers that you offer individual consultations, Madame Zaepffel."

"Something troubles you, I can tell," said Geneviève looking directly at him. "I sense distress. You must be careful." Hermann noticed the flicker of concern that ran across Peter's face. "I see individuals by appointment, and you will be most welcome to call. I use cards to sharpen my perceptions, sometimes the Tarot deck, sometimes those of Madame Lenormand."

Peter simply nodded to Geneviève and made no comment. He walked over to the hunting map and began to inspect it closely. "I know of the Tarot," began Hermann, "But I am not familiar with the cards of Madame Lenormand."

"She was fortune-teller to Marat and Robespierre, Captain Kaestner. The Empress Josephine and Czar Alexander consulted her often." Geneviève smiled warmly. "Her cards can be uncannily accurate. You must come to see me one day too. I will demonstrate their effectiveness if you will allow me."

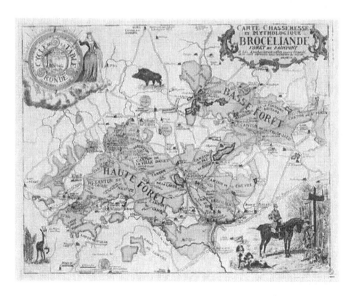

CHAPTER EIGHT

Geneviève turned off the lamp beside the fireplace. "I'm going to bed, my darling. Can I leave you to clear up?"

"Of course." René was already walking to the door to check it was locked.

She loved their bedroom, and above all she loved the four-poster bed which had been there since she was a child. Perhaps she had been born in it, she had never asked her mother. She sat at the dressing table and looked at her face in the mirror. Not bad, she thought, turning left then right to check that her skin remained taut. No wrinkles yet, but time passes and we will all become wrinkled and die.

She remembered the shocking way she could sense each person's mortality when she first became aware of her psychic powers. It was as if the future, the final state of everyone she looked at - young or old - was presented to her. Every face, however bright, however flawless, revealed its own transience. It became a mask she could instantly see through - to the skull that would be all that remained of it when it lay in the ground.

She sometimes wished she had never been given her gifts, but knew she should thank God and his angels for them. She was able to help so many thousands now. It still astonished her that she drew such crowds in Paris.

René entered the room, and seeing her at the dressing table walked over, bent down, and opened the clasp of her necklace.

"Thank you, my dear." She began to remove her earrings.

He smiled. "Another successful evening in our castle."

"I do like those men from Point-Clos, they have such breeding."

In bed, René made his usual half-hearted attempt to make love, but she knew he was tired and she needed time to think. "Not now, my darling. We are both exhausted, and it is time for sleep." She could feel her future now - so close it frightened her. She didn't want to, but she saw one image after another tumbling in front of her. She saw herself in the young German officer's arms. She was opening herself to him. She could feel his lips on hers, she could feel his hands running through her hair. This was wrong, she found herself repeating in her mind as she tried not to want him. He had such charm, though, he was so gentle and yet so assured. But he was much younger than her, ten or twelve years perhaps. She could feel his hands running up her thighs. She must pray. She began to silently recite the Lord's Prayer, and conjured up images, first of Christ on the cross, then of the Piéta. It was hard, it required concentration, but in the end it worked. She felt that shift in consciousness, that raising of her vibrations, she had first felt so many years ago when she was a child.

She had sat in church, and looking up one day at the image of Christ dying on the cross, she had seen him freeing himself, stepping forward to prove that he was still alive. Light was pouring from his heart and she began to cry, not out of fear or sadness, but out of happiness and the shock of seeing something she knew no-one else could see.

She and René had known each other ever since the time they had met in a restaurant in Rennes when she was in her twenties. She was with her father. René had struck her as a melancholy young man, but there was something about him that drew her to him, that opened her heart. She learnt that he had lost both his parents, had been discharged from the army as a young officer, and was now training to be an engineer in Paris. Her father invited René to visit them at the Manoir, and several weeks later there he was at the door, apparently 'passing through' - an unlikely idea that flattered Geneviève. No longer melancholy, as they walked in the forest, he confessed to her that he had dreamt of a house just like the Manoir, and of a girl who lived there, as beautiful as her. He was just a year older, and - she soon discovered - was both amusing and a born actor. After several visits that summer, he surprised her one day by telling her he loved her and wanted to marry her, but she kept him waiting for two years. Perhaps that was cruel, but she felt they were too young and he needed to finish his training. Once they were married, he came to live in the Manoir with her and her parents. He supervised the installation of a heating system for the house, and took over the management of the estate when her mother and father were both, with little warning, taken from her with tuberculosis. He was her rock, her foundation. But like her father, he had a temper. He always had to be in control. She turned in the bed. She really ought to go to sleep now. He might be a know-it-all, but he was almost always right, particularly in practical and financial matters, and Geneviève had come to respect that. She had promised to obey him the day she married, and she always would.

She must always be faithful to him too. She knew that. Although they were still fond of each other, with the passing of the years they had inevitably lost the ability to arouse each other's deepest passions, and now their intimacies were confined to the occasional encounter which was soon over, and which - to her at least - felt more like a duty she ought to occasionally fulfill than the expression of any real desire. Perhaps the fact that they never had children had influenced her, causing that delicious imperative she had experienced as a young woman to eventually wane. Or perhaps it was simply age and the price one pays for the comfort of familiarity.

She tried to sleep, but the images returned, and she could feel Hermann now, close to her, whispering in her ear, telling her that love was more important than anything in this world, that loved reigned supreme above all virtues, above all man-made rules, all promises and pledges. "In the end, it is only love that counts", she could hear him saying in that almost perfect French he spoke, which was tinged - just sufficiently to make it so attractive - with a German accent. If only she could be certain when she saw these images that seemed to be coming to her from the future. She was sometimes mistaken, she knew that. Sometimes she would pronounce from the stage at the Salle Pleyel, interpreting the flow of pictures, the strange sensations, and even as the words were out of her mouth, she would know that she was wrong - she had misinterpreted them, or perhaps an evil spirit had influenced her, despite her being guarded by angels. Perhaps this was not her future that she was experiencing now as Hermann breathed gently on her neck, running his fingers down her spine. Perhaps he was lying in his bed at Point-Clos imagining these scenes, and she was simply picking up his thoughts. Perhaps his astral body was here beside her, kissing her now - on her neck, her breasts. Instead of being alarmed at this thought, she found it excited her, even though she knew this was wrong. Oh, to be wanted, to be desired with a fervour that was uncontrollable! If she could command his attentions, how thrilling that would be. It would mean she was still as young as him really - at least in her heart, which was what counted.

CHAPTER NINE

Henri Gillard stepped out of the old Citroën, tightened his scarf around his neck, and breathed in the air of the place. It smelled good: of manure and of the fields. The dirt track that led through the village of Tréhorenteuc, a few miles from the Manoir du Tertre, was
thick with mud, even though the sun was shining. Easter was just a month away, but it was still unseasonably cold.

From across the road a small delegation emerged from the Bar-Tabac. Behind the usual greetings and smiles he knew he was being sized up, and he couldn't quite tell from their expressions whether they were grateful that a priest had finally been found for their remote hamlet, or whether they resented the intrusion of an outsider. Now, out of a sense of guilt, if not piety, he thought, they would feel obliged to attend Mass and feel obliged too to confess their sins. Or at least some of them.

Mme Harel led him towards her bar, "I think you will need a drink before seeing the rectory… Or several perhaps," she shouted over her shoulder.

Paul Croiset the Mayor and Jacques Barteau the baker took Gillard's bags and followed. Inside more smells: cigarette smoke, wine and beer long spilt. He took out his tobacco and offered it to the men. As they rolled their cigarettes and talked, Gillard casually slipped in and out of Gallo, the local patois, and it did the trick: he was one of them - a local boy, born at Guégnon. They could trust him and the conversation flowed.

"How are supplies? Wine, tobacco, food?"

Croiset was quick to respond. "We're lucky here, Father. We're used to growing our own. Most people keep chickens. The Germans sometimes requisition supplies, but we get tobacco from them. Wine can be hard to come by, but there is no shortage of cider. I just thank God we're not living in Rennes - they've never recovered from the bombing."

"Endless queues," said Barteau. "Even if you're lucky and have family in the country who are generous. But who can afford to be generous these days?"

"Perhaps it will settle down," said Gillard. "There are some who say we'll be better off in the end - and gain independence from France." A nervous pause punctuated the flow of conversation.

Croiset asked Gillard if he had seen any action, and the priest described his time in Crédin and the stories he had heard of bravery and incompetence as France was all too swiftly defeated.

Mme Harel poured each of them a bowl of cider, "Let's just hope it's over as soon as possible, and everyone can get back to living their lives in peace once again."

Croiset raised his bowl, "To Monsieur le Recteur!"

With a few questions, Gillard confirmed the information his bishop had given him. There were a little under two hundred parishioners here, and in addition to the Bar-Tabac, one shop, which was also the bakery. A school had been established in 1866, and as they spoke, fifteen children were being taught by their teacher, Mme Heriot, who was paid by the commune.

"I would be surprised if you lasted more than two years in this place, to be honest," said Mme Harel. "Both the church and the rectory are falling down, and there has been no priest in the village for the last year. Before that, none of them have stayed more than two years and most of them hated every minute of their time here."

"Not true, Henriette!" Croiset said. "One lasted six years - but if the good father manages to stay that long it will be a miracle."

"I hope I stay a good deal longer," replied Gillard. "In Vannes they explain this lack of staying-power by joking that the village is hardly Christian - that you're too close to the forest and that Merlin has got you in his spell."

"More likely the cider than Merlin," said Barteau, as they drained their glasses before walking back across the road to the rectory.

Once the men had dropped his bags, he was left on his own with Mme Harel, who took him through the simple two-storey building. Like most of the old houses in Brittany, it had thick stone walls and a fire-place large enough to sit in. Downstairs a basic kitchen adjoined the main parlour, and upstairs the space was divided into three rooms with an iron bed in each.

"There is no electricity, but you have these," said Mme Harel, showing Gillard the oil-lamps in the kitchen. "Mind you, we have so many power cuts you wouldn't notice much difference if you were connected."

From the back door she pointed to the outside lavatory and the vegetable patch overgrown with weeds. "Not much, is it?" she said with a shrug of the shoulders and a smile, which might have meant: 'And let's see how long you can put up with it.' Or, as Gillard decided was the case: 'But I think you'll cope. You're different.' She left him to return to the bar. He looked around at the bleak grey walls and the empty fireplace. 'So this is what they give me after eighteen years of dedication?' With that thought, he left the house, crossed the road and started walking towards the church. But then he remembered the set of keys given to him by the bishop, who had said only two words to him as he handed them over: 'Good luck'. They were in his suitcase. He turned around in the mud and walked back to the rectory.

As he left the building for the second time, it struck Gillard that there was something peculiar about this place. Usually a church occupied the centre of a village, but here it stood behind the main street, as if somehow unwanted or ashamed of its own existence. The priest had long adopted the habit of catching himself out whenever he noticed a negative thought, and so, turning around his first thought he arrived almost at once at a second: perhaps the church was hiding, not out of shame, but because it protected a secret.

As he turned into an alley that ran from the street behind Harel's bar and the row of adjoining houses, he was taken aback by the loud honking of half a dozen geese who seemed to have formed another welcoming party for him. This delegation was less friendly, strutting towards him as if they wanted him to go away, but he continued walking, inadvertently stepping in their droppings. "Bless you!" he said out loud, thinking of St Francis.

And there it stood: the small, unremarkable church of the village of Tréhorenteuc. Gillard had seen enough churches by this time to recognize the  problems it presented. He could see signs of weakness in the belfry, a leaning wall that suggested settlement, and he knew how it would feel and smell inside, damp and cold, as if God Himself had deserted the building and left it in the care of the lesser gods of earth and rain. The familiar creaking of the oak door, the scent of damp stone and wood. But a Presence. Something. His first thought: God has not deserted this place. He is here. Light from the stained glass window fell onto the altar and for a moment he paused, his dissatisfaction now far away. As he looked around, his eyes were drawn to a large monument that almost filled the north transept. A plaque revealed that it was the tomb of the church's patron saint, Onenne, whose statue lay uncomfortably upon it. As Gillard examined the statue he noted that it was old, undeniably, but the saint's stomach was swollen as if she was pregnant, which made no sense, since she was known for her chastity. The tomb itself was remarkably unattractive and completely out of proportion with the size of the church. He would have to see if it could be moved, or reduced in size. He turned and looked at the altar. The crucifix standing on it was unappealing too - the head of Christ wrong in some way that he found hard to put his finger on. It just didn't look like Christ. It would have to go.

He turned his attention to the pews, peering closely, pushing his fingernails into the wood where it seemed to be soft. As he'd expected, they were riddled with rot. He would have to find the funds to replace them. But at that moment he smiled. He had been so preoccupied with the physical state of the church he had forgotten to attend to the Spirit. He walked to the altar and knelt before it. He prayed that he would serve this parish well, that his life would be of use to the Lord, that His will and not his own would be done.

For a moment, he found the peace he had experienced many times before, but only ever fleetingly, and it vanished no sooner than it arrived - this time replaced by a memory: of facing Bishop Le Bellec for yet another enquiry into his beliefs. How many times did he have to assure him of his faith? For ten years he had submitted every one of his sermons to the bishop for approval before preaching, until finally he was summoned to the Bishopric to be given this post - quite clearly as a punishment for the way in which he dared to continue to uphold an interest in doctrines which, while not strictly heretical, went out of fashion centuries ago. Why did he insist on maintaining an interest in astrology, for example? Time and again he had been asked this question, and each time he had answered by drawing attention to the depictions of the zodiac in the windows of Our Lady of Notre Dame in Paris and Chartres. Time and again he had assured the bishop that he had never cast a horoscope, and that he was solely concerned with the way in which the zodiac depicted the eternal truths of the Catholic Church, and that his only sources of reference were the medieval Books of Hours. But Le Bellec never believed him.

Father Gillard shook his head, returning himself to the present - in the back of beyond, in the little church of St Onenne. At the age of forty-one, having served two busy urban parishes to the best of his ability, he had been sent here - to this 'piss-pot of the diocese', as his colleagues in Vannes called it. He felt a wave of anger, followed by a sense of repentance, and then acceptance. That process of moving from anger to acceptance, his spiritual director had pointed out, was the gift of the Church. Obedience, he liked to say, is not a passive act of weakness but the key to sainthood. Constantly yielding to authority melts the hard edges of the soul. Obedience forces the little will to collapse and the soul in consequence to be enflamed.

He would obey and God's will would be done. At the age of twenty-three he had entered the priesthood and sworn obedience, as well as poverty and chastity, and no one was ever going to make him break those vows.

Over the following weeks - in a surprisingly short time, it seemed to Gillard - he became accepted by the villagers. He began helping the mayor in his office and visited the school once, sometimes twice a week, to read Bible stories, or to talk with their teacher about the children in her care or the problems their families faced. People seemed to like him - he drank with them in Harel's bar, he was generous with his tobacco, he made sure his sermons were brief and avoided fire and brimstone. By late Spring, when he proposed a fête to include the revival of the old custom of blessing St Onenne's well, everyone seemed delighted: "We should start the celebrations with a Mass, followed by a procession from the church to the well. We can dust down the old banners, have Croiset playing the corne-muse, persuade the geese to follow us, and give thanks to our patron saint."

Preparations began at once. Trého, as the locals called the village, had recently acquired a nickname: Le Gigot, 'the leg of lamb'. While the citizens of Rennes and Nantes were scraping together the ingredients for every meal with ration cards and supplies bought on the black market, villages like Trého were seen as havens, stocked with meat, poultry, eggs and vegetables, hidden by greedy farmers from their fellow citizens and the occupying troops - or so the rumours went. And while this was certainly an exaggeration, eggs and butter were still in good supply, and Aubertin the baker was able to produce plenty of cakes and biscuits. Discreet transactions resulted in plentiful supplies of wine, cider, and chouchen, the local mead. Word was sent out to the surrounding villages. There would be boules, and the lads in the village were going to play a football match in the afternoon against the boys from Néant-sur-Yvel.

On the morning of the fête, tables were set up beneath the trees, the lawn opposite the church was decked out with bunting, and the sky offered the promise of a clear day. The church was full, and visitors arrived from far afield. In his sermon, Henri Gillard talked about the importance of hope and shared his plans for the refurbishment of the church. He spoke of the human need for beauty and of the way in which a church can offer a vision of paradise.

At the end of the service, a short, middle-aged woman walked confidently towards him. With blonde hair brushed away from her face, a clear skin and penetrating eyes, she had none of the cowed or time-worn aspect of his parishioners. She carried herself like an aristocrat. "Good morning, Monsieur le Recteur. Allow me to introduce myself: Geneviève Zaepffel. I come from the Manoir du Tertre, just outside Paimpont. I am so pleased to meet you, and I am delighted you have taken on this post. I do hope you stay here for many years."

"Madame Zaepffel, your fame has gone before you," Gillard replied. "I have read several of your books, and was most impressed. I sometimes use your 'Dictionary of Happiness' to provide me with inspiration."

"I am surprised to hear this. You are so kind."

A cluster of giggling children ran past. Gillard smiled. "We are not all trapped by convention, Madame Zaepffel. There are some of us, even amongst the clergy, who like to gaze at the stars."

Geneviève Zaepffel's face lit up. It seemed to Gillard that this one remark of his had acted as a password, which enabled them to recognize each other as kindred spirits. She invited him to pay a visit to the Manoir in the near future.

Their conversation was interrupted by the arrival of the geese. Croiset had become impatient and had led them over. Gillard took his cue, turned from talking to Mme Zaepffel, and signaled to the banner bearers to follow him, and the march began. The geese took the lead, strutting at the head of the procession as if they were in charge. Round the corner and into the main street

they marched, past the rectory and Harel's bar, the corne- muse blowing and the banners flapping behind them. The geese knew exactly where to go. In front of the Mairie, they turned into the lane that led towards the copse. There, protected by its guardians of ash and alder, Onnene's spring had been contained for centuries in an oblong basin formed out of blocks of stone, with seven steps that descended into the water.

The well had been cleaned for the occasion and decorated with flowers. Gillard directed his assistant to stand opposite him, to swing the censer over the water, while he climbed down the steps to give the blessing. As the puffs of white smoke drifted over the well, he spoke the prescribed words, but they seemed hollow to him, as if the well, as if St Onenne herself, were telling him: "You have no need to bless me. I bless you." He made the sign of the cross and then scooped up some water with both hands, and turning to the crowd behind him and above him, threw it over them, to the delight of all the children.

On leading the procession back, he was surprised to see two German staff cars parked beside Harel's. They must have arrived while everyone was at the well. Half a dozen officers sat at the tables. He recognized their uniforms - they were Luftwaffe men from Point-Clos, not soldiers.

"Good morning!" shouted one of them. The other officers smiled, and Gillard returned their greetings with a nod of recognition. The parade continued past them, back to the church. While his assistants disappeared into the sacristy to change clothes and deposit the banner and censer, Gillard stood at the church door, and watched with satisfaction as the crowd began to mill around the stalls. Croiset struck up on an accordion, the food and drink on the tables was uncovered, and soon glasses were being raised high in the air.

"I do congratulate you, Monsieur le Recteur, on reviving this custom," said Madame Zaepffel who had found him again. Before he had time to respond, they were interrupted by one of the officers, a handsome fair-haired man - in his late thirties, guessed Gillard. "Madame, how nice to see you here," he said, smiling at Mme Zaepffel and bowing courteously. "And Father, may I introduce myself? My name is Hermann Kaestner. I have recently arrived at Point-Clos." They raised their glasses. Mme Zaepffel told Hermann she was pleased to see him again, and that he would be most welcome to pay another visit to the Manoir. "In fact, why don't the two of you come for dinner next week? You are both new arrivals in this region, and I feel it is my duty to befriend you both. And besides, my dear René is away again, and I am beginning to feel lonely."

A day was chosen, and Mme Zaepffel disappeared into the crowd. Hermann turned to Gillard. "What an excellent idea to hold such a celebration." Gillard smiled in appreciation. "I imagine what is happening must be very difficult for you," Hermann continued. "No-one wants to be occupied by foreign troops, and none of us want the suffering and privations of war. But what can we do?"

"Get on as best we can." Gillard smiled to indicate he harboured no ill will. "And this is good to see," he said, turning to enjoy the scene around them. "And I do believe the football match is about to start." The crowd was moving over to the field. Hermann and Gillard joined them, and soon there was cheering and shouting as first one side, then the other, seemed to gain the upper hand. Gillard looked at the faces around him - Breton, French, German. They all seemed so carefree, so involved in what they were observing - why on earth did people have to fight each other? The score finished even, and as everyone drifted back to the centre of the village, Croiset began playing again on his accordion.

Gillard was standing in the shade of the church porch, talking with the teacher, Mme Heriot, and her husband, when Hermann interrupted their conversation to tell them that he and his fellow officers were returning to their base. He looked forward to meeting the abbé again soon at the Manoir.

Gillard resumed his conversation with the Heriots, but a few moments later Mme Harel came running towards them looking distraught. "Father, come quickly! Someone has let the air out of the Germans' tyres and they are screaming and shouting at the boys."

As Gillard turned the corner, he saw a small crowd gathered around the cars ahead of him. He could hear one of the officers shouting in French: "You think you can treat us like this? Don't you understand who is in control of your god-forsaken country?"

There was more shouting, and as he came closer he could see that one officer seemed more angry than the others. Gillard understood some German and was alarmed to hear the man saying to his colleagues, "We'll teach these idiots a lesson. I want three of them taken back to the base. We'll decide what to do with them later."

Hermann looked at Gillard, as if appealing for him to intervene. The abbé was surprised at his own calm as he offered a solution: "Gentlemen, perhaps I can help? Have a bowl of cider at the bar, and meanwhile I will make sure your tyres are re-inflated."

"We will not tolerate this kind of behaviour," began the belligerent officer.

"Thank you, Father," said Hermann, taking his colleague by the arm and guiding him towards the bar. "Come on, let's have a drink. We will show them we are beyond pettiness."

Gillard watched Hermann as he opened the door to Harel's, ushering his fellow officers in with a disarming smile. That worked well, thought Gillard, I like that man. And then he called out to the boys to fetch a pump as fast as they could.

CHAPTER TEN

Hermann was blinded for a moment by the sun glancing off the surface of the lake at Paimpont. He was riding fast - probably too fast - along the road to the Manoir on one of the motorbikes from the base. He was hoping to arrive a little early, to get a chance to be with Geneviève alone before the abbé arrived. But as he pulled into the courtyard, he could see that Gillard was already there - his car parked beside the rose bushes. Hermann touched the bonnet. It was still warm.

Once they were seated at the dining table, Father Gillard proposed a toast to friendship. Hermann looked into Geneviève's eyes and thought he caught within them a look of shared intimacy, even of complicity, as if they had both known each other for a long time.

Geneviève had cooked lamb with rosemary, and after they had eaten this, she offered them a selection of cheeses followed by a traditional dish - a Breton flan, made with custard and prunes. He and Gillard complimented her on her cooking - the meal was excellent. She gave an apologetic shrug of the shoulders. "We seem to be surviving reasonably well."

Hermann began collecting the plates, "After such a feast, the least we can do is help to clear the table." He carried them into the kitchen, accidentally brushing against Geneviève as she turned from the dresser. She smiled when he apologized but said nothing. They then moved to the fire-side. Geneviève explained that she was in the habit of lighting a fire most evenings, whatever the season. The walls of the Manoir were so thick, its location so shaded by the forest.

As the flames leapt up, she turned to the abbé. "Perhaps you will forgive me, Father, if I ask a delicate question. I only dare to do this because this evening you have shown yourself to be so open-minded and so conversant with spiritual matters - as you have also proved to be, Captain." They both smiled at her in encouragement. "The question I have, is why Catholic doctrine remains silent on the question of reincarnation - despite the fact that it is espoused by many of the world's most advanced spiritual teachings?"

"Some say that reincarnation was included in the official doctrine of the Church until it was abolished at the Second Ecumenical Council, but they are, I am afraid, mistaken," replied Gillard. "In all my researches I have been unable to find any proof that the church has ever advocated this idea."

"And you, Madame Zaepffel, do you believe in reincarnation? Have you ever had intimations of other lives?" asked Hermann.

Geneviève paused, as if hesitating to reveal an intimate detail of her life, but then, with a sigh, she began, "Many years ago I announced that I had been given my mission in a vision. I told my followers that St Judicaël had come to me and insisted that I dedicate my life to serving the people."

"Yes, I remember reading about this in one of your books," said the abbé. "You described how you had been lifted up out of your body as a young girl whilst you were lying ill in bed. I've always thought of this as a wonderful example of the astral projection the Theosophists explain so clearly."

"Exactly," said Geneviève. "But what I have not told anyone, and must ask you never to repeat to others, is my memory then of having entered the life of Judicaël's sister, Onenne, who is of course the patron saint of the church in Tréhorenteuc." She was silent for a moment. A hush fell in the room. Even the fire seemed to stop crackling. "As my body lay in bed in a fever, I was lifted up in my spirit and seemed to travel back in time to the seventh century. I was a child of the same age, there in the family home, which was also the royal court. My parents were the king and queen. I could see the great fire in the hall, my brothers and sisters were chasing me round and round a long table, and then I rushed outside, darting between the legs of the grown-ups. I could smell the stench of the pigs as I veered towards their sties, but then I slipped, and my brothers and sisters piled on to me. There were so many of them, and of course later I read about the family. I was the youngest of twenty-two. My poor mother! The experience was so vivid, so intense. Suddenly I was being rescued from the pile by the pig-keeper, who shooed the other children away, dusted me down and suggested I take a walk - to calm myself and pick some flowers for my mother.

"And there I was picking bluebells in the woods, as in a dream when all at once one finds oneself in a different location, as if it were the most natural thing in the world to be at one moment here and at another moment there. I lifted up the flowers and breathed in their perfume, and it was as if every part of me was singing 'Hallelujah' to God and all His angels. I was transported in an ecstasy, and although my body was lying in my bed here in the Manoir as a feverish little girl in the early years of the twentieth century, I was in my soul floating in the sky as a child of about the same age in the seventh century, being filled with the glory of Heaven."

"How very beautiful!" said Hermann. "What happened then?"

"I fell into a profound sleep, and from that moment I became less ill. But every night I had the most vivid dreams in which I would wake up but continue to dream, conscious of every detail. The next night, for example, I found myself being introduced by my mother the Queen to an old man, who radiated peace and holiness. 'This is

the hermit Elocan, Onenne. He has come to see you.'
And this was the first time I had been addressed by name
and knew for sure who I was. The old man sat with me
and told me of the wonders of God's creation, and he
sang psalms to me, and I remember that as he left I
wanted to go with him, and cried as the door was closed
behind him, my mother holding me close and consoling
me. I awoke that morning feeling bereft, filled with a
yearning to be with him again that was unbearable. But it
was a yearning for more than him, it was a yearning for
God that he had somehow managed to awaken in me.

"The following night I dreamt that this desire had
become so great that I, as Onenne, crept from my
bedroom late at night, and stole into the darkness,
determined to be united with the old hermit. My mother
had told me that he lived in the forest, somewhere
between the forge and the lake, and so I knew in which
direction to travel. I could see where I was going - the
moon was almost full. Sometimes I was startled by the
sounds of the night - an owl hooting, a fox scurrying
between the trees ahead of me - until at last I came upon
a cottage that I believed was his, and knocked at its door.
For a while no answer came, but in the end I could hear
the bolt being drawn aside, and the door opened to reveal
a woman who was of course astonished to find me, this
ten year old child, anxiously peering up at her. She took
me in, gave me bread and warm milk, and asked me what
on earth I was doing out so late and all on my own. I
couldn't, of course, reveal to her that I was a princess, but

instead spun her a yarn about how I had escaped from a cruel mother and father who would often starve and beat me. My new guardian took pity on me, and on tucking me up in bed, told me that I could help her in her work as a shepherd on the outskirts of the forest. I fell fast asleep in that warm cottage in the woods, only to awaken of course as Geneviève Lefeuvre, in my bed upstairs.

"The next night my dream simply followed on. There I was with the shepherdess, wearing the clothes she had given me, tending her lambs. But I was miserable. Not only had I left my mother and father, and all my brothers and sisters, without a word, for which I felt ashamed and guilty, but I also yearned to be with Elocan, as if he were my true father and my true mother combined. And now, to compound the discomfort of this child's heart, I had lied to this kind shepherdess. At such a tender age I had betrayed those I loved the most. I had no alternative, I felt, than to continue on my quest to find the old hermit."

Hermann sat further back in his chair. He hadn't expected Geneviève's account to last so long, and his mind had begun to wander. How long would it be before they would be making love? He imagined her refusing him, speaking to him in that assured, almost condescending tone, while he simply ignored her words and looked into her eyes, pulling her towards him. Geneviève seemed to have noticed his lapse in concentration. She stared at him with a surprised look, and then continued.

"Once again I found myself stealing out of a home under cover of darkness, compounding my sins by adding to the list of those whose love and trust I had betrayed. I was determined to find the hermit's hut, and walked for hours through the forest. Just before dawn, frozen to the bone, I came upon a dark brooding lake, swathed in mist. I thought I was within reach of Elocan, but just as my heart began to rejoice, a chill ran through me. There ahead of me stood a wolf. The mist arising from the lake, which I now know was the one we call the Fairies' Mirror, half enveloped the creature who bore its teeth at me with a snarl before disappearing into the bracken. I turned and ran, my heart pounding.

"When I reached the head of the lake, I climbed upward, not daring to plunge back into the forest, and soon I was up above the Fairies' Mirror. But I continued onward, past that rock known as Arthur's Seat, and down along the heathland path until I found myself on the outskirts of Tréhorenteuc. I knocked at the door of the manor house, and was welcomed in by a young groom.

"When the lady of the manor descended to discover me in her house, again I felt obliged to lie, and told her the same story of cruelty I had told the shepherdess. Feeling sympathy for me, she offered me board and lodging if I would look after the manor's geese.

"No sooner was I settled, than I sought out the village church, to give thanks to the Mother of God for having saved me from the wolf. And it was there in the old church that I found peace and confessed my sins."

Geneviève paused. She glanced towards Hermann, as if trying to gauge his reaction to her account, before leaning forward in her chair to add another log to the fire.

"You are a gifted story-teller, Madame Zaepffel," said the abbé, who took advantage of this moment to remove his jacket.

"Thank you. But this is no story, you must understand. I have lived through these events - even though I was not in my body." She cleared her throat, and continued. "My next dream was of taking care of the geese, carrying slops out to feed them, and shooing them away whenever they threatened to trample the flower-beds of my mistress. I felt warmly towards my charges despite their dreadful honking, but at a certain moment turned my attention away from them to appreciate the roses which were now in full bloom.

"Looking around to make sure I was not spied upon, I cut five of the most beautiful specimens, and making sure the geese were well occupied, made my way to the church.

"I entered the building, and knelt before the statue of the Blessed Virgin and presented my roses. At that moment once again I could hear all the choirs of heaven singing 'Hallelujah!' and I felt myself rising up off the ground, being filled with such a feeling of ecstasy that it was almost unbearable. And then I saw... And then I saw! An angel was on either side of me, lifting me up, and I could hear their wings beating, and I could feel the light and the love that they possessed radiating from them and pouring into my heart until I felt as if it was breaking open. At that moment, they gently brought me back to rest on the ground and I knelt there weeping, until I heard a sound, only to look up and see that my mistress was standing there by the door, tears running down her cheeks. She ran to me and clasped me to her, and between gasps for breath said, 'But who are you? Who are you my child?' And it was then that I told her that I was the daughter of King Judhaël and Queen Pritelle.

"After this, it was of course impossible for me to remain at the manor, and I was returned to the court amidst much rejoicing. I was forgiven at once, and although it was heart-warming to be reunited again with my family, deep down I was still not happy. I didn't feel at all like a Prodigal Daughter who was back where she belonged. Not at all, I'm afraid."

Geneviève sat back in her chair. Hermann and Gillard remained silent, listening to the voice of the fire, still wrapped in the atmosphere of her tale. After a while, it was she herself who broke the spell. "To this day, I do not know whether this means that I was this young saint in a former life, or whether the experience simply demonstrates how easily one can enter the memory of another's life."

The abbé stood and smiled warmly at Geneviève. "Only Our Lord, of course, can truly know, but thank you for telling us of your experience, dear Madame Zaepffel. I shall leave you now, and must thank you for an excellent evening in excellent company."

As the priest drove away in his ramshackle car, Hermann decided that he too should go, but Geneviève placed her hand on his arm and said, "Don't leave just yet. Let me show you my favourite tree. It's not far. The sky is so clear tonight, and the moon is full. We will easily find our way through the forest."

Hermann knew, simply by this touch on his arm and this invitation that they would soon be lovers.

They entered the wood behind the house and followed a path that led into Brocéliande itself. They walked in silence, Hermann content to follow Geneviève, the soft forest earth rendering their footsteps almost silent as they travelled through the woodland. At one moment there was a rustling in the distance, as if they had surprised a badger or fox.

"Look, my tree is just here," said Geneviève after a while, pointing ahead. Hermann walked forward a few paces to see a great oak standing like a king surrounded by his courtiers - smaller oaks who paid homage by standing back a little, forming a clearing which he and Geneviève now entered as if they were approaching a sacred grove of the druids, or the inner sanctum of a church.

She held up her hand to the oak in greeting, and then walked towards it and touched the trunk fondly. "I come here whenever I am troubled, or need solace or inspiration. He is my dear friend, my counsellor, my sage."

"He is truly magnificent," said Hermann, gazing up into the branches. "But tell me something, Madame Zaepffel, can you really see into the future?"

"Please call me Geneviève, and I shall call you Hermann. I have had the second sight since childhood. Sometimes it is a curse rather than a blessing. Sometimes I am wrong or a destiny changes and my predictions then prove incorrect, but for the most part, it seems that I have been given this power."

"But how does it work? Do you hear a voice in your head telling you these things, or do you see pictures that reveal the future?"

"Both, when it comes to knowing the fate of nations. But I learn the most about an individual's fate from either using the cards or from conversing with their Guardian Angel."

Hermann looked at her in surprise. "Do you really believe such beings exist? I know certain Christian and Islamic mystics believe in Guardian Angels, and Kabbalists too, but…"

"We all have a Guardian Angel, Hermann. Often I see these beautiful spirits standing beside or behind people. But only when I concentrate and I am in the right frame of mind. That is why I offer individual consultations, so that I can prepare myself to see them and receive their messages."

Hermann took a step towards Geneviève. "Can you see my angel? Will it tell you what will happen in my life?"

"I have not really concentrated on you, Hermann. It makes me afraid."

"Good heavens, why?"

Geneviève moved a little to one side, and all at once she was caught in a spotlight of silver, a shaft of moonlight illuminating her hair from behind. "Can you not feel what is happening between us?"

"Yes, of course." Hermann started to take another step towards her, but she held up her hand to stop him.

"Let me try to see your angel," she said, moving back and leaning against the oak. "Move over there, so the moonlight is behind you."

Hermann moved, and then stood still and looked directly at her. "Come closer," she said, half closing her eyes. "Ah yes! I see your Guardian Angel now. He places a hand on your shoulder. His wings - beautiful tall, golden wings - stretch out and around you. He loves you very much."

Hermann felt a gentle breeze from behind - so gentle he surely imagined it. "I can believe that energies flow to us from the moon and sun and stars. I have studied astrology. But I am not sure I can believe in angels."

"Your angel laughs and says one day you will believe in his existence." Geneviève opened her eyes fully and blinked, as if she was returning to the everyday world from far away. "Come closer." Hermann stepped forward. He looked into her eyes, and lowered his lips towards hers. They kissed, gently and slowly, and then he took her in his arms and held her close. For a long time they stood there, holding each other in the moonlight, without a word passing between them. He tried to think but he couldn't. All he could do was surrender himself to the moment. Eventually it was Geneviève who broke the spell of silence. "Common sense tells me this is madness, but I cannot deny the life of my soul. Our destinies are entwined. You know that." They looked into each others' eyes, transfixed for a moment, before turning back, Geneviève leading the way. When they reached the Manoir, they stood on the gravel beside the lawn, holding each other close. "Go now," whispered Geneviève eventually.

A few days later Hermann rode over to the rectory at Tréhorenteuc. He had enjoyed talking with the priest that evening at the Manoir, and had been excited to discover that he was well versed in more than simply church doctrine. He appeared to know a great deal about astrology and numerology, and seemed keen to discuss these subjects with him.

Gillard suggested they take a walk to the lake that Geneviève had described in her dream, the Fairies' Mirror. It was a mild afternoon, the sun's full strength deflected by a scattering of light cloud. He led Hermann up to the high point above the village. "You see how Trého lies just at the edge of the forest? Because of the topography, when you're in the village you don't realize how close it is. And over there, to the southwest," he said, pointing, "lies the coast and the Gulf of Morbihan."

Dropping down a little through the gorse and juniper, they came to a plateau of grooved slopes of granite schist lying above the lake. A natural bench had been formed out of stone that looked out across the forest. "Here is Arthur's seat. Let's sit here and I'll tell you about this spot."

They sat in silence for a while. Gillard closed his eyes, and it seemed to Hermann as if he was doing this not because he was tired, but because he wanted to feel his way into the landscape and its story. "As you know, the whole of this region is steeped in prehistoric monuments," he began, his eyes still closed. "Back in those days, thousands of years ago, the avenues of standing stones by the sea at Carnac were raised, and the great mound of Gavrinis was not marooned on an island in the gulf, but lay on a wide and fertile plain."

Hermann allowed himself to travel back in his imagination, following Gillard's voice. "And not far to the north of Morbihan, we come to the forest of Brocéliande, which at that time was far larger than it is now. And here in this forest, on the high points, the old ones buried their dead in great cairns."

Gillard now opened his eyes and looked directly at Hermann, and as he did so, his voice changed from that of a storyteller guiding his listener on a journey, to a more conversational tone: "And there too I suspect they buried their powers, their magic in some way. Who knows? Perhaps they charged stones with incantations and buried them deep in the earth. Perhaps they stood in circles on the high points, around their dead, and chanted to the gods to protect them forever, to enchant the forest so that no-one would desecrate their holy places. Whatever they did, the enchantment remained... Can you feel it?"

To many people, thought Hermann, that question would seem strange, but he and Gillard were birds of the same feather and somehow they both already knew this. "Sitting here I feel as if time no longer exists," he replied. "It reminds me of the area around Externsteine in the centre of Germany. But why Arthur's seat? King Arthur?"

"Yes, precisely. You see when the Britons fled the Anglo-Saxon invaders and later the Normans, many of them sailed in their boats from Cornwall to Brittany, which is why a part of this region is called Cornouaille. These Britons brought with them not only their monks and saints, but also their old stories. The country around here became soaked in the legends of King Arthur and his knights, and the search for the Holy Grail."

"In Germany we love those stories too. You know Wagner's Parsifal, I suppose?"

"Of course I do! In a while I will take you down to Klingsor's palace, or at least that is how I like to see the valley below."

They sat in silence once more, and then, as a flock of birds flew below them along the valley from east to west, Gillard spoke again: "It must be wonderful to fly in a plane."

"It is. I joined the Luftwaffe because I love flying. There is a freedom you feel up in the sky…"

"That you have never felt on Earth?"

"Well, that is not quite true. I used to feel it sometimes with my Wandervögel friends, when we took off into the countryside and slept out under the stars and swam in the rivers and lakes. Then I felt free."

"Ah, I have heard of this movement, the wandering birds - young people walking the countryside in groups singing the old songs and shaking off convention. It sounds magnificent."

"Sadly it was all closed down when Hitler rose to power. Although…" Hermann leaned towards Gillard with a conspiratorial smile, "…there are some who defy the ban and still roam the countryside - they call it 'wild hiking' - no-one's going to stop them feeling free."

"I would imagine no-one's going to stop you feeling free either."

Hermann smiled and nodded. "I think you're right. I blame my father. Freedom is his highest value - he was a Wandervögel in his youth, and is keen on all those life reform movements: people trying to improve housing and education, campaigning for clothing reform, agricultural reform and so on."

Gillard took a pouch of tobacco from his pocket, rolled two cigarettes and handed one to Hermann. As they sat together smoking and admiring the view, Hermann's mind went back to the early days of his training in the Luftwaffe. He remembered crossing the courtyard at Oberschleissheim and entering the flight office.

"Anyone going up?"

A senior pilot, Arend, looked up from one of the desks and said "Want to practice diving?"

"Sure."

Within minutes they were seated in the Stuka, Hermann as pilot, Arend behind him in the rear gunner's seat. "The trick with diving is to hold your nerve, as you know." Arend shouted through his mike, above the noise of the engine. "Remember that even if you black out, you'll only go out for three seconds at the most - by which time you'll be up and away and out of trouble."

As the Stuka raced down the run-way, Arend shouted again: "Take her up to 4,000 metres." The control tower cleared them to fly north-east. It was a fine day, the sunlight glancing off the snow-capped Alps in the distance, and by the time the plane had reached its cruising altitude they were high above the Isar. Hermann looked down on the meadows that flanked the river.

"OK. Time to go!" shouted Arend.

Hermann eased the drive lever forward, set the trim flaps, closed the coolant traps, pulled back the throttle, and the plane obediently rolled and tipped into a 60 degree dive that sent them hurtling downward.

The Jericho trumpets mounted on the wings started their scream. They had no practical function - they were there just to terrify those on the ground, but for the pilots it added to the thrill. Hermann knew the automatic dive recovery system would kick in at 450 metres, but what if it didn't? He looked down and saw a group of boys - there must have been about five of them - running along  the river bank. And then the dive bottomed out and the aircraft was soaring upward and he could feel himself being pressed into his seat by the G force. Then there was grey, then stars.

He must have blacked out for only a second or two. "Shit!" he shouted over the radio -- "Look what I found the other day," said Gillard, interrupting Hermann's reverie, as he took out of his pocket a small sculptured figure in bronze of a naked woman, her hands raised in supplication or blessing. "It is clearly Gallo-Roman. She must be Venus."

Gillard placed the figure in Hermann's hands, and he turned it over, marveling at how well it seemed to have survived the passage of time. "Where did you find it?"

"Just beyond the well, digging in the rectory field - my half-hearted attempt at agriculture."

"Well, they have found the Venus of Willendorf in Austria. This can be the Venus of Tréhorenteuc. Are you going to hand it over to a museum or a university?"

"After the war is over," said Gillard. "In the meanwhile I shall hide it somewhere to keep her safe."

"What a good idea. But perhaps you should tell someone where it is hidden. You remember the story of St James's bones in Compostella. They hid them because they thought that English marauder Francis Drake might steal the relic when he attacked Cadiz."

"Exactly! And then whoever did this died and the bones were lost for centuries. You're right. I'll tell you, Hermann, where I bury it."

Hermann knew at once what had happened - that in saying this, Gillard had voiced his trust in someone he scarcely knew. He felt privileged to be trusted by such a good man.

He returned the statue to Gillard with a smile. They both stood up and then began to follow the path that dropped down through the gorse towards the Fairies' Mirror.

Once they reached the lake-side, Gillard turned to Hermann. "We have come now to the Valley of No Return of the Arthurian tales - or the Valley of the False Lovers, as it is also called. According to legend, the wicked sorceress Morgan created this spot. She lured any knight who so much as harboured a thought of infidelity into this valley of hers, promising every kind of earthly pleasure. Once they had passed those trees over there, they found themselves trapped and were unable to escape. This valley is, in other words, a prison for those who betray the ones they love."

"What a beautiful prison," said Hermann, looking around him. The surface of the lake was indeed like a mirror, dark and still. Birch, juniper and beech trees grew alongside the water and clung to the rocks on either side of the valley. He thought of his desire for Geneviève. He had been told to get close, but no-one had ordered him to fall in love with her. He leaned over, and peered into the water. He could just make out his face reflected back at him, but it seemed dark and troubled.

CHAPTER ELEVEN

That night, Hermann was supposed to be writing his report to Krause in Berlin. But he couldn't get Geneviève out of his mind. There was something utterly fascinating about her - about her confidence, the way she believed so surely in her powers, the clarity in her gaze as she looked at him, the way she had kissed him, with shyness at first but then with passion.

The next morning he kept their appointment promptly. Great masses of grey and white cloud piled on top of each other to create the illusion that the forest was surrounded by mountain ranges, and through this newly enchanted landscape he flew along the road on his motorbike towards the Manoir. They kissed at the door, and Geneviève led him into the sitting room. She gestured to the circular table that stood to one side of the staircase. He sat facing her. "I am so pleased you have come. I shall use the cards of Madame Lenormand."

Hermann knew that divination could sometimes yield uncanny insights, particularly when using the Tarot. Geneviève began to shuffle the cards, then handed him the deck. "Hold this now to your forehead. Ask any question you like, silently in your mind, shuffle the deck, and then return it to me." Taking the cards from Hermann, she proceeded to lay them out in four rows of three cards each, face downwards.

"This first row tells us about affairs of the heart." She turned over the first card. "Here you have the number six: a cloudy sky. This tells me your love life has been troubled in the past. It has not brought you much happiness."

"This is true," said Hermann, looking briefly at the card before returning his gaze towards Geneviève.

"And here, in second position, is number nine: a bouquet of roses. The card in this position in the spread tells me about your current situation." She looked up and directly into Hermann's eyes with a strange broken smile, as if she could not quite bring herself to feel happiness. "You are in love."

Hermann nodded and started to open his mouth, but closed it again and swallowed.

"The third card, in the position of the future, is the stork in his nest." She paused, gazing at the card with a fixed expression. "But the card is upside down. This means your love will not bear fruit." There was an awkward silence. They both stared at the card. "If the card was upright it would signal birth, something new.

But reversed, I'm afraid it means the stork falls from his nest. There is no future for this love of yours." She abruptly stood up, and walked to the window, standing utterly still, her back to Hermann.

He waited a few moments, and then walked over to her. He wanted to turn her round and pull her close to him, but he held back.

She began speaking in a strained voice, as if on the verge of tears. "I'm afraid I cannot continue. This has never happened to me before. I have always finished a reading, but I cannot go on." She turned around to face him, but stepped back. "It is wrong," she simply said.

"The card reading?"

"No. What is happening between us is wrong. All that I said to you in the forest. I am a married woman, you must understand. I cannot allow my feelings for you, or yours for me, destroy our lives." She touched his lips with one finger. "Say nothing. Just go now." She walked to the door that led out into the garden, which was also used as the main entrance to the house. She held it open.

Hermann walked towards the door until he faced her. He paused, then bowed to her in a stiff, formal way and immediately left.

On his way back to Point-Clos, he pulled off the road, to give himself time to think. He wasn't going to let a card reading get in the way of his feelings, or his work. He was irresistibly drawn to Geneviève, he was starting to fall in love with her - whatever that might mean - and he wanted to find out who she truly was, whether her psychic powers were genuine, whether she was indeed one of the greatest seers of all time, as her followers clearly thought, or whether she was just fooling people to make herself feel important. But he knew, as he sat there on his bike, that above all he wanted to surprise her one day and break through her reserve - to hold her close to him, and to make love to her.

The next morning he woke early, and as soon as he was dressed, went straight to the flight office to ask for clearance to fly over the Manoir, and then, as the morning sun began to burn the mist from the trees, he walked over to his plane, disengaged the Jericho trumpets, and climbed into the cockpit. He knew that Geneviève was alone in the house. He would show her how much he felt for her.

Wheeling over the aerodrome, he waved to his friends taking their early morning dip in one of the swimming pools, and within minutes, he was there - the slate grey of the Manoir's roof catching the sunlight as he dropped towards it.

First he swooped low and sped straight over the lawn out towards the horizon. When he reached the fields he turned the plane over, flying upside down towards the house, and then - just as he could see the shutters of her bedroom window opening - he flipped the plane upward, soaring high in the air before dipping down again towards the fields that lay beyond the lawn, to fly one loop and then another in the sky in front of her.

He was jumping for joy in the sky - the happiest man in the world. He steadied the Stuka now, and flew slowly and directly towards the house so he could see her standing at the window. He skimmed the roof, turned the aircraft around again towards the fields, and performed a perfect barrel roll, laughing out loud as he dived and soared like a dolphin playing in the ocean. Finally, he flew back towards Geneviève, waved at her, and then disappeared once more over the roof of the house as he headed towards Point-Clos.

One day he would figure out how to fly a double loop that would leave a vapour trail looking like a white heart drifting in the clear sky. He just needed the right conditions and more practice. The cards were wrong. In the world of Spirit, they were as free as birds on the wing. Their love would last forever.

CHAPTER TWELVE

By August the abbé had been installed in the parish for six months. During this time his thoughts had been preoccupied with the renovations needed for the church and the rectory. Then one morning, as he was inspecting his vegetable patch, an idea came to him that struck him as being so obviously splendid, he immediately ran across the street into Mme Harel's bar and announced it to her as if it was already decided: "We are going to turn the rectory into a cinema!"

"Has the abbé gone mad?" was Mme Harel's immediate response. "Have a strong black tea and come to your senses, Father."

He hadn't gone mad - it was one of the best ideas he'd ever had. Even the cantankerous old Hervé, already on his first drink of the day, who opposed everything as a matter of principle, was forced to concede it was a masterful plan.

"When I was thirteen," Gillard told them, "my father took me to Rennes to see 'L'Affaire d'Orcival'. It was my first visit to the cinema. I will never forget the magic of that night. A week later my father was dead - killed in a riding accident, just at the outbreak of war." He stopped for a moment. It was unlike him to talk about his childhood. He drained the cup of tea Mme Harel handed him, and looking over to Hervé, continued, "A film opens our horizons, brings wonder into our lives. It'll be just what we need to keep up our spirits."

Two weeks later a couple of the young men from the village hacked away at the thick stone wall of the rectory to run a cable bringing electricity to the building. Gillard persuaded them to also create an opening between the main room and the kitchen, wide enough for a projector's beam. He then made the journey to Vannes to buy the equipment. He had recently inherited his godmother's estate and not only could he afford this, he could now pay for much of the restoration of the church and rectory with his own money, but he wouldn't tell anyone that. He would risk the sin of omission and apply to the Bishop to fund the works, while quietly supplementing any funds he received with his own.

On his return from Vannes he asked Mme Harel for the whitest sheet she could find to be hung at the end of the room, and over a dozen villagers stood in the dark, watching over and over again the test film supplied with the projector.

Gillard watched as they stared eyes-wide at the screen, delight on their faces. 'Here,' he thought, 'in a forgotten corner of Brittany, on the edge of the great forest, almost at the end of the world, we are about to change the life of this sleepy old village forever.'

A bureau on the Avenue Ulm in Paris rented films at a reasonable price, and after only a week of anticipation, the first film arrived, in two great reels carefully packaged in a cardboard box wrapped in brown paper. War might be raging across Europe, but a small parish in the back of beyond could still receive its parcels in good time.

He designed a poster…

THE ACROBAT

We proudly announce the inauguration of the village cinema with the showing of Jean Boyer's famous film 'The Acrobat'.
The Rectory 8pm Saturday 15th August
Admission 20 centimes. Children free.

On the Saturday it was all hands on deck. Every single chair from Harel's was carried across the road to the rectory. The bar had extra chairs in storage, which they used on those few occasions there was a wedding or christening, and these were brought over too. That evening virtually the whole village was present: the children sitting on the floor, their noses almost touching the sheet. Every chair was occupied, and small groups of three or four people were squeezed into the window bays.

Just as Gillard began working his way towards the screen, to formally welcome everyone and announce the film, Madame Zaepffel with her husband René entered the room. "Monsieur le Recteur, I do hope you don't mind us arriving without tickets. We only heard the news yesterday and simply couldn't keep away. I don't believe you have ever met my husband - he is away so often."

"I am sure we can squeeze in another two," said Gillard, greeting the couple and soon finding two extra chairs. He was then obliged to clap loudly to attract everyone's attention. He announced the film and extinguished the lights. The beam shot across the room and the magic began.

When the film came to an end, the cheers were deafening. He had been right - it was one of his best ideas. As Monsieur and Madame Zaepffel left, he shook their hands warmly. "I have some good news to share with you. I have designed a new window for the church. A master of stained glass has been working on it in Vannes. We will be installing it next week - you must come and see it."

Gillard enjoyed company. What could be more pleasing than such an evening - the whole village gathered in his rectory - or time spent in Harel's bar surrounded by friends, cider flowing, no shortage of tobacco or jokes? And what could be more fulfilling than ministering to those who were in need: the anguished, the dying, those whose faith hung by a thread? And yet he craved solitude too. And he found it, not by praying alone in the rectory or in the church, but by walking out on the hills or in the forest, and by taking his battered old bicycle out into the countryside - exploring the region, discovering wayside crosses, forgotten holy wells and standing stones, heathland or woodland seemingly untouched by the passage of time.

It was on one such excursion that he discovered a source of building materials for the renovations he planned for his church. On clear days, from Arthur' seat high up above the Fairies' Mirror, he had noticed a range of red cliffs on the far horizon. One weekday morning, on waking to discover a basket of food left by Geneviève beside the rectory door, he decided to explore these cliffs. He added a bottle of wine to the bread and cheese in the basket, and set off along the road heading north.

At the top of the hill he stopped to survey the panorama of dark green forest, touched with a strip of reddish-brown revealing the ridge beyond. Realizing the pre-historic site known as the Monks' Garden was just behind him, he dismounted and walked over to where it lay beyond the bracken a few metres from the road. Quite why this cluster of stones arranged in a long rectangle - all that remained of an ancient long barrow - was called the Monks' Garden he didn't know. Perhaps monks really had grown herbs and vegetables within the boundary of the stones, but more likely it felt safer to refer to such a place in Christian terms. 'We should call it the Druids' Garden', he mused to himself as he rolled a cigarette sitting on one of the largest rocks. 'One day I should measure these stones and this rectangle. Perhaps the Divine Proportion is hidden within them - after all, weren't the masons who built the great Gothic cathedrals the inheritors of such secrets from the druids?'

Taking to the road once more, he found that it meandered through the forest, dropping down for a while before climbing up again, until the tree-cover thinned and he found himself cycling across a great swathe of heathland with views in every direction.

An hour later, as he approached the ridge, he decided to turn off the road to follow a well-worn track that ran straight towards the cliffs. This, he soon discovered, led directly to a quarry where two men, their rough clothes covered in red dust, sat eating sandwiches in front of a hut. After the usual greetings, Gillard took out his bottle of wine. The men found mugs while he laid out his supplies.

He asked them if they would show him how they worked. Several cigarettes and a finished bottle later, they moved somewhat slowly towards the cliffs and he watched with fascination as they prised a great chunk of red shale from the quarry face. They split this into smaller blocks, and then with surprising speed - or so Gillard thought - they chipped away at one of these to produce a piece of stone of exactly the size he would need for his church.

One of them handed Gillard his mallet and chisel, inviting him to fashion a building block out of one of the rough chunks that lay at their feet. He needed help - it was harder than it looked, but there was something deeply satisfying about this activity, something primordial. And he thought of the way the freemasons saw this work as 'perfecting the ashlar' - a metaphor they used for refining character and soul.

Before beginning the long ride home he discussed costs with the men, and asked if he could return, joking that one day he would throw in the towel as a priest and join them for good in their quarry beside the forest.

CHAPTER THIRTEEN

Over a hundred military gliders were kept at the base, and Hermann enjoyed his work of training the pilots in advanced techniques. But despite the large number of planes and officers stationed at Point-Clos, surprisingly few combat missions were being flown. The coastal bases were considered adequate for dealing with the allied incursions, and the resources at Point-Clos were being held in reserve. Hermann had time on his hands, and as often as he could, he practiced aerobatics in a Stuka. To get a good vapour trail he needed a cold and moist atmosphere. It was often damp in Brittany, but it wasn't yet cold enough. He would have to wait till the Autumn or Winter, but in the meanwhile he could at least perfect the manoeuvre.

He wanted to see Geneviève. He thought about her every day. And he needed to send a detailed report to Krause that offered more than the initial overview he had already provided. When he next called at the Manoir,

Geneviève told him that René had just left. She appeared more distant and would only let him stay for a short while. He called again the following day, and this time she seemed to lose her reserve. They took tea outside, and talked about their childhoods and memories of summer holidays. On parting, she allowed him to kiss her on the lips, and for a moment she surrendered to him before turning away.

He told her he would like to dine with her at the weekend, and it was on that August evening, before they had even begun to eat, that he drew her close to him and began stroking her neck with the tips of his fingers, making her shudder with delight. "How can love between two people ever be wrong?"

She stepped back from him. "You forget I am married, Captain."

Hermann gazed at her, not knowing what to say, admiring her resolve, excited by the knowledge that hidden beneath her rejection lay a secret longing for him.

It took several more visits before she capitulated. One evening, when the weather seemed unnaturally warm and close, she finally gave in to his attempts to make love to her. Neither of them felt hungry, and so they decided to take a blanket and a basket with just wine and glasses out on to the lawn. As Venus appeared in the darkening sky, Hermann told her that he wanted to undress her, and then he simply leant forward and began to kiss her tenderly, until - as he could feel her body arching towards him - he moved one hand towards the buttons of her blouse. This time she offered no resistance, and he began to remove her clothes slowly, stopping every few moments to smile and look into her eyes, kissing her again before continuing in his quest to discover more of her body, until at last she lay naked beneath the stars. He stood and began to unbutton his shirt, saying, "What if someone sees us?"

"You should have asked that before you started, Hermann. They won't. Nobody can see us here." She sat up and began removing his belt and pulling at his trousers. She stood, and they held each other in the moonlight, at first without moving, and then as if possessed, searching out every part of each other's body with their lips and hands, until they finally fell on to the blanket.

When they had finished making love, and Geneviève was lying back, looking up at the night sky, Hermann took his glass of wine, and slowly tipped a little over her breasts. He smiled at her, kissed her, and then whispered softly into her ear, "And now I shall have to drink every drop of this."

From that moment, every barrier of inhibition or separation between them seemed to vanish. René had been posted to St Nazaire and was not due back for weeks, possibly months. Inland there was little evidence that a war was going on, but on the coast the allies had begun bombing ports and factories, and engineers were needed more than ever now, as fortifications were enhanced and bridges rebuilt after attacks. Hermann decided to take full advantage of René's absence, and he began to call at the Manoir whenever he could get away from the base.

They made love almost every time they met, and he was both surprised and delighted at the way in which Geneviève's sensual appetite seemed as demanding as his own. Although he was starting to feel that he loved her more than he had loved any other woman, he was also acutely aware of the fact that he was observing her on behalf of the Ahnenerbe, trying to find out as much as he could about her. He sometimes wondered how he could feel so comfortable looking openly into the eyes of someone he was deceiving. Love must surely exist in a realm beyond truth and falsehood.

Every so often René would return on leave for a short while, and at first Hermann tried visiting, simply as one of a number of officers from the base who consulted the Druidess of Brocéliande. Several times he was invited to dine, but it made him feel ill at ease, and he told Geneviève not to invite him any more.

When René was away, and he could stay at the Manoir in the evenings, he would sit by the hearth and read his favourite poets out loud, or ask Geneviève to tell him about her prophecies and experiences of clairvoyance. He would make mental notes of these and write them down as soon as he returned to the base, but more often than not, he would find her predictions recounted in the pages of the bulletins she had let him borrow.

In the evenings when he remained at Point-Clos, Hermann played cards with his fellow pilots in the mess and drank at the bar, or he excused himself and read alone on his bunk, or sat in the office Ernst allowed him to use, writing letters to his parents or Milly, or typing out his reports to Krause, assuring him he was not failing in his duty, and that he was alert to any new prediction the Druidess of Brocéliande might make.

In early September, as they ate together in the dining room, Hermann asked Geneviève if she would like to attend Mass with him in Tréhorenteuc. He wanted to see the new window that had been installed in the church, and he also wanted to see Gillard again. Although he was not a Catholic, and hardly a Christian in the conventional sense, he occasionally felt a yearning to sit quietly in a service, trying to sense the Divine, even though his attempts were usually unsuccessful, and he found himself instead picking holes in the sermon or reacting against the doctrines expressed in the bible readings.

"No Hermann, I won't come. There is already gossip about horizontal collaboration, as they call it. People are talking. They've seen you here I'm afraid. But it's not just you - people resent the fact that I entertain officers here." She looked defiantly at him. "I'm not concerned - I know how to defend myself. The Manoir is surrounded by light. Even so, I have no wish to be humiliated by smirking faces. You go without me."

So Hermann attended Mass alone that Sunday, even though members of the German armed forces were not allowed to attend church services in occupied territory. He was on a mission for the SS, he reasoned, and no-one of importance would find out or even care.

He had looked inside the church before, on the day of the fête, but hadn't found it particularly interesting: the usual run-down affair with  dull windows and a few painted wooden statues. Now, as he walked in that Sunday morning, he noticed a difference. The tomb that had taken up so much room

 had completely vanished, and as he moved to the back of the church to sit discreetly behind the congregation, he saw - on an old oak cross-beam near the font - a number painted in gold: 1.618. And there, on the southern wall, was the new window, which depicted a scene from Chrètien de Troyes' account of the Holy Grail appearing before the knights of the Round Table, providing each knight with whatever food he desired.

As he sat through the service, he tried to behave as respectfully as he could - standing and kneeling with the congregation, although he decided it would be wrong to take communion as if he were a Catholic.

He was the last to leave, and Gillard, waiting for him at the porch, invited him to the rectory. As the abbé poured a glass of wine for each of them, Hermann asked about the significance of the number painted on the beam.

"It is the Golden Mean, Hermann - the key to Divine proportion and harmony. I am gradually rebuilding the church and as I do so, I ensure that every measurement possible conforms to this ratio."

"Of course, Leonardo's Divine Man. It's a proportion found in the human body, and in all of nature, isn't it?"

"Exactly. And since a church is a representation of the body of God, of Christ, it should show the same proportions."

"The old cathedral masons knew this secret, I believe."

"They certainly did, and I see no reason why even the humblest chapel should not follow this principle. I intend to make my church a temple of the Holy Grail, built upon this Divine Proportion, and filled with images that reflect the sacredness of that legend, and its connection to our landscape and our local heritage."

As Gillard spoke these words, Hermann was back at his final briefing with Krause in Berlin. After speaking to him about Paris, the Obersturmbannführer had begun telling him enthusiastically about Reichsführer Himmler's plans for a new headquarters for the SS and the Ahnenerbe. It was to be created in a castle in Westphalia. At its heart would be a grail sanctuary...

Krause had picked up his pipe. Clouds of smoke rose into the air, caught in a beam of sunlight that ran between them, as if the angels themselves were trying to separate Hermann from this man who was about to change his destiny forever.

"You might wonder why we have chosen this spot - Wewelsburg - so far away from Berlin. Our reasoning is clear, Captain. Remember the old story: the Battle of the Birch Tree?"

"Ah yes, but I can't remember the details."

"The legend is based upon an old prophecy that the hordes from the East, who attacked Europe under Gengis Khan, will attack us again. And it is at Wewelsburg in Westphalia that the Battle of the Birch Tree will be fought - the final decisive battle that will lead us to triumph over all the world. In searching for this spot, predicted by the legend, we discovered that Wewelsburg is aligned with Externsteine and some of the most powerful energy lines that run across the land. Wilhelm Teudt helped us with these calculations before the Reichsführer decided to break his links with that inspired but - how shall I put it? - flawed man."

"Do you know?" continued Krause, looking at Hermann warmly as if they were by now the best of friends, "The Reichsführer once confided in me that he wished the Englishman Alfred Watkins could replace Teudt. After all, he had also discovered the existence of ley lines, as he called them, and was undoubtedly less infuriating  than Teudt." Laughing at his own anecdote, Krause then showed Hermann a photograph of the castle. "Notice its unique shape. Teudt's calculations reveal that the north tower is the Omphalos - the exact centre of the world: the new world of the Reich. It is the tip of the Spear of Destiny - the sharpest of points! Look how the triangular footprint of the castle makes this clear. We shall add a shaft to this blade of the spear - a long rectangular building that will house the most senior officers. The castle itself will remain an inner sanctum, accessible only to the SS generals and their guests. A grail room will be set aside for meditation and study. Nearby we shall build the SS Reich Leaders' School, with barracks and munition stores built around inner courtyards in a wide fan that overlooks the valley."

Krause looked up from the photograph to gaze directly into Hermann's eyes. As if to drive his message directly into his heart, he leaned forward and tapped Hermann's chest several times with his forefinger as he said, "You are a lucky man, Hermann. One day you will be standing in Wewelsburg, proud that you are a member of the SS." ...

"What else do you envisage for your church?" Hermann asked Gillard, realizing he would have to tell Krause about the project.

"I want to make it into a building which, in every detail, evokes the power and the mystery of Christ's grail. You see the way the chalice is coloured green in the new window? That conveys the idea given in the old stories that the grail was originally an emerald worn by Lucifer, before he disobeyed God and the emerald was loosed from his crown and fell to Earth. There it was picked up by Adam and Eve and passed on, from generation to generation, until it came into the hands of Joseph of Arimathea, the uncle of Jesus. And it was in this emerald, carved into a chalice, that Joseph gathered the blood of Jesus before laying him in his tomb. I want to replace the eastern window with an image of this emerald-green grail at the centre - worshipped as the living symbol of our Lord and his blood that was shed for us all. And I want paintings depicting the legend hanging on the walls, and even a series of pictures for the Stations of the Cross that lead towards this revelation in the east."

"What a splendid idea! Let me raise a toast to your project." Hermann lifted his glass. "To the grail chapel!" He felt so close to Gillard and to Geneviève, whom he imagined now, sitting in her study, thinking of him perhaps, talking to angels. What harm could come from telling his superiors of the activities of two friends whose interests were purely benign? How could Geneviève's desire for world peace and Gillard's plan to create a grail chapel ever be used for ill?

CHAPTER FOURTEEN

Autumn was a good time to write. As the nights started to grow longer, and the trees began to shed their leaves, it was easier to spend time indoors, to resist the attractions that summer always seemed to bring. Geneviève should have been concentrating on the book she was supposed to be writing, but she wasn't. She couldn't. She kept remembering the times she had made love to Hermann. It was as if she was building a collection of the most exquisite films in which every detail of their exchanges were recorded. The little jokes, every caress, the loss of control as they reached the heights of ecstasy. The sound of him crying out, which thrilled her, because she knew she had caused this with the way she had moved her body. His smell, the way his muscles tautened as he thrust into her. It was all so delicious she could hardly bring herself to sit at the typewriter. And she loved the way he kissed her too, and spent time talking to her as he stroked her stomach or fluttered his hands over her breasts. He was considerate in ways that René had once been.

Dear René, what was she to do? She must trust her guides, trust her intuition. God moves in mysterious ways after all, and who was she to disobey her Guardian Angel? There was a divine law in place, it seemed, that ensured no seer could truly know their own future. She remembered the life of Madame Lenormand, whose cards she used. She had accurately predicted the fate of Napoleon and his Empress Josephine, but was taken completely by surprise when she was imprisoned herself in the Bastille.

Would she end up living in Germany with Hermann? Would René perhaps die tragically, and after a suitable time of mourning, would she marry Hermann and continue to live in the Manoir? Could they all perhaps live together in an 'arrangement' - a ménage-à-trois? After all, others had done this. But this was all madness. She couldn't bear to think about it. In fact, she wouldn't think about it.

She took a deep breath, left her desk and went downstairs to make herself tea. Back in her room she began to apply herself. She would call her book '1943 - Year of Hope' - that was a good title, people needed something to cling on to in these dark times. Its subtitle would be 'Prophecies 1937 to 1946'. René could summarize her prophecies for the years 1937 to 1941, and this could form the bulk of the book. All she really had to do was write an introduction that would galvanize people's interest, and then write some closing words which would offer hope and comfort. But there was also the matter of her giving prophecies for the years to come - up until 1946. Perhaps she should attempt to write these in quatrains like Nostradamus?

Whatever she wrote, she would have to get a license to have the book printed. Paper was hard to obtain, but it was possible. Books were still being produced, and René was so good at arranging these things. It would be her most successful book ever, of that she was sure.

She began typing. The most obvious point first... obvious to her, but clearly not to most of her countrymen. We have a clear choice between doing good or ill, between obeying the voice of the Spirit or succumbing to materialism. The choice is quite simply between faith or death. If people really want to go on fulfilling the demands of their selfish little selves, their egos, rather than opening to the spiritual world, then only death can liberate them. But the way of faith, of the Spirit, is open to all. She has, after all, dedicated her life to showing people this way. But how many have really listened? They are enmeshed in their desires, their obsession with material goods and comforts. People must wake up and listen or it will be too late.

There, that took hardly any time at all. Only a few pages were needed to make these points. She often marvelled at the way, once she was settled, the words would flow through her, whether through her hands at the typewriter, or through her mouth when addressing thousands. Of one thing she was sure, the Spirit really did move in her. Her destiny was clear. She had a mission to fulfill.

And now to the second chapter. She would start by showing people in general terms how the prophecies she had made in the past came to be fulfilled. René's summaries would then follow. She closed her eyes, and prayed for guidance, for an image that would open the gates for the words to flow. And there she was, standing on the stage at the Salle Pleyel in December 1938. Seated in the audience, just a few metres from her in the front row, was the son of the Prime Minister and a member of the British royal family. She mustn't mention his name in the book. She remembered entering the trance and there before her was a frightful scene. A dark slick of tangled and tattered flags lay upon a sea of bodies. These bodies were alive, inhabited by the ghosts of men who had died fighting for their country. In great masses they heaved and moaned as they tried to raise their standards, but each time they tried, their flag was pulled down by another horde of spectres. But then a mist appeared, and there was just brightness, and then she saw only one flag - the tricolore, whose stripes faded as a swastika appeared at its centre, sewn in red, white and blue by an invisible hand. The way of conflict was sheer folly, only bloodshed and untold suffering would result. There must be peace between the two nations of Germany and France. She could see now the map of Europe being re-arranged, borders were changing, dissolving. Together, for the good of all humanity, our two nations will bring the United States of Europe to birth. There will be a new flag, the old money will be swept away and there will be just one currency used throughout Europe. She could see a coin now, like a great sun, the goddess Europa gazing triumphantly from it.

More images came: men of many nations fighting in Spain, coloured people from lands unknown to her, deserting their homelands and coming to Europe, a long revolution sown by racial hatred dissolving the United States...

The sound of an engine in the distance interrupted her writing. A tractor perhaps, but the harvest was over. It was coming closer now. Oh, but of course! She rushed from the room, down the stairs, and flung open the doors to the garden, just in time to see the belly of Hermann's plane flying directly over the roof.

She ran across the gravel and out on to the lawn. She wished he wouldn't do this, it was so frightening, but so thrilling at the same time. She hated it when he dived. He always began by soaring upwards, higher and higher until she could hardly see him as she shielded her eyes from the brightness of the sky, and then he would suddenly pitch his plane forward and come rushing directly down as if he were heading straight for the earth. She had asked him what would happen if he couldn't stop the descent.

"Don't worry, my darling. It's all automatic. Even if I black out, the plane will carry me back up in the air to safety. The technology is fool-proof - it's been tested thousands of times." He kissed her. "You have no idea how wonderful it feels to be up there, playing about in the sky - it's like dancing in the open air, but on the grandest scale. One day I will take you up and you will see." He spread his arms out wide and walked slowly away from her, then wheeled around and rushed towards her. "Don't you want to fly like an eagle through the air?"

She had teased him then, pulling him towards her and whispering in his ear that he was more like a peacock, who wanted to show off to attract his mate, than a lone eagle in the sky.

Now he had finished his display, and he was flying back, straight towards her. Once he reached the lawn, he began to fly around the house and the garden in a great circle. Around and around he went, and as he did so, he flew so close to the tree-tops that they started to shed their leaves in great cascades. She was laughing now, opening her arms out wide, and turning round too, to follow him and to catch one leaf after another as they came tumbling in front of her eyes - each one a message of love in burnished gold. And every so often she could see him, just a glimpse of him, waving and laughing. At one moment his plane swooped so low she caught her breath. 'No, Hermann! Not so low my Wandervögel!' And then his engine changed pitch. He soared upwards to clear the roof of the house, and was gone.

CHAPTER FIFTEEN

Hermann called at the rectory by chance, hoping that Gillard would be in. He was in luck, and soon they were taking the familiar route, cutting through the back of the village and around to the high point, to Arthur's Seat, which that afternoon looked more like the magician Merlin swathed in a grey wizard's cloak, than any ancient king hewn out of rock.

By now this had become a routine - every few weeks Hermann and the abbé walked in the forest. They would stop by the old forge on the lake-side, or sit on Arthur's seat to take in the view, to smoke cigarettes, and to talk about the old stories, the legends that seemed to inhabit every part of the forest. When Gillard wasn't speaking, he was a good listener. He seemed genuinely interested in Hermann's life, asking him about the books he read, about his education, his childhood. And when he was speaking, particularly about the old tales, his eyes seemed to shine. He knew every one of the characters of the

Arthurian legends in detail - the bumbling Sir Kay, the innocent young Perceval, the evil Mordred, Arthur's treacherous son, the beautiful but flawed Queen Guinevere, or Geneviève as she was also known, Lancelot her lover, who betrayed his friend the king. The ideals of these knights inspired Gillard, and one day as he was talking about the bonds of chivalry that existed between these companions of the Round Table, Hermann had all at once seen the connection. Here was a priest, a member of a brotherhood of celibate clergy, fascinated by another brotherhood: of noble knights engaged in acts of heroism - men who could express their romantic and aggressive urges, fighting evil, courting maidens. Hermann could imagine forsaking aggression, but not the world of love with all its carnal delights. Perhaps that explained a certain sadness he sensed in the abbé.

What would Gillard think of him making love to a married woman while her husband, ignorant of his betrayal, was away from home? Was Hermann Geneviève's Lancelot? She certainly loved René as Guinevere loved Arthur, even when she lay in Lancelot's arms. How could any good come from this? Even as he tried to dismiss the thought from his mind, he saw himself in Geneviève's room, unbuttoning her dress as she stood with her back to him. He pulled the dress from her shoulders, and began to kiss the back of her neck, his hands caressing her breasts. Looking up to turn her around, his eyes fell on the framed photograph of her wedding. She and René seemed so proud, so happy. But then, as she turned to face him, nothing else mattered. Love is the supreme value, beyond all human morality, beyond the jealousy and possessiveness of the ego. We cannot understand these things, he told himself, as he pushed her gently on to the bed.

Now that they were once again on Arthur's seat, looking out across the forest that stretched to the horizon, Hermann turned to Gillard. "Perhaps it is impolite of me to ask, but before you entered the church, did you ever know the love of a woman?"

"No-one has ever asked me that. No-one has had the nerve, or perhaps I should say the honesty, to voice a question that I suppose must occur to many people when they meet a priest." He paused, then smiled. "You know Hermann, in your case I find the question a compliment. It comes from a sincere interest in your fellow man, I feel."

Gillard looked into the far distance for a few moments, then turned to Hermann again. "Before I was ordained, when I was studying canon law in Paris, there was a woman." He shook his head now from side to side. "Perhaps one day I will tell you. It was not easy, and I was not a brave man. Not a good man either. Shall we walk?"

They headed north on a track that ran through the heather and bracken, the valley with its lake of the Fairies' Mirror gradually disappearing from sight as they kept to the high ground.

"Tell me about your plans for the church. Tell me again why you want to dedicate it to the Holy Grail."

"O, Hermann, because it is the symbol of everything we seek in our souls: the gold of the alchemists, the love of God. In the days of the druids, the symbol that stood for all this was the cauldron. It was an image of the Mother Goddess. And then in the Christian era this symbol was transformed into a chalice, the cup that caught the blood of Christ. And since the church lies in this landscape so imbued with the stories of the knights of the Round Table and their search for the Holy Grail, it makes sense to have a Grail church here. I would like it to become a place where pilgrims and seekers can pray, before they set out into the land to search for the grail themselves."

"That's a beautiful idea." Hermann knew he was being dishonest. He was trying to find out more about Gillard's plans because he had been told to send as much information as possible to Berlin. Krause had used that favourite phrase of his, 'a subject of interest at the highest level'. But he was also genuinely intrigued on his own account. "You said you were going to use the Golden Mean."

"Yes, that's the real key - the way you can change any building into a sacred vessel. The Platonic philosophers were right - God works with numbers, and the ratio of the Golden Mean is the secret code that underlies the way the universe is constructed. The proportions of our bodies, the veins of a leaf, the structure of seashells, and of flowers and seeds, all are governed by this ratio. And for a building, it is the perfect proportion for the human body to inhabit. People will feel comfortable, at home in the church - at one with their surroundings. That is the most important, the fundamental change, that I am making to the building as it stands. And then, within this hidden structure that of course no-one will notice, I will add more obvious signs and symbols to elevate and inspire those who visit the church. I'm going to paint above the entrance, 'The door is within.' They will go inside and of course they'll find no physical door within, and will realize it is encouraging them to search within their own hearts and souls. And then we will have more windows depicting scenes from the legend of the Holy Grail, and I want to use mosaics too. I have designed an image of the Grail for the floor, just in front of the altar. And I am designing another one that will cover the whole of the western wall. Christ will be depicted as a white stag, surrounded by four red lions. They will have haloes, to provide the clue."

"That they are really human - the evangelists?"

"Exactly. And there will be a single columbine flower tucked away for the initiates to smile at."

"I am clearly not an initiate."

"In sacred art, everything is symbolic, Hermann. Colours, shapes, numbers - they are all there within art and signify deep truths, or offer clues to lead the seeker onward. The background of the mosaic will be gold, to offer the clue that the alchemical mysteries are being depicted. Merlin's Stone, located in the forest nearby, will be placed prominently beneath the stag to symbolize the

Philosopher's Stone. Just above this will be the single columbine I mentioned. With its violet colour it symbolizes the dove of the Holy Spirit. Columbine is an androgynous plant, and hence symbolic of the union of the male and female principles. It was used as one of the signatures of Leonardo Da Vinci, and was a favourite of Dante. When someone who knows their symbology looks up at the mosaic, it will trigger all these thoughts in their mind."

"Ah, I see now."

"The idea is that everything in the church will speak to you. One door after another will open, as the associations build upon each other. I want the church to be a school and a place of worship - not only for novices, but also for people who understand, people who know about the golden chain of the Perennial Tradition that stretches back in time to include the Christian mystics, the alchemists, the old temple builders, the Freemasons and the Rosicrucians. And for these initiates, I shall place other signs in the church. I am planning a circular window in the sacristy with the symbols of the zodiac, and inspiring phrases written above the doors and on the walls. By studying religious art, I have come to understand that there are exact correspondences between the images the artists have depicted, the colours they have used, and the numerology that is hidden within their designs. And so we are back to the Golden Mean again - the significance and power of numbers. Our souls, our bodies even, seem to respond to this Golden Mean as if to some hidden impulse or vibration, harmonising us, calming us, opening us to the influence of the divine."

Gillard had spoken with passion and enthusiasm. This was his life's work, and Hermann could sense this clearly. They walked in silence for a while. A flock of wild geese flew high above, reminding Hermann of the dream Geneviève had told them both, that evening beside the fire in the Manoir. "I couldn't help noticing the tomb of St Onenne has been removed."

Gillard laughed. "Yes. It was an ugly affair wasn't it?"

"Well, yes. Monstrously ugly in fact, but isn't she the patron saint of the church? Can one simply remove an entire tomb of a saint?"

Gillard stopped to roll two cigarettes, and then, as they both lit them from the same flame, he said, "I don't really believe she existed." He stepped back and blew a column of smoke into the air. "There's no mention of her in Catholic hagiography, and the story of her life, which Madame Zaepffel recounted, is simply a local legend confined to a few square kilometres of Brittany. With all due respect to our new-found friend, I imagine she heard about the legend at her mother's knee, and then simply dreamt of it one day."

"You mean the saint was simply a fiction of the early church here?"

"Ah, my dear Hermann, how can anything be simply a fiction as you put it? Is not everything a peculiar blend of fantasy and reality - our minds colouring everything we see with our prejudices and preconceptions? We hear a few words of gossip at Madame Harel's, and in only a matter of days the innuendoes have become hard facts, the rumours have become engraved in stone. And then we argue over what is true and what is not true. Originally my intention had been simply to reduce the tomb in size, but once we dismantled it, and dug beneath it, we found no remains. This confirmed a theory I had already begun to develop.

"When Christianity first reached these lands, it was common for my predecessors to lure the people away from their pagan practices by inventing saints. These saints would replace the local spirits - sometimes simply taking on the same name - the goddess Brighid and the god Dionysus became St Brighid and St Dionysus for example. And so I think the same thing happened here. Shall we keep walking? Look we can drop down to the river this way." They took a fork in the track that led down to the valley and to the Aff, which flowed south towards the Fairies' Mirror. "I believe our church stands on a site that was sacred before the coming of Christianity - sacred because of a great ash tree that had healing powers attributed to it. It became the centre for cult worship - by the druids no doubt. And how does St Onenne emerge out of this? Well, her name derives from a Celtic word for the ash, so I think the early Christians adopted and personified this cult of the healing ash tree. Instead of praying to a tree spirit for healing, they began praying to a saint with the same name instead. They might well have kept the tree in place for some time, before it fell to make way for the first church to be built, perhaps out of the sacrifice of its own body."

"This would explain why you found nothing in the tomb."

"Exactly. They say her bones are buried in a casket beneath the church floor, but I haven't seen anything, and if there is such a casket, I'll bet you the remains belong to someone else." Gillard shrugged. "The women in Trého used to pray to that old statue that lay on top of the tomb, but what were they asking for? To have the life in their wombs terminated, or the results of their drinking habit magically wiped away. It was all very unsavoury. Even so, I know there have been grumblings, complaints about the tomb's removal to the bishop and so on, and I do understand the value of myth and legend, which is why we will have new windows that commemorate her and her fellow saint."

"Who is that?" asked Hermann as they reached the lake.

"A person who had the virtue of actually existing," smiled Gillard. "The thirteenth apostle, St Eutrope."

"Surely the thirteenth apostle is Judas Iscariot?"

"Not in Brittany, Hermann. You forget you are in another universe here." They laughed. "I suppose it is rather strange. Thirteen is considered such an unlucky number. But it's because he brought the gospel here. As a young man he travelled from Persia to Galilee, and there he encountered Jesus and was entranced by his preaching. He was even present at the feeding of the five thousand. His story is one of the treasures of this region. After the death of Christ he brought his message to Gaul and converted many people, including the daughter of the Roman governor."

"Not the governor himself?"

"No, sadly not. He was so angry that Eutrope had converted her - she was only thirteen years old - he had Eutrope killed."

"Poor fellow. So he became a martyr?"

"Yes indeed, and I am commissioning a stained glass image of him for the transept, and we will make a chapel for him. His life is rather interesting. When we get back to the rectory I'll show you an account of it. And in a way it will prove my point about Onenne. There's no such record of her life, only a legend that is more folklore than anything else."

Back at the rectory, Gillard handed Hermann a large leather-bound book, and then set about laying a fire. Hermann looked at the frontispiece: 'The Golden Legend or The Lives of the Saints, Jacobus de Voragine, Archbishop of Genoa, 1275.' He turned to the page where Eutrope's life was recounted: 'In the realm of Persia, Saint Eutrope was born and came of the most excellent lineage of all the world, the son of the admiral of Babylon...' He read of Eutrope's journey to Galilee, where he witnessed the feeding of the five thousand with five loaves and two fishes.

Gillard lit the fire, and went in search of glasses and wine. He was soon back.

"It's rather marvellous to read such an account, isn't it?"

"Yes, it is impressive. It's easy to imagine one is there. I've almost finished. I've got to the bit about him throwing flowers as Jesus passes by on an ass in Jerusalem - the Palm Sunday story." Hermann continued reading for a few moments. "But the end here. Surely not..."

"What do you mean?"

"Well, listen. He hears of the crucifixion, and is upset. He hears of the resurrection and is overjoyed. That makes sense, but then: 'And all the Jews that he found in his country, for anger he destroyed, because they of Jerusalem had put our Lord to death'. "

"Well, I suppose we don't really know if that's true. It's probably an exaggeration."

"But how can a person who starts a massacre be called a saint?"

Gillard sighed. "Perhaps this is just legend, Hermann. I always take the details of these stories with a pinch of salt. No-one reads these old saints' lives any more."

Hermann stood up. The sun had set by now and the room had grown dark.

"Well can you pick and choose? You don't take the other details of the story with a pinch of salt, I'd imagine. I had many friends who were Jewish when I was young. An old rabbi used to visit us in Berlin quite often. He was a good man."

"Yes I do understand Hermann. It is very unfortunate. There are good and bad apples in every race, but the fact remains that St Eutrope is the patron saint of this parish, and I need to balance the feminine element introduced by St Onenne with a masculine one. Their chapels will face each other - Onenne's tiled in turquoise to remind us of the sea and Eutrope's decorated with red tiles, so that the elements of fire and water face each other. The astrologers will understand."

CHAPTER SIXTEEN

Geneviève leant back. The words weren't flowing. She had been hunched up, trying to concentrate, trying to see with her inner eye. But all she could see was Hermann. She was so deliciously happy. She could hardly believe it sometimes. She would walk through the house singing. What a beautiful, magical place she lived in. She had been so lucky with her life. So many people had suffered. So many people consulted her whose lives were in ruins - their health compromised, their livelihoods threatened, their marriages a sham. And yet here she was, utterly in love - not only with Hermann, but also, she felt more and more, with her darling René. It must surely be her karma. As an evolved soul, she could love more than one person. Her heart was large, as vast as the universe. If only all humanity could open their hearts in this way. She had read that the early Christians accepted multiple wives, perhaps husbands for all she knew. It was only later that the institution of monogamous marriage was introduced.

The druids certainly allowed it, and she had learnt that St Patrick, on converting all Ireland, had ordered his scribes to write down the old druid laws so that he could study them. And there it was clearly written that a man could have many spouses. Their rights were determined, honour was maintained. How civilized, how generous, were these old sages. But alas, she was not living in those times. Perhaps René would understand, if she told him at the right moment. After all, he admired the German race. He wanted France to ally itself with Germany. He could perhaps open his heart enough to truly know that it is possible to share our love more fully, without the petty jealousies of ownership. If he knew she still loved him. If he knew what a fine soul Hermann was, surely he could allow him into their lives?

But then, with a wave of despair, she realized the hopelessness of this thought. She sensed herself as René standing in the bedroom. He had just walked in, determined to surprise his Queen Geneviève with a bouquet of roses, and there she was lying naked on the bed, Hermann caressing her, parting her thighs with his hands, kissing every part of her body with a fervour that astonished even her. But as this was happening, she wasn't sighing with pleasure, but was standing there - in René's shoes, in his clothes, the sweat on his brow, the roses in his hand, his heart pounding. She could feel the horror, the shock to his heart. It was unbearable. It was impossible.

But she couldn't stop thinking about it. It was as if she and Hermann had created such electrifying images it was impossible to turn away from them. More and more, she had discovered in the last few weeks, she could see only the past, nothing of the future. And however much she knew she was hurting René, she couldn't help reliving her memories over and over again, her body revelling in the sensations that were almost as vivid to her now as they were when she first experienced them. She was no longer looking out from René's eyes now, but was looking down instead on Hermann's head between her thighs, and she was feeling his tongue flicking in and out of her, then round and round in dizzying circles. And there she was, whirling round and round in the garden, the golden leaves falling.

How could she work, how could she gaze into the future, if he insisted on doing this to her? How could she detect the quiet, subtle signals of fate when, from virtually the moment he had met her, he had picked her up like a violin or a cello, and would play her over and over again so exquisitely?

But every so often her virtuoso would suddenly stop. Why did he do that? Just when she was about to faint with ecstasy. And he would ask her what she saw in the future - for Germany, for France, for England. And she would try to make him carry on, but he would just laugh and run one finger slowly up her leg, or dig his fingernails into her buttocks until it hurt, or trace a circle with his tongue around her nipple, and say 'Come on, what have you seen?'

And she would sometimes feel so desperate for him to continue she would make things up, or to be exact, she would extrapolate from what she had already seen on stage in Paris, or while seated here at her desk before he had come into her life and disturbed her tranquility.

And now she was trying to compose quatrains that would reveal the future for the readers of her next book, and nothing sensible would come to her. No prayers, no requests to her Guardian Angel were answered. How different it was in New York, when she had seen quite clearly their President, that man Roosevelt, at the helm of his country until his death, or when she had seen the face of Mussolini with a cross marked on his brow, and she had warned all of France of his aggressive intentions.

The door bell rang. She ran downstairs.

Hermann laughed as he held her tight and lifted her off her feet to swing her from side to side. "Did you know I was coming?"

"I had no idea. You have robbed me of my powers, you wicked man. But I don't care. I no longer want to know the future - I want to be continually surprised."

"I'm starving. The food at the base has become even more dull than it was before. I'm not sure why."

"There is some cold chicken. Let me make a salad."

Hermann sat in the kitchen while she prepared their lunch.

"I was with the abbé the other day, you know, and I must say he rather disappointed me."

"Why is that, my darling?"

"Perhaps I shouldn't tell you this, but he believes St Onenne never really existed - that her story is just folklore, a legend that masks a primitive cult of tree-worship."

"How very odd and ridiculous."

"Well, he can explain it all. He thinks your vivid dreams were simply the product of your mind, replaying a story you heard as a child. But it's not really that which bothered me, he's entitled to his opinion after all, and I can see his point - apparently Onenne derives from a word for ash tree, and so on - but it was what he told me about his plans to create a chapel for another saint: Eutrope."

"Ah yes, the thirteenth apostle."

"Yes, exactly. What a horrific man."

"What on earth do you mean? He brought Christianity to this region."

"Yes, but he ordered the killing of all the Jews in his country."

She didn't reply for a moment. It would sound too extreme, too cruel, but Hermann must believe this, too, surely. She brought the salad over to the table. "Sometimes the sword of justice must fall with utter determination, however harsh this might seem to us, don't you think?"

"What do you mean?"

She began to lay the table. "You've surely heard of the way it is the plotting of the bankers, the conspiracy of the Jews and the Blosheviks and Freemasons, that has led us to this terrible war?"

Hermann said nothing, but looked at her quizzically, as if he was waiting for her to say more.

"René has explained it so clearly to me, that we are now engaged in a struggle between two races - the Aryan and the Semitic. And it is the Aryan race that will triumph."

Hermann shook his head. "But I was speaking about Eutrope's massacre - something that occurred, or supposedly occurred, almost two thousand years ago."

"The battle between the light and the dark has been fought since the beginning of time, my darling. We must always struggle against the darkness."

They ate in silence. Hermann seemed lost in thought. When she had finished, she stretched out her hand and ran it through his hair. All at once she felt like his mother. Of course the idea of a massacre upset him, the world is indeed a vale of sorrow. She stood up and walked around the table to him. She bent down and whispered in his ear, "Let me take you upstairs now. I will soothe your brow." She unbuttoned his shirt and ran her fingers over his chest. "I will make you cry with pleasure."

CHAPTER SEVENTEEN

As autumn changed to winter, the allies stepped up their bombing raids along the coast, and the base which had been quiet for so long was now frantic with activity. Hermann saw very little of Geneviève or the Abbé Gillard - he was only able to snatch visits infrequently. Point-Clos was on full alert, and he began flying regular missions to support the coastal air bases in defence of the factories and U-boat pens at St.Nazaire and Lorient. He would never defend a massacre or the hatred of an entire race, but he had learned to accept the need to fight, and now he found that he enjoyed more than ever scoring a direct hit, watching smoke pouring out of an enemy plane that would pitch violently out of the sky and plummet towards the sea or land. And as if his relationship with Geneviève was somehow a mirror image of what was occurring around him, the increasingly frenetic and violent world he found himself in became reflected in the way he behaved with her. It had begun, perhaps, even before the allied attacks had intensified, when he had started trying to coax information out of her. Krause was becoming increasingly impatient, and Hermann found that if he teased her, tortured her even, by arousing her, caressing her and then stopping whatever he was doing, holding her down just as she seemed about to climax, she would give him just the sort of information he wanted: "Beware of the Italians' loyalty. Mussolini cannot be trusted. The campaign in the East will succeed". And then one day he discovered that if he spanked her, not too hard, but sufficient for her to cry out, she would give him more information - not to stop him hitting her, but quite the reverse - to make him continue. And so he would kiss and caress her, then order her to bend over and begin beating her, until all of a sudden - and the timing had to be right - he would stop, and bending close to her ear, would ask "More?" and she would beg for more, and he would say, "Tell me about the English," or "Tell me what will happen next year," and she would hurriedly say: "The English will be defeated and will ally themselves with Germany," or "The Spring will bring great hardship, but the Reich will triumph," and then he would reward her, spanking her more, and then turning her over and pushing inside her until they both collapsed on to the bed, laughing and sighing together.

This was the seed he had sown, but the harvest was one he could not have foreseen. The more he made love to Geneviève in this way, the less he found he loved her. Her stupid ideas about Jewish conspiracies had annoyed him, but then the world was full of such stupidities - even Gillard wasn't immune to them. The Vichy government was as anti-Semitic as his own. Everywhere the Jews were the scapegoats of people's envy and anger. Who was he to fight against the tide? But at the same time he was angry with himself. He could feel he had no moral strength, no ground inside him that allowed him to stand strong and tall against what was so clearly wrong. He knew he should be compassionate and loving to all beings, but he had to face facts. He was flying a plane designed to kill people, he was fighting for his country, he was an adulterer, he was lying to his lover, he was lying really to his friends and fellow pilots, because no-one knew the truth. He was deceiving Krause because he didn't believe in the Ahnenerbe's dream of racial superiority, and he was betraying Gillard because he was spying on him for Krause. He was in every respect the most despicable of people. And now, on top of it all, he found himself enjoying being with Geneviève, not for her warmth or her caresses, but because he could exercise complete power over her. He could control her, fly her like his Stuka. And he did this, not against her will, but in conformity with her desire. She wanted to surrender. It was a game they both willingly played. With every slap she would soar, and he could feel her climbing higher and higher, and then he would stop and withhold his touch, and he would feel her dropping into free fall, until with a sudden perfectly timed slap she would soar again in the sky, until at last with a series of quick thrusts inside her, he could bring her crashing to the ground. But in all of this, despite the excitement they both felt, despite the information he was able to obtain for Krause, he could feel his fondness for her silently slipping away.

He knew what it was - the battle between will and love. There was a thrill and a beauty in the exercise of power that was in some way opposed to the experience of warmth, tenderness, care, empathy. He sensed this most strongly one afternoon, when he decided he would obtain more information by taking Geneviève to even greater heights of ecstasy. He arrived at the Manoir with a bouquet of paper roses he had found for sale in Paimpont, and as she thanked him and drew the flowers towards her, he leaned forward and kissed her neck. She slipped her hand into his, squeezed it, and led him upstairs. The staircase creaked and groaned as it always did. She opened the bedroom door. He closed it behind them.

He told her to take off her clothes and stood, arms folded, watching.

She moved towards him. "Let me undress you, my darling."

"No, I will remain dressed. Take off your clothes and stand facing away from me."

He waited as she stood there naked, trembling in the afternoon light. Slowly he walked towards her, paused for a few moments, just breathing in and out on the nape of her neck. He then took his right forefinger and lightly touched her lower back, just above her buttocks, then ran it slowly up her spine to the top of her head.

"The serpent awakes," he whispered in her ear. She would know what that meant - the serpent Kundalini that occultists say runs as a current of energy through seven chakras from the base of the spine to the crown of the head. For most of humanity the serpent sleeps, but it can be awakened, can uncoil and rise up through the body, bringing with it illumination and ecstasy. He fluttered all the fingers of his right hand now over her buttocks, and then ran his forefinger up along the cleft between them, and then again up to the top of her head. She shuddered.

He stepped back and slapped her hard. She gasped. He waited, then again ran his fingers over her buttocks, up her back, and around to her breasts.

He leaned forward, and spoke quietly but firmly into one ear. "Tell me what will happen with our campaign in the East."

"I have told you before. There is nothing to worry about."

"I want to know more. Look harder. Look now into the future."

"Oh my darling, how can I when..."

He slapped her again, then stroked the inside of her legs between her thighs, and then slapped her another five times before stopping.

"More?"

"Yes, of course... please..."

"Then tell me more." He took a chair and told her to sit down. He began undressing. "I am very patient. I have all the time in the world and you will tell me."

"Alright. The campaign in the East will suffer great hardships, but by the late Spring I see the flags of the Reich flying in Moscow."

Hermann was naked now as he stood in front of her. He bent down, and they kissed. "Tell me more," he said firmly, taking her hair in one hand and pulling it backwards so that her head tilted upwards. He could smell her fear and excitement. "When exactly will this be?"

"June. It will be in June,"

"Good. America now. Tell me the fate of America."

His cock was so hard now, and she could see this. She stretched out her hand to touch it, but he pushed her hand away. He could wait.

"They have made a great mistake entering the war. They will regret this. Their country will be torn apart by racial hatred. There will be riots in the streets."

Hermann moved behind her, one hand still holding her hair tightly. He bent down and played with one of her nipples.

He whispered in her ear. "Tell me again when the war will end."

"1945. 1946 at the latest."

"You have said Germany and France will lead a union of European nations. How many nations will join this union?"

"Seventeen. They will sign an accord in Paris."

"Good. Get up on the bed. On all fours."

They both knew how this would end. She climbed on to the four-poster. He stood and stroked her thighs, flicking his fingers gently around her vulva. He then said, "Tell me what you see in Europe. What are the images that come to you?"

He raised his hand, and was about to slap her when, quite unexpectedly, Geneviève sat up. He could feel the spell was broken. She began crying into her hands.

"Oh my god."

She was sobbing now, uncontrollably. "What do you see?" He climbed on to the bed and cradled her in his arms.

"I see great ovens with bodies and parts of bodies in them. Limbs, faces, hands. Smoke pours from these ovens. It is like hell on earth. There are children in them. Adults. It feels like the end of the world."

"Where is this, Geneviève?"

"I cannot see."

"Who is doing this?"

"I cannot see. My guides cannot tell me."

They sat there on the bed, Hermann holding her, trying to comfort her. Their game, his mock interrogation, seemed grotesque to him now, unworthy of both of them.

"Lie down," he said, covering her. "I will bring you some tea."

As he drove back to the base, he knew what he must do. He must reclaim the love he had felt for her, that tenderness he had begun to destroy. He needed to show her that he really cared for her, that he would always treasure her, even though he could not always agree with what she said or thought.

The late afternoon sun was already moving towards dusk. If he hurried he would be over the Manoir as the sun was setting. He ran over to the Stuka, fired up the engine, and after clearing with the control tower, was soon soaring high into the air.

'Love conquers all,' he told himself. This time he would manage a heart. He climbed to the right height for the rapid descent towards the field in front of the house. His timing was perfect, the sun was dropping towards the horizon, layers of light cloud reflecting the sunset in brilliant pink and gold. Once he reached 4000 metres, he pushed the drive lever forward, pulled back the throttle, and rolled into the dive, only to hear the scream of the trumpets he had forgotten to disengage.

CHAPTER EIGHTEEN

"My god, what is that pilot doing?" René Zaepffel was standing beside Geneviève at the bedroom window. She had no idea what to say. Her heart was pounding. Hermann's plane recovered from its dive and within minutes was gone. Eventually she said quietly: "They must be getting bored at Point-Clos." She turned to René. "It is such a surprise to have you back here, my darling."

"It was worth the journey just to see the look on your face when I arrived at the door," smiled René.

"Let me make some supper, you must be hungry."

"I am, darling. I will light the fire."

The house grew dark as the sun began to set. They soon discovered there had been yet another power cut, and René began lighting candles in the kitchen and dining room. As they sat to eat, they were surrounded by shadows, but the candles cast their warm light on their faces as they looked at each other across the table.

Geneviève smiled warmly at her husband. "I do enjoy these power cuts. The light is so much more romantic."

They ate together in silence for a while until René looked up from his meal. "What if we are wrong, Geneviève?"

"About what, my dear?"

"About the course of the war. Have you heard what is happening on the eastern front?"

"I have no idea, no. But my spirit guides have told me that the National Socialist flag will soon be flying in Moscow, and in every corner of Russia." She looked at René. He was still handsome, she thought, but she sighed. "I do wish you had more faith in me."

"You can never trust rumours, of course, but my colleagues tell me we are incurring heavy losses and are losing ground. They say Hitler has made the same mistake as Napoleon, and it will be his downfall. I say nothing to them, of course, you never know where allegiances lie, but it worries me sometimes."

"I am convinced, my darling, that in the end the forces of light will triumph. There will be great suffering, we know. But I have seen with my own eyes - and you know this - the hosts of spirits, all those who fell in the Great War, standing like a vast army surrounding one proud standard-bearer holding the flag of the New Europe. And it will be France and Germany who will lead this New Europe into an age of prosperity and peace. You must believe this, René. I do."

She helped herself to more of the vegetables she had cooked, before handing the serving spoon to René.

"I do, of course, my dear. It's just that sometimes, when I am far away from you and feel out of touch, away from your light and your love, I remember those months you were in prison at the beginning of the war, before the Germans came to liberate us."

"Ah yes. But what an experience that was, what a test of faith! In the end they had to release me because what I had said was true. They had their spies and their informers, malicious gossips who sat in the Salle Pleyel and twisted my words, but look what happened! I was freed, and the whole awful experience is now just a dream." She realized she had never told Hermann of the way the French police had arrested her at the outbreak of war, suspecting her of Nazi sympathies, of collaborating with the enemy. But it was undignified. One cannot speak of everything that has happened.

"What if…"

"We are protected, René. The cards are sometimes wrong - or rather my interpretation of them is sometimes misguided - but what I see when I am lifted out of my body in trance is never wrong. Good will triumph. The light will descend. Each country will have its moments of crucifixion. You and I, my dear, may have our moments on Calvary, but that, after all, is how Christ works in us - transforming the darkest matter in our souls into light through suffering."

Geneviève brought her glass of wine to her lips. In that moment she saw the face of Hermann looking into her eyes. She was lying back on the ground, the dark starlit sky above. He was moving inside her with such force that she could only surrender to his rhythm, opening her heart and her body until she somehow became him utterly, and he became her. And then he cried out, just once. And his eyes closed, and it looked to her as if he was dying, as if he was in great pain, and for a moment she was frightened, and then he opened his eyes and shouted out, "Consumatum est! It is finished!" and began laughing. They were Christ's words on the cross when he finally died, she knew that, but she wasn't shocked. Instead she too laughed with happiness and relief, holding him even closer.

She looked at René. He was staring at her. Perhaps now was the moment. Perhaps this would be their Calvary - not their arrest as collaborators, their farce of a trial, their disgrace and execution - but here at the dining room table. Here, with their meal growing cold before them, with the food they had just eaten undigested in their stomachs. Perhaps this was the spear she would thrust into his heart, and he too would say, "It is finished, it is over," picking up his plate and hurling it across the room.

And then he would turn from her, and the moments he stood there would seem to last forever, and she would want to go to him and take hold of him, and beg for his forgiveness, but instead she would stand there, horrified at what she had done, at what she had said. And he would turn back, and with a coldness that would terrify her, slap her across the face, and picking up his glass, drink from it slowly as she stood there, reeling - her world turning, her life vanishing, disintegrating beneath her.

"It is not we who control our lives, our destiny. You know that, my darling." She reached across the table to take René's hand in hers. "The stars, our Guardian Angels, God Himself, rules our lives, and the lives of nations. We can only be their servants."

"How much you reassure me." René was smiling at last, clearly feeling the warmth in her words, in her touch.

"Shall we take our glasses upstairs?" she said, stroking the back of his hand with her fingers, hoping she could wash away her fears with love, that she could heal the wounds that in her heart she knew could never heal.

CHAPTER NINETEEN

Hermann received the order to report to Ahnenerbe headquarters on a cold grey morning in December. Ernst handed him the message that had just arrived and waited while Hermann read it.

"I have been summoned back."

"What a surprise. Are you pleased?"

"I'm not sure. I miss the old country - I miss the mountains, the air. But I'm starting to like this place."

"You certainly seem to be liking the locals." Ernst gave only the slightest of knowing smiles. He looked at the list of flight movements posted on his wall. "We have a Junkers 52 that Berlin is reclaiming. It leaves at 1800. Not the most comfortable way to travel, I admit, but if you must go..."

Almost a year had passed since Hermann last stood at the gates of the Ahnenerbe compound in Berlin.

"My dear fellow!" Krause almost shouted as he greeted Hermann in his office. "I have good news for you. I hope you don't mind that I told you nothing in my cable, but I always think a little mystery makes life more interesting. Our Reichsführer Himmler is very pleased with your work." Krause paused as if to let the compliment sink in. "He wants to congratulate you in person, and the plan is this... Sit down, sit down!" Krause leaned back in his chair. "What an extraordinary stroke of luck that your priest has come up with the same idea as ourselves. And I must admit, he has gone about the task with a good deal more efficiency than we have managed to muster. But that is all about to change, thanks to you. Sometimes all that is needed is a little information. Just a detail, an idea. Your reports on the church in Brittany arrived at precisely the right time - and your remarks on the Golden Mean were just what were needed."

"It is hardly a new idea," said Hermann.

"There is a war going on, Captain. You cannot expect the obvious to be always obvious in such situations. Remember Hahnemann and his theory of Homeopathy - minute doses, Captain, minute doses! We are perhaps guilty in the Reich of always thinking of the grand gesture, the use of maximum force, when Hahnemann has shown us that the smallest of adjustments can, in the end, yield the greatest results. We are grateful to you, Captain, for your information, and we have taken the opportunity of a celebration that is shortly to take place, to provide you with a visit to our future headquarters." Krause stood up and looked down on Hermann, his face beaming. "You are going to Wewelsburg! We are all going. Von Knobelsdorff, the Castle Captain, is to be married and we shall fête the happy couple. It is the solstice in two days' time - perfect for a wedding. We leave tomorrow."

The drive to Westphalia took their car west from Berlin through the broad, flat expanse of the Mark Brandenburg. Here and there were patches of snowfall. The sky was clear. For hours, it seemed, they passed countless lakes, shining in the sun, separated by great stretches of pine growing in the light sandy soil. Despite his sense of annoyance at being so summarily ordered home, Hermann could not suppress the feelings of joy that rose in him as he looked out at the countryside sweeping by. There was a freshness and a brightness here that was rare in Brittany. Thinking back to his time at Point-Clos, it all seemed strangely unreal: the shadowy forest, the cold Manoir, his nights making love to Geneviève.

As they turned south towards Seesen and Paderborn, the snow-clad peaks of the Harz mountains came into view. The wide sky, the foothills clad in beech and oak, the rocky gorges Hermann knew lay hidden in the ranges, they all made him feel again that sense of freedom he once knew as a Wandervögel. He wanted them to stop the car, stop so he could get out and start walking into the hills - walking away from everything that now restricted him. What had happened to his life? He had once felt so free, but now he could feel the world closing in on him, as if he was bound to a destiny he could no longer control.

In the late afternoon they arrived at the castle. Captain Von Knobelsdorff emerged from the southeast tower and saluted them as the car slowed to a halt beside him.

"The lucky man himself!" cried out Krause as he slammed the car door behind him.

Von Knobelsdorff led Hermann into the tower, and up its stone staircase to the first floor. "We think you should have the grail study room, if you don't mind sleeping on a camp bed surrounded by books." He lowered his voice as they passed a door marked 'King Henry's Room'. "The Reichsführer arrived this morning. This is his room. He is resting now. Your room is adjacent, so we shall speak quietly."

Three of the walls of the grail study room were lined with books. "I can see you are a man of culture," said Von Knobelsdorff, as Hermann tilted his head to read their spines.

Hermann took down a volume whose title intrigued him. "Books and mountain air are all I need for happiness."

"I will leave you to it, then," said Von Knobelsdorff, closing the door quietly behind him.

Hermann sat in the armchair by the window, and turned to the book he had chosen: 'Crusade Against the Grail' by Otto Rahn - an account of a young man's journey to the Pyrenees to explore the history of the Cathars, whom some believe were guardians of the Holy Grail. As he turned the pages, he experienced a growing sense of recognition, as if he himself had written the book a long time ago. It occurred to him that the abbé must surely have read it.

An hour passed, and there was a knock at the door. Krause had come to take him on a tour of the castle. Walking silently past the Reichsführer's room, they descended the stairs, crossed the courtyard, and approached the north tower. Krause stopped at the doorway to show Hermann the inscription carved above it: 'Domus mea domus orationis vocabitur'.

"My house shall be called a house of prayer," said Hermann slowly as he translated the text from his schoolboy's memory.

"There was once a chapel here," explained Krause. "And it remains a sacred place for us too." He opened the door, and invited Hermann into a large circular hall that occupied the entire ground floor - the SS Generals' Hall, the Obergruppenführersaal. Twelve windows, set in columned niches, filled the room with daylight. In the centre stood a massive round table, made of oak, with twelve finely carved chairs arranged evenly around it. Beneath the table, although his view was partially obscured by the legs of the chairs, Hermann could just make out the image, depicted in dark green marble floor tiles, of a stylised sun with jagged rays.

Krause pulled two chairs out from the table. "Let us sit at the centre of the world, Captain. To appreciate what I am going to show you in a  minute, you must first understand the function of this room. Here the leaders of each of the twelve divisions of the SS will gather at the Round Table to decide the fate of the world. As a student of esoteric disciplines you will, of course, understand the reason for our organization having twelve divisions. Seated here around this table, the twelve generals will be like the knights of the Round Table, filled with the noblest and purest of thoughts. They will defend the people. Like the knights of old they will embody the ideals of chivalry and virtue. They will radiate a strength and a power that reaches to the farthest corners of the world." Hermann ran his hands over the surface of the table. It was a fine example of craftsmanship. But how incongruous all this talk sounded in the modern age - of knights of the Round Table and chivalrous deeds. Krause carried on: "And, of course, around the castle there will be the farms, the schools and hospitals, the garrisons that will defend and support the families of the SS officers who will form the pure nucleus of the Aryan people - the noble warriors who will police our new world, who will defeat the Asian horde, who will purge the world of corruption."

Krause stood abruptly and pointed to the marble tiles beneath the table. Hermann stood too and looked down. "A sun-wheel, Captain, with twelve spokes - each spoke symbolizing the power of one of the generals who will meet around this table. Notice the position of the central sun. It is situated directly above a golden swastika we have placed in the ceiling of the crypt. I will take you there now." He led Hermann outside, into the courtyard.

"Before I show you the grail chapel we are building in this sacred place, let me explain to you its purpose." Krause took a silver case out of his pocket, and offered a cigarette to Hermann. As they both stood in the courtyard smoking, Krause continued. "The Spear of Destiny will stand in the Generals' Hall. It is said that whoever owns this spear controls the destiny of the world. This spear lanced the body of Christ and his blood was captured in a chalice. And it was this blood that was magical! I speak symbolically, of course, but symbols are powerful, are they not? You are well versed in symbolism, so you know this. A soaring tower gives us a feeling of strength and power, a pond in a garden soothes us, and in some ways it acts as the counterpoint to the tower. We need such a counterpoint here. A man needs a woman, a blade needs its scabbard. The Spear needs its grail, Captain, which is why we are creating a chapel, a temple, call it what you will, dedicated to the Holy Grail in the crypt that lies beneath the Hall."

Krause led Hermann back into the tower, and down a flight of steps into the basement. He pushed open a heavy oak door: "We have you to thank for this, Captain."

Hermann stepped into a dark circular room, lit only by pale shafts of light coming from a series of small windows high on each wall. Half a dozen prison workers were sitting against one of the walls, pick axes beside them.

"What the hell is going on?" shouted Krause.

"They are taking a break," said a guard who emerged from the shadows, cigarette in hand. "It's heavy work, the rock is hard."

"How much more do they have to do?" asked Hermann, who was beginning to feel bilious.

"A further ten centimetres in the central area..."

"We shall then run a gas pipe to the centre of the crypt," interrupted Krause. "This will feed a perpetual flame which will burn in eternal memory of those who have fallen for the Reich, and in particular for those officers of the SS who have been killed in the course of their duty. In the light of the sun above, in the Generals' Hall, the knights will rule the world. In the darkness here below, their mortal remains will be guarded in the place of the grail when their souls have flown to Valhalla. In addition to the flame that will burn forever in memory of our dead, there will be pedestals built here for twelve urns, and a chest that will hold the rings of SS officers fallen in the course of duty." Krause then pointed to the floor and ceiling, and then around the domed crypt: "The Golden Mean, Hermann. What a difference it makes."

Hermann looked up at the golden swastika on the ceiling, and then at the floor beneath it, where the prisoners had been hacking at the rock. He imagined the perpetual flame burning in the centre of the darkness. And then, to his surprise, he saw an image of an angel blowing out the perpetual flame, and of skull-faced wraiths wearing the uniforms of SS officers, gathering around the brazier, inhaling gas into their ghostly forms and collapsing on top of each other, until the room was filled with their bodies and he could feel himself choking. "I am leaving," he said abruptly and made for the door. He only inhaled again when he got outside.

Krause looked at him with concern as he closed the door behind them. "I am feeling unwell at the moment," said Hermann.

"Our Reichsführer is also somewhat ill today. His physician, Herr Kersten, will be arriving tomorrow. Perhaps we can arrange a consultation for you?"

"Thank you, but it will pass - something I ate perhaps. I'll go to my room. Nothing a good night's rest won't cure."

As Hermann lay in bed trying to sleep, he thought again of the question that had troubled him as they had driven to the castle: how it was that he had lost his sense of freedom and become entangled in such deceit. He thought back to the times he and his family had spent their holidays at Freilichtpark, of how he had found his freedom too with his Wandervögel friends, taking to the hills and forests whenever he could. And he remembered the time he hitchhiked alone to Ascona in Switzerland. He began to smile as he recalled that adventure. Why had he allowed himself to be drawn, without a thought, into the position he found himself in now? 'Without a thought, of course,' he found himself saying out loud, before he fell asleep.

The next day, Hermann woke early in his castle bedroom, and - remembering it was the morning of the solstice - went to the window, opened the curtains, and looked out on the new day. The sun was already climbing above the hills, but a thin layer of grey cloud obscured its light, so that it resembled a pale moon trembling behind the clouds, as if afraid to show its face. He got back into bed, and after trying unsuccessfully to fall asleep again, turned to Rahn's book, propping himself up against the hard wall with several pillows.

Still feeling nauseous, he decided to avoid breakfast, and planned to leave his room just before the wedding was due to begin. He couldn't face having to make small talk, and hoped he could simply join the crowd when it was due to gather in the courtyard below. Just as he was about to leave, Krause knocked at the door and entered without waiting for his response.

"How are you feeling today? It's almost time - are you coming?"

"I'm feeling better now, thank you," replied Hermann. "I was just about to join the throng."

In the courtyard, several dozen SS officers stood talking in small groups, some with their wives or mistresses by their side. Krause took Hermann straight towards a small group standing with Von Knobelsdorff by the entrance to the east wing.

"Reichsführer, it is with great pleasure that I introduce you to Captain Hermann Kaestner of the SS-Ahnenerbe." In his early forties,  the man with a receding chin, tightly clipped moustache and pale unhealthy-looking skin turned to face Hermann, and smiled broadly through his glasses. After exchanging 'Heil Hitlers', he took Hermann's hand in both of his and shook it effusively. How soft and small his hands feel, thought Hermann, as he looked into Heinrich Himmler's grey-blue eyes.

"We are delighted with your work, Captain," said Himmler, leaning towards Hermann and lowering his voice, as if speaking in confidence. "I have asked that you be seated beside me this afternoon." Hermann bowed slightly in acknowledgement. "I have read your file," said the Reichsführer, before turning to Von Knobelsdorff and Krause who were talking together beside him.

The wedding was to take place in the Great Hall that connected the southwest and southeast towers. The Reichsführer, followed by the SS group commanders, filed into the hall, the other officers and guests behind them. Once Hermann was seated, he noticed that all the women in the hall were wearing black, as if they were attending a funeral. They must have chosen this colour to match their partners' uniforms. The hall itself reminded him of the drawing room of the Manoir du Tertre. The walls were oak-paneled, with runes carved into discs placed along the panels at regular intervals. In one corner a wooden staircase led to a minstrels' gallery.

A short plump man, SS-Oberführer Klein, squeezed tightly into his black boots and uniform, stood in front of a long table which was decked with displays of flowers and fruit, and great sprigs of oak leaves. Two paintings of runes - white against a black background - stood in frames beside the flowers. Klein raised his hand for silence. A group of musicians entered the room - three men and one woman - and walked to the front of the assembled company. They bowed to Klein and climbed the staircase to the gallery. As they began playing, Hermann recognised the music at once: Brahms' - 'A Rose is Gently Blooming'.

After a few moments, Klein gestured to the guests to stand up, and as they did so, Von Knobelsdorff and his bride entered the hall and began walking along the central aisle towards Klein. They stopped a few metres in front of him. He smiled and bowed towards them.

"It is the winter solstice!" began Klein, in a portentous voice. "And here our fragrant bride arrives like the new-born sun."

Herman remembered the morning's pale light and looked again at the bride. She too looked pale - and a little fearful. She was the only person in the room wearing white. She turned to Von Knobelsdorff, who must have been at least ten years her senior and smiled at him nervously. "The goal of every union is perfect balance: for equality of soul between man and woman. And yet, in our world of work, and now of war, it is the man who must carry the spear and the woman who must carry the burden of hearth-work and child rearing. Gertrude Höner, are you prepared to support your husband in all his labours to glorify the Reich?"

Gertrude almost shouted out her reply: "I am!"

"Have you attended the Bride School and received your certificate?"

"I have, and it is here," she said, more quietly. A woman stepped forward and presented a scroll to Klein. He unfurled it with a flourish. There, beneath a symbol of the Germanic Tree of Life, was her name followed by a series of vows she had made upon graduation, which he proceeded to read out: that she would be loyal to Adolf

Hitler, Heinrich Himmler and all the leaders of the Nazi Party unto death; that she would remain at all times a sustainer of the Germanic race; that she would become proficient in cooking and housekeeping, sewing, washing and ironing, childcare, nursing and home design; and that all children born in her marriage would be raised in accordance with the ideals of the National Socialist German Workers' Party.

When he came to the end of the list, there was enthusiastic clapping.

"Captain, I must now turn my attention to you - loyal husband to be! Do you wish with all your heart to be married to Gertrude Höner?"

"I do!" replied Von Knobelsdorff, clearing his throat afterwards with a cough.

"Do you bring the rings to seal your bond?"

"I do!" said the Captain, turning to the man who stood beside him. The officer clicked his heels and turned forty-five degrees in one movement, so that he stood between Klein and Von Knobelsdorff, and was able to hold out the small wooden box that held the rings.

Klein turned to the bride. "Do you Gertrude Höner swear to be the faithful and loving wife of Captain Manfred Von Knobelsdorff?"

"I do!" said Gertrude.

"In that case, I hereby declare you to be man and wife, and that you shall wear these rings in token of your vows until death." Klein turned to Von Knobelsdorff and nodded. The Captain took a plain gold ring from the box held out by his comrade, and slid it onto Gertrude's finger. He looked directly at her, smiled, and bowed his head. She then took his ring, the SS-Ehrenring, the death's head ring, and placed it on his outstretched finger. The couple kissed. The crowd clapped. The musicians began playing, and the two of them walked back along the aisle, arm in arm, smiling and nodding to friends and colleagues to either side of them.

Once they had left the hall, Klein asked the musicians to stop playing, so that he could make an announcement: "Ladies and Gentlemen, there will be a brief pause whilst we transform this hall into the feasting chamber! Please vacate the room now, to assist us in the preparations."

Hermann slipped away and returned to his room. He was already half way through Rahn's book and wanted to finish it before he left. Two hours later he heard a commotion in the courtyard. It was time for the wedding lunch.

"You are over here," said Krause, gesturing to Hermann to come to the head table that had been used for the wedding. White plates with a single swastika at their centre were laid with cutlery decorated with runes. "These have been created especially for the castle," explained Krause. All but one of the oak sprigs had been cleared from the table, but the two framed images of the runes remained facing the room. Behind them stood the Reichsführer by his chair, surveying the scene.

"Ah, Captain Kaestner, welcome to the high table. I trust you enjoyed the ceremony?"

"I did indeed, Reichsführer."

Once all the guests were seated, a hush swept through the room as if everyone knew what was about to happen. Heinrich Himmler stood up and raised his arm. Everyone else stood up and shouted "Heil Hitler!" in unison.

"Please be seated again, my friends," began Himmler, who remained standing. "I know you are all hungry and are keen to begin feasting and toasting the newly-weds. But let me say a few words by way of congratulations to the happy couple, and in recognition of that greater hunger we all feel - for the victory of our Führer and for the triumph of the Third Reich!" The audience clapped loudly. Himmler gestured for silence. "You - Captain Von Knobelsdorff and Frau Von Knobelsdorff - stand in the vanguard of a new era. You are amongst the first of those couples whose union has been consecrated, not by some spurious rite of a cruel and depraved church, who tortured witches in the dungeon of this very castle, but by the rite of the SS-Eheweihen - a rite of purity and dignity unsullied by centuries of religious oppression. Today those blessed by our rite are but few, but in the future there will be thousands of SS families who will look to you pioneers with gratitude and admiration.

"You see these oak leaves here? These come from the trees sacred to our forefathers, sacred to our pagan heritage. They have blessed your union. And your union has been blessed, too, by being consecrated on a most auspicious day: the winter solstice, when the sun begins its triumphant conquest of darkness." Himmler paused and turned to the newly-weds. "We raise our glasses to you both - to your health and happiness!" Everyone stood once more and raised their glasses, calling out: "Prost!"

Once again, Himmler gestured for all to be seated. Hermann thought he had finished the speech, and moved his plate closer in anticipation, but then he realised that on the contrary, the Reichsführer had only just begun.

"Your union, my friends, is blessed not only by an auspicious time, but also because it has been held in an auspicious place - here, in this magnificent castle that stands at the sacred junction of lines of power that run in every direction, to all four corners of the Earth. This castle stands at the very centre of the dream of the Reich, where in future days our children will live to defend the Aryan people against the Asian horde, as the prophecies have foretold.

"This is why I must encourage you - this radiant couple here, and all of you seated here in this audience - to worship at the altar of motherhood, to worship blood and soil: the pure blood of Aryanism, the pure soil of the Fatherland. It is our duty to bring this purity into the world through our children - not only so they may enjoy the delights of life on Earth, but also so they may defend the Fatherland and spread the gospel of National Socialism throughout the world. This is why we have created the

Ahnenerbe as a division of our beloved SS. And here to my side sits one of its brightest stars." To Hermann's astonishment, Himmler had turned to him, and now the entire room seemed to be staring at him. "Captain Kaestner, I am now pleased to say, before this assembled company, on this auspicious day of the solstice, that you are hereby promoted to the rank of SS-Obersturmführer, in recognition of your achievements - and more importantly, of the potential you display for future responsibilities within the very highest ranks of our noble order." With a broad smile of acknowledgement, the Reichsführer bowed his head to Hermann, and then turning back to his audience, began clapping vigorously. The entire room broke into applause. Hermann stood, closed his eyes and bowed. His heart was racing. He sat down, and as the applause died down, Himmler began speaking again: "The SS-Ahnenerbe is painstakingly uncovering every aspect of our glorious past, every muscle of that great being that stands as our primal ancestor: the Übermensch, the Superman of the Aryan people. Those who serve this just cause - the officers of the SS-Ahnenerbe - deserve as much recognition as those who struggle on the battlefield to advance the triumph of the Reich.

"To fulfill our people's destiny, we have insisted that every woman who wants the privilege and the honour of marrying a member of the SS, must first enrol in our Bridal Training Programme. I agree entirely with Frau Scholtz-Klink, the leader of this programme, when she tells us, and I quote: 'Women must be the spiritual caregivers and the secret queens of our people, called upon by fate for this special task. Motherhood is divine. You need us, you depend on us. We are participating in the resurrection of our people.'

"My friends, only a strong family life will create a powerful and pure nation. Let us raise another toast to the happy couple, but this time in the hope that many fine and healthy Aryan babies will be the fruit of their union. To your children!"

"To your children!" shouted the smiling crowd.

"Before we turn to our food - and I know you are all even hungrier now than when I started - I want to finish with a closing remark. You see these two runes here?" The Reichsführer pointed to the pictures that stood in their frames before him. "You will be familiar, of course, with the double victory rune of our order. But perhaps not all of you know that although the symbol seems to represent two bolts of lightning that will strike anyone who dares to stand in our way, this SS rune also symbolizes the all-powerful sun which rules over the Earth." Himmler picked up the frame and, turning to the couple, continued, "Frau Von Knobelsdorff, there is a good reason for calling our wedding rite the Eheweihen - the initiation. By virtue of this rite, you have been initiated into the family of the SS. The double bolt of lightning will always protect you. The rays of the sun will always warm you." He bowed to Gertrude, returned the frame to its position, and picked up the other image, showing it first to the room.

"The second rune we display at our weddings is the Hagall rune. This is the symbol carved into the SS-Ehrenring, proudly carried now by the Castle Captain. It is the mother symbol of our runic alphabet, the foundation stone of our beliefs." He picked up the frame and showed it to the bridal couple: "Captain Von Knobelsdorff, this rune conveys our unshakable faith in the ultimate victory of our philosophy. By virtue of this rite your memory will be preserved for eternity. Upon your death, your Ehrenring will be enshrined forever in the crypt of this castle. Your immortality is assured!"

Himmler returned the picture to its place on the table and began clapping. Everyone joined in. He sat down, and stared straight ahead for a few moments, before turning to Hermann. "I should have finished with another toast."

"It was an excellent speech," replied Hermann. "Everyone is so hungry they want food rather than drink."

"I could tell you were not expecting your promotion, Captain - or rather I should say SS-Obersturmführer."

"That is true…" began Hermann.

"When the war is over," Himmler lowered his voice, leaning so close that Hermann could smell his breath. "I want you to take over Krause's department. He will be ready for retirement by then, and we will need fresh blood." Glancing at Krause, who sat to his other side, but was deep in conversation with another officer, Himmler continued: "A life in Berlin, regular foreign expeditions - I envy you."

Hermann was about to speak, to think of a way of declining the promotion, of saying he preferred the life of a pilot, but Himmler returned to the subject of his speech: "I wanted to talk about the bridal cup - that strange tradition we have of pouring wine onto the dress of the bride, but I find the custom crude and unnecessarily wasteful. Nevertheless there are links, they say, with the story of the grail, and that subject has fascinated me for many years. You too, Captain, I understand, from reading your reports."

"It has indeed, Reichsführer. And being posted to Brittany, so close to an area associated with the grail story, has been a great privilege."

"The Abbé Gillard must be a man of considerable learning."

"It has been a pleasure to share his company and to learn from him."

"I have no sympathy for the religion of Christ, as you must have understood from my speech, but I do know that a seam of truth runs through that religion, and still burns like a dim flame amongst certain of the clergy. I would like to visit your man's church one day and converse with him, and with the prophetess Zaepffel - she must be an extraordinary woman."

"She is certainly that," replied Hermann.

"When I was in Barcelona two years ago with our Führer, conferring with General Franco, I made a visit to the Abbey of Montserrat. Do you know it?"

"I have heard of it, but have never had the pleasure…"

"I was on a quest for the grail," continued Himmler, who now seemed oblivious of his surroundings, and had not yet touched his food. "It really is in a splendid location - high up on the edge of a jagged mountainside an hour or so from the city. I had no interest in the Abbey itself, following as it does the Order of Dominic the Inquisitor. Instead I was like a bloodhound, following a trail started for me by that man Otto Rahn, whose book so fired my imagination."

"'Crusade Against the Grail'?"

"Exactly - that's the one. A work of genius." Himmler broke into a broad smile, clearly delighted that Hermann knew of it. "As you must know, then, he took the clue, given by Wolfram von Eschenbach, that the grail was kept in Montsalvat. Rahn thought that pointed to Montségur in the Pyrenees, but I had read that it was in reality further south - in Montserrat. I was sniffing. I found nothing. Perhaps Rahn was right."

"His thesis seems compelling. I have just started reading the book here."

"Ah good! He is no longer with us, of course. You knew that I presume?"

"Rahn is no longer alive?"

"We recruited him to the Ahnenerbe. He was our bright star - like you. We also promoted him to Obersturmführer. But then we found out that he was a homosexual, and - too late - a Jew." Himmler turned to

Hermann and looked directly at him. "You are not a homosexual are you Captain?"

"No, I am not."

"It must be rooted out, Captain! The vice is everywhere where men gather and cannot control themselves. Discipline is essential."

Hermann nodded, searching in vain for a way to move the conversation to a new topic.

"Rahn held such promise for us," Himmler said. "Or so we thought. He killed himself just before the outbreak of war - simply walked out into a snow storm in Austria. We had punished him lightly for his sodomy - a spell of guard duty in Dachau - nothing you or I could not endure with ease!" Himmler smiled, and turned at last to his food.

Hermann took the opportunity to eat too, filling and re-filling his mouth as often as he could, to make it clear he could not speak.

"This salad is excellent, is it not?" Himmler looked jovially around the room. "One day the entire SS will be vegetarian and tee-total - a life of purity and inner strength."

Krause turned to them both and explained that all the vegetables were grown by the prisoners at the nearby Niederhagen concentration camp, which provided labour for the castle.

Hermann left the hall as soon as the meal was over. He returned to his room, and instead of thinking about the consequences of his promotion, as he knew he should, he decided to finish his study of Rahn's work. Although the book had started with an exploration of medieval German poetry, this soon led to the romantic poetry of the Troubadors, and thence to Occitania - a region of France south of Brittany - where the heretical teachings of the Cathars and Albigensians flourished, until, in the early 13th century, Pope Innocent III authorised a crusade against the heretics that resulted in cruelty and slaughter on a massive scale.

All the while, as Rahn detailed the viciousness and ingenuity of the alliance between the Catholic church and northern France, who wanted to crush the political and economic power of Occitania, he was weaving another story like a bright thread in the tangled darkness. In the region's labyrinthine network of caves, with their vast underground cathedrals, deadly ravines and freezing black lakes, the Cathars were able to hide from the crusaders for years, worshipping in secret, and guarding their most treasured possession: the Holy Grail.

As Hermann read about the Cathars, he learned that they rejected the trappings of wealth and power which they believed had corrupted the church. Instead they led an ascetic life, believing that the world of the body was corrupt, and that suicide was permitted in certain circumstances.

Hermann saw in his mind Rahn struggling through the snow, traumatised by his experience of being arrested and then told to guard prisoners in Dachau. He imagined him walking and walking until cold and exhaustion took hold, the snow falling all around him.

Although the Cathars allowed suicide, even encouraged it in certain situations, wrote Rahn, they insisted that it be done not out of fear, but from a state of 'perfect disengagement from matter'. They could kill themselves only in a moment of mystical vision - filled with a sense of divine beauty and generosity. Did Rahn stand in the snow, wondered Hermann, letting go of his body in a state of ecstasy rather than trauma?

The Cathars taught that we only start to live once we die, and so only a person who fully wants to live can be allowed to commit the act which they termed the 'Endura'. Perhaps Rahn had decided to begin his life rather than end it, thought Hermann, realizing that in the last few months in Brittany he had been experiencing a sensation of his own life ending - closing in on him, so that he no longer felt in possession of it. He longed for some sort of rebirth.

The Cathars apparently accepted five ways of committing suicide: through poison, starvation, cutting the veins, hurling oneself off a cliff, or taking a hot bath and then lying down on cold blocks, to catch pneumonia. Perhaps, thought Hermann, Rahn took a hot bath before walking out into the snow.

He closed the book and looked from the window to the hills. And then the memory returned to him. He was twelve years old, seated in the dining room between his mother and sister, while across the table his father and their dinner guest discussed the ancient Indian religion of Jainism. Heinrich Lüders, a professor of Indology, began to describe the Jain practice of Sallekhana - voluntary suicide - and then, remembering that children were present, asked his mother whether she felt the topic suitable for 'sensitive young minds', as he put it. This alerted Hermann, of course, who was determined to remain with the adults. "You may leave the table now, dears," his mother had said, and his sister had grasped the opportunity to escape at once. But he insisted on remaining. "I am old enough!" he declared, and he was allowed to stay.

A Jain, he learned that night, can ask their spiritual superior for permission to end their life, and if this is granted they simply stop eating, and finally, cease drinking too. The Jains have no priests, and so a monk or nun or spiritual teacher must be consulted, and permission is only given if a person's obligations to their family have been satisfied, or old age or illness will soon end their life in any case. But perhaps there were exceptions, thought Hermann. If a Jain monk had been told that Rahn was about to be unmasked as a Jew, that he had guarded his own people in a concentration camp, that his sexual life had been uncovered and condemned, perhaps that monk, like an old Cathar priest well acquainted with the grief of this world, would have gently nodded with a look of compassion as the young man stepped out into the cold of the night.

CHAPTER TWENTY

"There is a flight leaving for Point-Clos tomorrow from the Fourth Division airbase at Bad Saarow," said Krause the next morning over breakfast. "You can spend tonight there."

Bad Saarow, tucked around the northern end of the Scharmuetzelsee, just a short drive south-east of Berlin, had been a fashionable spa town during the Roaring Twenties, with film stars, artists and politicians, and celebrated sportsmen like the boxer Max Schmeling, living beside the lake. They had all been attracted to the town's rural surroundings so close to the capital, and by its reputation as a place for rejuvenation and healing. At the Bad Saarow spa you could soak in thick dark mud, warmed and pumped into baths. And you could float in ancient sea-water drawn from the depths into elegant pools. Like the Russian poet Maxim Gorky, who stayed at the spa for a year when suffering from TB, you could follow the treatments of Dr Grabley, a specialist in water therapies, or - like Winston Churchill who stayed in 1930 - you could play a round of golf, or watch an international chess tournament.

"You can pretend you are a film star or a famous boxer," continued Krause. "I, meanwhile, must return to Berlin - some of us have work to do."

Hermann knew of the place as a favourite resort of the rich and famous, but had never visited it. He joined a group of officers who were leaving Wewelsburg that morning to return to the Bad Saarow complex. During the drive, he learned how the resort had been transformed by the war. The local clinic had become a military hospital, the Fourth Air Division had built an airstrip and established itself alongside the anti-aircraft artillery school. The concentration camp north of Berlin at Sachsenhausen had provided most of the labour for these projects.

"There is even a branch of the Ardenne Institute outside the town," said one of the men travelling with Hermann, Wolfgang Schrader. "Some say it's a weapons research institute. All top secret. You can't get anywhere near it."

Hermann fell asleep in the car as they drove past the lakes of the Mark Brandenburg, waking only when they arrived at the base. Everyone piled out and began walking towards one of the buildings. "This is your treat, Hermann," said another of the men, laughing. "Krause told us not to mention it until we got here - he said you like surprises. He's arranged for us all to have an evening of R&R courtesy of the Fourth Division. That means hot mud, hot water and hot women."

"We'll leave our things here," said Wolfgang as they entered a dormitory, "then go straight to the spa. It's closed to the public, but not to us."

As they walked around the lake it started to rain. Grey clouds hung low in the sky, and the place, far from looking like a glamorous resort, seemed tired and past its prime. The paint was peeling from the villas whose gardens ran down to the shore. Uncleared gutters, filled with leaves, spilled rainwater against mildewed walls.

The spa, too, looked neglected, as if it had been closed for business for years. On entering the building, though, that impression vanished. A woman at a reception desk checked their booking, and showed them to the treatment rooms. They showered first and then entered a room in which another woman, dressed in a grey uniform, was filling a small pool with black mud, using a hand pump connected to a pipe that disappeared into the ground. "Oh god, will you pump me like that, nurse?" shouted out Wolfgang.

"Behave yourselves boys, otherwise I might just make sure the mud is boiling when you get into it." She gave the sort of half smile that women give when teased by men. Hermann could never tell whether such smiles concealed contempt or pity.

One by one the men piled into the pool, but he hesitated. "Get in up to your neck, Obersturmführer!" shouted one of them at him in a voice of mock command. And so he did, sinking down into the pool, enjoying the feeling of his body being enveloped in the warmth and darkness.

"I could shit in here and you would never know," said Wolfgang.

From the mud-bath, via the showers, they moved to the sea-water pool with its high-vaulted ceiling. "So this is where Käthe Dorsch and Viktor de Kowa swam?" echoed Hermann's voice across the water

"Yes, all the stars were here," said Wolfgang. "And now it's just for us: the masters of the master-race."

Hermann needed to get back to Brocéliande. He didn't belong with these people. His destiny lay in that forest, not at Krause's desk in Berlin, bound forever to the madness of the Ahnenerbe. He floated on his back in the warm salty water, his body becoming more and more relaxed while his soul began to flounder in the darkness.

"Time for the sauna!" shouted out Wolfgang, and once more they were in the showers together, and then seated in the close warm silence of the sauna room.

Wolfgang looked at Hermann. "Forgive me asking, Hermann, but how could we all not notice?" In saying that, he deliberately lowered his gaze to stare at Hermann's groin. "You're not a Jew-boy are you?"

Hermann looked directly at Wolfgang. He wanted to hit him, but he could only feel a sense of dread in the pit of his stomach. "Oh for God's sake! Sometimes you just have to circumcise a boy. You know that."

"If Rahn could get away with it, why not another favourite of our esteemed leader?" Wolfgang laughed, but the laughter sounded hollow to Hermann. "The girls might not like it when they see it."

"I'm not coming with you. I'm tired. I'm not in the mood."

"Oh come on, they'll do anything. You can hit them about - a little, not too much of course. Or you can get them to smack you about, if that's what you prefer. They're up for anything - as long as you pay them well."

"No. Not my idea of fun. I'm tired. I told you."

"Those Jews have got it coming to them, you know," continued Wolfgang as if he wasn't finished with Hermann.

"What do you mean, Wolfgang?" asked another of the men.

"We are not supposed to talk about it, but so many know now." He hesitated for a moment. "Gas," he finally explained, sweeping his hand in front of him as if he was flicking aside dirt or flies. "It's quick, and followed by incineration. They're building more ovens in the camps now to cope with the load." He opened the door of the sauna stove and threw a log into the flames.

No-one spoke. Hermann waited until he could bear it no longer. He stood up and told them he was walking back to the base.

Before he knew it, the aircraft had landed and he was standing again in the cold damp air of Brittany. Everything was starting to seem more and more unreal. When in Berlin his time away had felt like a dream, a jumble of memories: making love to Geneviève, flying in the air above her house, walking with Gillard in the countryside, and now the few days he had passed in Germany seemed dream-like too - driving through the snow, remembering his youth of freedom, the castle with its dismal crypt, his promotion by Heinrich Himmler after that pompous wedding ceremony. But then the dream had turned into a nightmare. He kept seeing Wolfgang laughing as he talked about the ovens, throwing a log into the stove as if it was the body of a child. He had to tell Geneviève. This is what she had seen when she collapsed in tears on her bed. This is what his people were doing.

He threw his bag into his room and walked over to the bike compound. None of the bikes seemed to have enough petrol in them. He took one and rode over to the pump. He hoped no-one would see him - he didn't want to talk to anyone now. He rode to the Manoir as fast as he could. She had to know. However she or René felt about the battle between the Aryan and Semitic races, the massacre of St Eutrope - the nonsense she had talked about - she would be appalled to know the truth.

He knocked at the door. And then he saw through the window pane René Zaepffel walking towards him.

"Good morning, Captain. How nice to see you here. Please come in."

Hermann wanted to turn and walk away. What was he to say?

"Good morning. I wondered if a card reading might be possible with Mme Zaepffel? She really is so gifted."

"She is indeed, Captain. But I'm afraid the future must wait a while before it is revealed. She has gone to visit her aunt in Paimpont, and is not expected back until this evening. But do come and dine with us soon. I shall be here for several weeks and it would be a pleasure to entertain you. Do tell Commandant Ernst that you and he would be most welcome."

On leaving the Manoir, instead of riding back to the base, Hermann turned north and headed for the Fontaine de Barenton - an old spring, known as Merlin's pool, which lay in the forest beside the hamlet of Folle Pensée. He needed to be alone, to come to terms with the horror of what he now knew.

He had walked there once with Gillard. They had been standing by the Fairies' Mirror, and the abbé had asked Hermann if he felt like a longer walk - to visit what he believed was the site of an old druid college. They then followed a path that led beside the lake and deeper into the Valley of No Return - up past further smaller lakes and ponds connected to each other by the stream that once fed the old mill. By a gnarled and moss-covered oak, they struck away from the stream and followed a narrower track that led into the darkness of the forest. Eventually they reached a small clearing.

From where they stood, Hermann saw only a cluster of stones ahead of them, but as they got nearer he could see the pool, contained in a basin formed of large granite slabs. It was big enough to bathe in, and every so often bubbles of gas rose through the still water, bubbles that were once used as a form of divination by the local women looking for the husband of their dreams.

Gillard peered down. "When will the war end?" he whispered. 'In three years', announced three bubbles that struggled to the surface.

"This is the site of the college I mentioned, Hermann. And in the world of legend this is where Merlin was entranced by Viviane, the Lady of the Lake, and trapped in a crystal sphere. He wanted only her affections, she wanted his special powers. Even in old age, it seems, we chase dreams and are fooled by love."

Leaving the bike in Folle Pensée, Hermann walked to the pool. Why was it so hard to think clearly? A blackbird called to him from a tree, sunlight filtering through the branches. He sat on one of the stone slabs beside the spring. He was trapped, like Merlin, in some form of nightmare. He couldn't get the thought of thousands of people, men, women, children, whole families, being herded together, gassed, burned. He started shaking his head over and over again until he caught himself doing this, and stared down, instead, into the darkness of the water.

What was the point of telling Geneviève - how could he anyway, now that René was back? And what had she meant by the 'sword of justice'? Perhaps she would feel all this horror was regrettable but necessary to win the battle against the Semitic race. What insanity that was, as if race mattered at all. He might be half Jewish, for all he knew. Perhaps his mother had made love to a Jewish friend - after all, his family were all free spirits in their youth. Perhaps that was why his parents sometimes had the most furious rows behind closed doors, why the old rabbi had circumcised him.

His sense of self, of who he really was, was starting to unravel. There was nothing to hold on to. No centre. Desire had made him blind. In the pit of his stomach he knew now that he was guilty of the worst form of pride, born out of a sense of superiority - a belief that he was more intelligent than the people who controlled his destiny. He had always thought the mission of the Ahnenerbe to prove the supremacy of the Aryan race absurd. His error had been to think this didn't matter, that he could still work for them, ignoring their stupidity, and remain untainted by it all. His error had been to not really think at all. And all the time he had ignored the anti-semitism that was fomenting everywhere around him, as if he believed that, like the three monkeys who cover their ears, eyes and mouth, he could maintain his innocence as long as he ignored evil. At least Geneviève had the sincerity of conviction, whereas he was a hypocrite - his actions separated from his beliefs by a lack of compassion, a refusal to engage with questions of morality.

He stood and looked around him. Perhaps he should talk to Gillard, confess everything to him, tell him that he loved all of life, all people, wherever they came from, that he worked for the Ahnenerbe, and that he did this, not because of its obsession with racial doctrines, but because of its interest in history, ideas, research. Surely someone would have to be dead not to feel excited by the thought of expeditions to lamas in Tibet, shamans in Siberia? But to confess everything would mean telling Gillard he had betrayed his friendship, that he had been spying on him and had sent details of his plans to Berlin, that he had betrayed René and Geneviève.

All of a sudden the whirling of thoughts and feelings stopped, as if a wind had suddenly dropped. And then just one thought came riding into his mind: there is another person you have betrayed - your own self, the image of who you are and what you hold dear. Your humanity, Hermann, your soul.

He had gone too far down this path now and there was nothing to be done.

CHAPTER TWENTY-ONE

Gillard was sitting at his favourite table in Harel's. The door opened, and in walked Hermann. Gillard waved: "Ah, there you are! I thought I might have seen you over the weekend. I have just been telling Madame Harel about the Stations of the Cross, my dear friend. A rather serious subject, perhaps, given our surroundings and the time of day, but please join us."

Mme Harel winked at Hermann. "Some crêpes for you, Captain?"

"The idea behind walking the Stations of the Cross is to help you take the same journey as Christ - from suffering to resurrection," continued Gillard, nodding to Mme Harel on Hermann's behalf, since he failed to answer her request. "It is supposed to help you - to make you think, not despair." Gillard offered Hermann a cigarette. Mme Harel returned from behind the bar with bowls of cider and a plate of crêpes, made with salted butter.

"Are you well, Hermann?" asked Gillard, who thought his friend seemed unusually distracted.

"I think so, but a good deal has occurred recently."

"Time marches on, doesn't it? Even in a quiet little spot like this, where nothing seems to happen." Gillard smiled. Keen to pursue his chosen topic, he continued, "It is a mistake to think of each station merely as a depiction of a stage in the historical journey of Jesus to the cross. Remember that religious pictures are forms of ideographic writing - they use images and colour to convey spiritual concepts and experiences. I want to commission a set of paintings for the church depicting the Stations in the local landscape, with local figures: you and me, Monsieur and Madame Harel, as many of us as possible, to reinforce the idea that these images are about us, about how we overcome the trials and difficulties of our lives: how Christ can live in us…"

"I don't think you should depict me," interrupted Hermann. "I don't think a German officer should be invited to take part in such a project."

"But you are part of the community now. People like you here."

"You have handsome features, Captain," said Mme Harel, pouring them more cider. "You shouldn't hide your light under a bushel."

"But we have invaded your country, for heaven's sake!"

A moment's silence followed. Then Mme Harel spoke: "Well, we certainly don't blame you for that, Hermann."

Gillard simply shrugged his shoulders, then carried on: "I am sketching out each image, making notes of the colours I want to use, and of the number symbolism that should be conveyed."

"Who will you get to paint them?" asked Mme Harel.

"I don't know yet. I think the next step will be to take photographs of the settings: the manor house, the Valley of No Return, and so on. Then we should have photographs taken of all those who wish to take part, wearing the appropriate clothing and striking the right poses. We can make up costumes for them and store them afterwards. One day we can use them to put on a Passion Play."

Mme Harel took their empty plates from the table. "Where do you get your ideas from, Father? You are wasted on us here."

Gillard waved the compliment away. "The Realists have been using photography to help them with their compositions since the last century. I'm really not that original. When the photographs are ready I will approach an artist, and he will have all he needs to get started." Gillard stopped talking, lost in thought. He sighed to himself, and then began again: "I had forgotten for a moment there was a war going on. I suppose it may not be so easy to get photographs developed these days."

"I think I can help you with that. We have a photographer at the base," said Hermann. "He's a good man, and has access to a darkroom."

"Can I meet him?" asked Gillard. "Perhaps I could come to the base? I've often wondered what it looks like."

When Hermann arrived a few days later to take Gillard to Point-Clos, he told him that the Commandant had at first refused his request. "Of course the priest can't visit the base. This isn't a tourist attraction!" Ernst had thundered. The following day, though, he had sought out Hermann: "I owe you an apology, Captain. I had completely forgotten an instruction I received from Berlin some time ago, stating that individuals with a standing in the community should be encouraged to visit the base under strict supervision." With just a hint of irony in his voice he had continued, "Apparently allowing visitors to see our aircraft will demonstrate the invincibility of the Reich and the futility of resistance."

Gillard smiled and climbed into the sidecar of Hermann's motorbike. "I hope you convinced him I'm not a spy."

"The English and the Americans don't have a chance," Ernst told the abbé proudly as he showed off his planes: sixty Dornier bombers, forty Junker troop carriers, twenty-four Stukas, a dozen Messerschmitt fighters, and more than a hundred military gliders. Hermann accompanied them as Ernst took Gillard over to his tree nursery to explain his plans for an arboretum at the base. In the Crimea, he told him, they would plant thousands of acres of forest, to reproduce the landscape of their homeland for the Germans who would settle there. "Wherever we go we will plant forests, not just for their beauty and the wood that they produce, but for the benefit of our children and future generations."

In the officers' mess they met the base photographer, Peter Koch, who had dined with Ernst and Hermann at the Manoir soon after Hermann had arrived at Point-Clos.

"Let me show you my work, Father," said Peter, opening a folder of prints. There were scenes of farmers gathering hay, local churches and landscape shots, as well as portraits of officers and photographs of aeroplanes.

"You clearly have a gift for this," said Gillard, impressed by the quality of his pictures. "Would you be free next Sunday to take some landscape photographs? And then perhaps a week or so later, for photographs of the villagers? I'm assuming Hermann has told you about our plans?"

"He has indeed, and provided we are not needed here, I will look forward to being of use to you on Sunday. Hermann will you come with us?"

"Of course."

"Now all I must do is pray for sunshine," said Gillard.

By Sunday it seemed as if his prayers would be answered. Scattered clouds were stretched high above them, and looking to the west Gillard could see a bank of clear sky that widened even as he gazed at it. He stood outside the church, fulfilling his duty as the congregation left: congratulating some, commiserating with others, gently admonishing a few for their lack of attendance since he hadn't seen them for a while. But his heart really wasn't in it. He wanted to be up there on the heights and in the forest, supervising the photography, choosing the best angles, like a director of one of the films he was now showing regularly in the rectory cinema.

Peter and Hermann were waiting for him outside Harel's. "We've only just arrived," said Peter.

"The weather is perfect. It's cold, but clear, which is what we want. Shall we go straight away or would you both like a drink?" asked Gillard.

"Let's get going," said Hermann, looking at his watch.

They went first to photograph the manor house in the village. Peter worked fast, telling Hermann where to set up the tripod, measuring the light with his meter, and then taking just one image from each position. Gillard suggested viewpoints, but this was hardly necessary - Peter was clearly good at this. They walked to the Valley of No Return to photograph the lake. Gillard led them up to Arthur's seat to take pictures of the vista, the seat itself, and the Fairies' Mirror below.

"Let's refresh ourselves at Harel's now," said Gillard, as they walked back to the village. "And then if you have the time, we could drive into the forest and I could show you some other sites you might like to photograph."

As they sat in the bar eating toasted ham and cheese, Gillard confided in them another project he had recently dreamt up. "I have been thinking we could offer postcards for sale of local places associated with the legends - and of the church itself and its new windows. What do you think? Could we fit in some work on this today?" Before they had the time to reply, he carried on: "We could even release a guidebook once the war is over and it's easier to get things printed."

"That sounds like an excellent idea," said Peter, glancing at Hermann, who was gazing into the distance with a frown. "What do you think, Hermann?"

"Oh yes, a good idea, of course," said Hermann.

Once they had finished eating, Gillard asked them, "Which way is it going, do you think?"

Peter imitated a French shrug of the shoulders: "The best response is provided by your fellow countrymen, father. We don't shrug much in Germany, but we should." Gillard insisted on paying Mme Harel, and they set off on their next mission, to take photographs for the postcard series. Peter drove the bike, Hermann sitting behind him, Gillard in the sidecar.

"I feel I'm getting into the cockpit of one of your planes," he called out as he climbed in. They drove first to the hamlet of Folle Pensée, just half a kilometre or so from the Fontaine de Barenton, the site of Merlin's Pool. After photographing the pool in the afternoon sun, they walked up to the old burial site of the Hôtie de Viviane and stopped on their way back to Trého at Merlin's tomb - the remains of a dolmen that lay close to the road.

"It's become too dark now," said Peter, looking at his light meter as they stood in the clearing around the stones. "I'll come back another day for this."

"Thank you so much," said Gillard when the officers dropped him off at the rectory on their way back to the base. "I look forward to you both coming back soon. And Hermann, I almost forgot to ask. I do hope you will agree to pose for us as Christ, my dear friend? I think you have the right face for it."

Gillard had already sketched out his ideas for each of the Stations. Although he knew it would provoke the Church hierarchy, he wanted to weave in traces of the Arthurian and Grail legends. In the Ninth Station he would have Morgan le Fay, often depicted in the Arthurian stories as a witch and enemy of the Round Table, dressed in red to symbolize the sin of Lust. In the Thirteenth Station he would show Joseph of Arimathea receiving the blood of Christ in the emerald grail cup.

In the Twelfth Station he would show the sun radiating on the horizon behind the crucifixion scene. He would ask the artist to paint it with the sun at the same level as Christ's solar plexus. Asking Hermann to pose for this scene might seem odd, he thought, but it wasn't that unusual. Many European photographers had used live models to depict episodes from Christ's life, and he had read that in America, the photographer Holland Day had himself posed for an image of the crucifixion, and the artist Thomas Eakins once strapped a young man who had agreed to model as Christ, wearing only a loin cloth, to a cross mounted on the roof of his house in Philadelphia.

Over the coming weeks Gillard approached the villagers he had in mind. The school-teacher, Mme Heriot, would make a perfect Morgan. To his surprise she readily agreed. Perhaps she was unfamiliar with the legends? Or perhaps she had only read of Morgan in Chrétien de Troyes, who depicted her in a positive light as a healer. He noted, to his shame, that he failed to fully explain that she would be representing a cardinal sin. He made a mental note to clarify this with her as soon as he felt up to the task.

In the meanwhile it was a question of getting Peter to photograph her and the other villagers who would fulfill the roles of centurions, Pharisees, the Virgin Mary, Simon of Cyrene, and Veronica who washed the face of Jesus.

A group of women took on the job of organizing the costumes, meeting in the rectory to work together sewing and stitching. Old dresses and curtains were pressed into service, Mme Heriot brought over her sewing machine, and Gillard busied himself advising them and admiring their work. Once they were finished, Peter agreed to spend a full day on the project, and a few days later he arrived early one morning with Hermann, just as the abbé was taking his breakfast. Peter was excited and talkative, and was looking forward to exercising his skills, but Hermann said little. He set up the tripod and attached the Rolleiflex to it while Peter went outside to check the weather, soon calling out: "The sky is clearing, Hermann, and it really is unusually warm for this time of year. We can move outside!"

Moments later, Marie-Thérèse Heriot arrived to be photographed as Morgan le Fay. She was wearing a scarlet dress with slender shoulder straps. Her hair was normally tied back, but today it fell sensuously to her shoulders and she wore a lipstick that matched the colour of her dress.

Peter and the abbé both complimented her on her appearance. "Stand here, Mme Heriot," said Gillard, "and imagine that you are looking down on our Lord who has just stumbled as he carries his cross. Look at this stone here - he would be about here for you."

Peter took several photographs, and was satisfied these would be sufficient. Gillard could tell Mme Heriot was disappointed. So much work had gone into preparing for this moment, and within minutes it was all over. He reassured her that more photographs would be taken later. "Please stay with us. Help us decide which position each person should adopt, and try to put them at ease."

"And I can help with refreshments too," replied Mme Heriot, clearly relieved she could prolong the time she was able to wear her dress and be seen by the other villagers. Her husband came across and sat down to watch, seeming at once both amused and irritated by the whole business. Soon the rest of the models turned up, along with their husbands and wives, and some of their children too.

Mme Heriot put on more of the coffee substitute they had now grown used to, and Mme Harel fetched bread from the bakery. The abbé walked away from the gathering crowd in the rectory garden, to survey the scene from a distance. He wanted to savour this moment, to take his own mental snapshot. It was like a village fête, a pantomime and a photographic session for a magazine all rolled into one. In one corner Hervé was being prepared as Joseph of Arimathea: one woman combing his beard, another applying rouge to his cheeks as she tried to suppress her laughter. In another part of the garden Peter was photographing a centurion.

"Stay in your costumes please!" called out Gillard. "In addition to taking photographs of each of you, for the artist to copy your features and your costume, we will also try arranging you in tableaux. And when we have finished, we will take a group photograph."

By midday everyone else had been photographed, and it was time for Hermann to take up his pose. Gillard had decided that the Christ of Tréhorenteuc should wear the simplest of loin cloths. He thought the majority of paintings and sculptures adorned the Son of God with far too much cloth. Michelangelo, Cellini and El Greco had all disposed of any covering. There was a sound scriptural justification for this, he knew, but a naked Christ would be a step too far for his little grail chapel. Even so, he could follow in the footsteps of Thomas Eakins and, as if in expectation of the revelation of Christ's full humanity, the loin cloth would be drawn to one side to expose his thigh so that the entire length of his body could be seen.

Inside the rectory Gillard showed Hermann his drawing, and asked if he could accept being photographed with so little clothing. "It may seem a strange idea, Hermann, blasphemous even, but since the invention of photography this has become an accepted practice. I hope you are not offended by my suggestion?"

Hermann stared back at Gillard. "I cannot do this now - not with all these people here. Let me come back in a week or so."

For several weeks Gillard heard nothing from Hermann. He himself had a cold and was obliged to conduct two funerals for elderly parishioners who had both by chance died on the same day on the outskirts of the village. But now he was feeling well again, and had spent the morning helping out his stonemason friends at the quarry. Mme Harel called at the rectory in the afternoon, looking worried: "Hermann was here this morning, asking for you. He told me to tell you that he will come with Peter tomorrow to pose for the photograph. But he was in a strange mood, Father. He was distant - thin and drawn, as if he hasn't seen a decent meal in weeks. He has grown a beard, though, which suits him."

"He must be getting into character," replied Gillard as he lit a cigarette. For a moment he felt concerned for his friend. Hermann had certainly been very subdued recently, but that was no doubt due to the sadness of losing friends in combat. "If only this war would finish. Thank you for relaying his message."

CHAPTER TWENTY-TWO

Hermann and Peter arrived early at the rectory. As the abbé opened the door, he looked shocked. "Are you well, my dear friend? You look so gaunt - as if you haven't eaten for a long time. But I must say the beard does look splendid."

Hermann simply nodded. "Thank you. I'm ready now." He wanted to say more. He wanted to fall into Gillard's arms. To tell him everything. But he knew he couldn't. He knew he had to go on. "There is just one thing I would like to ask," he managed to say.

"Of course, Hermann. What is it?"

"Could we take the photograph inside?"

"Yes, how foolish of me," said Gillard. "Of course, that is far more sensible. Peter and I can bring the cross in from the garden while you undress upstairs." He walked over to the dresser and picked up a short length of rope and a piece of linen. "Your costume," he said with a smile. "It's not much, I know. But here is the sketch I have made, showing how I would like the loin cloth to fall. You will find a mirror up there."

While Gillard and Peter carried in the cross, Hermann undressed in the abbé's bedroom, which was sparsely furnished - just a wardrobe, a chest of drawers, an iron bed. A small crucifix hung on the wall above the bed. As Hermann came down the stairs, Gillard and Peter were talking earnestly together beside the cross, which now stood against the wall that was used as the cinema screen. The white sheet hung behind it. "No leave it, it will help with the light," said Peter.

Gillard turned to Hermann. "You look splendid, although perhaps the cloth should be drawn a little further aside so that more of the thigh can be seen. You realise the Fisher King reference, I suppose? No wound, of course, that would be wrong - but at least the eye will be drawn there, and there will be some who will understand the allusion."

"Ah, yes," said Hermann, remembering the detail in the grail story that the Fisher King, guardian of the Holy Grail, is wounded in the thigh.

While Peter busied himself with his camera and tripod, Gillard began to tie Hermann's wrists to the arms of the cross, his ankles to the upright.

Peter began moving the lamps that Gillard had brought down from the bedroom to create the right play of light and shadow on Hermann's body. Gillard tightened the last knot and stepped back. Hermann closed his eyes. He felt a little faint, but he knew that was the effect of the fasting. He had read that the spiritual exercises of Ignatius of Loyola, the founder of the Jesuits, involved imagining being crucified oneself, and he tried to do this now - straining against the ropes, longing for Gillard to actually take a spear and pierce his side so that he could feel the pain of the world in all its intensity.

The cords that Gillard had tied around his ankles and wrists started to bite into him, and Hermann focused on these four points of sensation as if nothing else existed in this moment.

"We have almost enough light," said Peter, "but not quite enough."

"I'll light as many candles as I can," said Gillard, looking in the dresser. He brought out a candelabra and placed it on a table near to Hermann. He took out candles from a drawer. Just then there was a sharp knock at the door. Gillard crossed the room, and opened the door just a little. "Could you come back later?"

"Father, my husband is leaving tomorrow and has been asking to see you for weeks. I do hope you don't mind?" It was Geneviève's voice. She almost pushed past Gillard and entered the room. Hermann could hear her gasp as she saw him on the cross. He could see René behind her, mouth open, looking directly at him.

"Excuse us please," said Gillard. "We are taking the last photograph for our project of illustrating the Stations of the Cross. We will only be a moment." He began directing them out. "If you could go over to Mme Harel's we will see you there shortly." Hermann closed his eyes.

The situation was so absurd, he wanted to cry out in laughter and fury at the stupidity of it all.

Gillard lit the candles. Peter began adjusting the camera position, moving his tripod further back. Hermann felt faint again. He breathed in deeply and pushed against the cords that held him. He knew Geneviève had gone but he could feel her now staring at him. She was gazing at him in horror or pain, he couldn't tell which, but then he felt her look change, and he could sense the love in her eyes. All at once he was filled with desire for her. He imagined her kneeling in front of him, and he remembered how she used to suck at him as if she was trying to pull every last seed out of his body, as if she would carry on well after he had come, until he cried out in agony, "Enough, enough!" And to his alarm he sensed his cock starting to swell as he thought of this. He saw himself now, hunched over his desk, writing his reports to Krause - telling that idiot about every dream and plan of his friends. He had betrayed not only these people he knew so well, but himself too - his integrity, his honesty, his freedom he had so casually relinquished. For weeks he had been tormented by the knowledge that he was utterly trapped, complicit in a regime that was now abhorrent to him. And here he was, an absurd spectacle, almost naked, unable to move, unable to tell anyone the truth. He bit his lip to draw his attention away from his groin, but the thoughts kept coming, flooding in on him as if this moment of shame was the moment he had waited for all his life - the moment in which, at its lowest point, in anguish over what he now knew, the vessel of his ego could at last shatter into a thousand pieces.

And then it seemed that all the barriers, which contained everything he had ever thought and felt, came crashing down, and he was drowning, straining there against the ropes that tied his legs and arms, holding his head as high as he could against the rising waters. And he could feel his cock again and it was becoming harder, and he was on a battlefield now as men stuck their pricks like bayonets into women and children - pushing again and again into bodies arching against them, legs pulled violently apart, disease and agony following their every movement like angry ghosts.

He saw that man in Bad Saarow throwing a log into the fire of the sauna. He imagined the horror of the ovens being fed with bodies.

In his heart he called out to God, to his Soul, to whatever was greater than him, and all at once he was there in the crypt at Wewelsburg, the perpetual flame now burning at its centre, its light hardly reaching the walls of the mausoleum, its reflection glowing darkly in the golden swastika high above. With one great surge of will, he broke free from the cross, the ropes snapping as he stepped forward, and with a single scream he blew out the flame.

There was a flash. "Just one more for luck!" said Peter.

"Thank you so much," said Gillard smiling, as Hermann opened his eyes. "I do appreciate all your help for something which took so long to organize, and then was over so quickly." He began to untie the cords that held his ankles and wrists. Peter was removing his camera from the tripod.

He was left to change on his own. They wanted him to join them in the bar, but instead he walked to the church and sat there alone in the dark. When enough time had passed, and he sensed Peter would be ready to leave, he slowly stood up and walked outside.

CHAPTER TWENTY-THREE

It had been a restless night - too hot and the air close as if awaiting a storm to crack it open and bring freshness again. When Gillard awoke in the rectory he felt ill at ease. His dreams had been troubling, but they slipped from his memory the moment he tried to grasp them as he sat on the edge of the bed.

There are poplar trees in the sky, he found himself thinking in his half-awake state. Is it in Heaven that all darkness is banished, or is darkness always beauty there, like the night sky? He shook his head, stood up and began to dress. He walked outside to the toilet shed, and then - after a brief tour of the vegetable patch - went inside to have his breakfast. Why are there days like this, when for no apparent reason one feels sad, and a little fearful, as if all is not right with the world?

It was then that he heard it. One single thud - quite far away in his estimation.

The plane came out of a clear blue sky. Geneviève had heard its engine some minutes before as she stood at her bedroom window. She did this every morning. After tea in bed she would get up, open the windows wide, and gaze out at the garden below and the forest on the horizon. She would admire her roses too, when they were in bloom. They were so well established they reached even higher than the first floor.

She too had not slept well and her dreams had been troubled. René had left her alone once again, and she felt uneasy standing there 'counting her blessings', as she called her morning ritual of reciting to herself every reason why she should be happy.

And then Hermann came flying low over the house as he had a dozen times before. She looked up and could see every detail of the undercarriage of his plane, and she began to feel angry. However many times she told him that it scared her, he still believed he could thrill her with this sudden invasion of her tranquility.

Once over the field that bordered the front lawn he began his climb. She imagined him laughing as he pulled back the joystick and her anger was gone. He had a freedom in his laugh that she loved. She had missed his visits recently, but knew he was avoiding her because René was at home. No doubt he was needed at the base too. Perhaps he would have more time for her again now.

The plane shot upwards and performed a perfect loop, and as it did so she could see a white trail of vapour following behind. It flew into a second loop in almost the same place above the field. She gasped out loud. He had done it. The white heart hung motionless in the air.

The Stuka turned, swooping into yet another dive. But then, just when it should have recovered and soared upward, it seemed to accelerate, and with a terrible fierceness headed straight for the ground. There was an almighty bang as if a bomb had exploded, and in an instant all she could see was the wreckage of the aircraft bursting into flames. A plume of black smoke rose into the air. She thought she saw the figure of Hermann engulfed in fire.

She wanted to run outside, but couldn't. She was frozen to the spot. The heart slowly dissolved into the morning sky.

Everything has stopped now. It is finished.

CHAPTER TWENTY-FOUR

August 1963

The psychiatric hospital at St.Avé, on the outskirts of the medieval town of Vannes, an hour's drive south of Tréhorenteuc, was built in the nineteenth century. But even in the 1960s it still retained a certain elegance, despite its modern outbuildings.

"I am so pleased you have come," said Dr Romelin, showing Geneviève to his patient's room. "Father Gillard, why don't you take advantage of this visit to get some fresh air, and show Madame Zaepffel the gardens and the lake? It is such a fine day."

Despite the sunshine, they had the grounds to themselves. Tall parkland trees provided shade, carefully tended white gravel paths wound through herbaceous borders, a blaze of colour - purple and yellow pansies in neat rows, bright orange marigolds framed in triangles of trimmed box. They began walking towards the lake. Geneviève apologized to Gillard for not having visited him or his church for so many years, conveyed her husband's greetings to him, and expressed her hopes that his health would soon be restored. Gillard listened without saying a word, and then stopped on the gravel path, and turned to Geneviève.

"Do you ever wonder if Hermann really existed? That may sound odd, I know, but sometimes, when I think of him, I can no longer see his face..." His voice trailed away, but then continued: "I have never asked you this before. Perhaps it is impertinent of me, but it is so long ago now, and we are both growing old. I realized early on that you were lovers, of course. But were you really in love with him, or was it just *une folie de guerre?*"

"Well," said Geneviève hesitantly, her eyes widening in surprise as she looked away from him, "I'm not entirely sure. Of course sometimes I thought I was, or felt I was, but then there were times when I was lying in René's arms and it would all feel so unreal, or so childish, as if my attraction to Hermann were simply the adolescent fantasy of a middle-aged woman who should have known better."

They began walking again until they reached a bench beside the lake that faced the sun. A family of ducks, disturbed by their arrival, swam swiftly away from the shore.

"Did Hermann kill himself or was it an accident? What do you think?" asked Gillard. "You know the talk of the village, I suppose." He regretted saying this the moment he finished his sentence, but the damage had been done, and perhaps it was better to voice these things.

"I really do not know, Henri. But tell me," said Geneviève, turning to face him, "Did you like Hermann?"

"Like him? I loved him! Not in the way you did, of course, but I loved him nevertheless."

"He admired you very much, you know. Those long walks you took in the countryside together, they were so important to him - he spoke about you often. I sometimes envy him. He died suddenly, Henri, but we are dying slowly. It must have been awful of course - those last moments in the flames."

Gillard held his face in his hands for a moment, and then stared into the water. "It must have been terrible," he agreed, trying hard not to imagine the scene. "Can I ask you something?"

"Of course, what is it?"

"I can't get this out of my mind at the moment, but perhaps you can help me. Why is it, do you think, that our lives took such a wrong turn once the war was over? You were imprisoned and humiliated. I was thrown out of my job and my home. Did we deserve it? Are we paying for our sins?"

For a moment Geneviève looked shocked, as if a priest, of all people, should know the answer to such questions. She turned her eyes to the other end of the lake, as though she wished she was far away. "Before the war, I was told in a vision that I would suffer imprisonment for my beliefs, but I would be saved. All I needed was faith. And three times, they threw me into prison - once, at the outbreak of war, and twice once the war ended. But every time I concentrated on the light, I prayed fervently, and my only concern was to help others. I consoled my fellow prisoners and tried to give them hope - as much as I could." Geneviève looked directly at Gillard. "Our lives didn't go wrong, Henri, and you will get through this. We are all tested in different ways. My prison was external - you have created a prison in your own mind. But the doctors will help you. You will recover."

Gillard shook his head slowly from side to side. He felt as if he was trying to free it of thoughts that clung to him against his will. "Thank you. Perhaps you are right. But I do wonder." He paused for a moment. "Have you never regretted deceiving René?"

"It is all so long ago now. The past is best left to rest."

"And what about your books and prophecies? Have you never regretted what you wrote? Even after seeing those films of Auschwitz and Buchenwald?"

"How can you say that, Henri? I never condoned such things, you know that. In fact I saw those horrors in my visions. I simply didn't know where they were, or who was causing them. Both sides committed atrocities. I only ever wanted peace amongst nations."

"You thought that the Jewish people were the enemy, though, didn't you? Along with the communists, the Jesuits and the Freemasons."

"Many people thought that way in those times. The forces of darkness were all around us. René and I sincerely believed that Germany and France would unite and lead the world to peace."

"But…"

"I abhor the suffering as much as you do."

Gillard sighed, looking out towards the lake. He then began to talk quietly, as if he was speaking to himself, "Who am I to cast stones? All I know is that I feel deep regret. I used to think that perhaps our salvation lay with Germany, that Brittany would be made free, that those wonderful ideals of the Romantic philosophers and poets would liberate us all. Who could fail to be inspired by the words of Schiller and Rilke, by the music of Wagner? But it all crumbled to dust in the madness of war. I feel out of place wherever I am now. I feel used up, empty. I sometimes wish I was no longer alive. I have even thought of ending it all."

Geneviève leant forward and held for a moment both his hands in hers. He wished he could return her warmth, to meet her gaze with gratitude in his eyes or in his words, but he felt as if his soul was paralyzed, unable to move or speak. He stared into the lake in silence. The family of ducks had become used to their presence and was once more paddling nearby. A breeze picked up, travelling across the water, rippling its surface, finally reaching them as they sat together on the bench. He rubbed his eyes. "I'm so sorry, my dear, but the pills they give me have the unfortunate effect of making me extremely tired in the afternoons. I'm afraid I must go and lie down."

Geneviève accompanied him to his room, promising to return soon. He lay down on the bed and gazed up at the ceiling, but the walk had stimulated him and he couldn't sleep. He lay there for almost an hour, and then decided to write in his journal. As he opened it, he came across its first entry, which he had read many times over. Written soon after his first stay at the hospital, it reminded him of how deeply affected he was by being dismissed from his position as rector of Tréhorenteuc.

Saint-Avé, April 10th 1963

These last few years have been so filled with darkness I still cannot detach myself from the weight of their memory. My judgement, I know, is affected, and I cannot trust myself to make the right decisions.

Listen to poor little me, the angry priest who was tormented by his superiors then ignored in the piss-pot of his village for twenty years, before being thrown onto the scrap heap!

In the Bay of Pigs the Americans and Russians have brought us to the brink of nuclear war. And in the face of all this darkness, how do I - the great Abbé Henri Gillard, creator of the grail chapel, saviour of the world - how do I react? Do I organize prayer groups or vigils as the world holds her breath while Kruschev and Kennedy play with our lives? No! Like some angry child, I ignore the advice of my friends, turn my back on my parish, and make the journey to Paris as if I were some Prodigal Son expecting to be welcomed into the arms of a forgiving father.

How can I even begin to tell my story to you: innocent bystander, curious student of the grail or of local history? I have to fight through a veil of despair and confusion to communicate at all. There's the darkness of the forest, Geneviève with her cards and her prophecies, Hermann in his Luftwaffe uniform, those evenings we spent by the fire in the Manoir, the terrible end to it all - and it's all such a jumble and seems so long ago now.

How ironic it is that our happiest times were during those days of the war, as if that bitter struggle somehow woke us all up and made everything more intense, more urgent. Nothing now feels powerful or vivid to me. Merlin even enters into my dreams telling me to come into the forest, reminding me that he too went mad. But he didn't have to suffer the sterility of this place, he didn't have to be drugged into forgetting by smiling men in white coats.

Self-pity is unattractive, thought Gillard, about to tear the entry from the book, but then he remembered Dr.

Romelin's advice to keep writing, never censoring, never destroying anything. "Just keep going," he had said. "You need to get it all out of you, you need to express it." For years he had kept notes of all the slights he had received from disapproving clergy, prying bishops. But then one day he had burnt the lot, thinking himself free, until, years later, a poison-pen letter arrived, unsigned, accusing him of bringing the Church into disrepute, telling him he should never have removed the tomb and statue of St Onenne. And so he had stuffed the letter into his pocket, and without a word to anyone, driven straight to Paris. If he wasn't appreciated in Trého, he would work elsewhere. For two months he stayed in the city, visiting one office of the church after the other, asking for a transfer to another parish. He applied for a post abroad as a missionary, he applied for social work in various branches of the labyrinthine world he had chosen to enter at the age of twenty-three. But the bishop was playing his end-game. The word was out: don't trust that man Gillard, he's mad. He's filled his church with immoral images. He's depicted lust by getting the local teacher to pose as a harlot in one painting, our Lord is almost naked in another.

And what was he to write in his journal today? That an old friend, Madame Zaepffel, the Druidess of Brocéliande, had come to visit him, after an absence of almost twenty years. That, as always, such gaps of time melt away in moments, as if they had seen each other just weeks ago, as if Hermann, too, would soon appear from the shadows, to join them on the bench beside the lake, to tell them how he had miraculously survived.

Geneviève drove out through the hospital gates slowly, Gillard at her side. She felt like a mother now to a man who seemed so broken. True to her word, she had returned, having telephoned Dr Romelin to ask if she could take his patient on a visit to the great inland sea in the Gulf of Morbihan. He told her he was delighted she would make such an effort.

Gillard gazed out of the window at the prim suburban villas that lined each side of the road. "When I was first taken to the hospital, I was very unhappy, as you know. But even in my despair I felt a lifting of my spirits as I was driven out of the confines of Brocéliande - as if I was breaking free from a spider's web that had entangled me for years. I now prefer the landscape here - the wide skies, the views of the sea. It sometimes seems to me as if the forest exerts a malign influence on those who live there."

There was little traffic on the road, and she speeded up a little - she preferred driving fast. "I cannot agree with you, Henri. The forest was my cradle and it will be my grave. I draw my inspiration from the trees and will never leave. But I do agree with you that it is good to spend time away from it - it is so much lighter here."

They were soon in open countryside. Yes, she thought, there is more light here. The vegetation is different too, the soil sandy not red, the trees standing less densely together. There was room to breathe here.

By the time they arrived at the port of Locmariquer, on the southern side of the great inland sea, it was midday. The fishing boats had returned with their catches, and oyster baskets were being stacked on the quay. As they walked along the harbour, the smell of newly-caught fish mingled with the fumes of oil and diesel from the engines of the ferry boats setting off for the islands. They studied the menus of the three restaurants which faced the sea. After some discussion, they chose the first they had seen, taking a table with a view of the water. The place was empty, they were the first customers of the day.

As they sat, Gillard smiled for the first time. "It is remarkably kind of you to bring me here, Geneviève."

She returned his smile. "I have always loved this town - the way it looks out to the islands."

"Perhaps we should have been fishermen or restauranteurs."

"We could arrange this for our next lives. I hope it's true that we have more than just one chance to get it right."

"You mean reincarnation?"

"Exactly. You remember our conversation all those years ago, with Hermann, beside the fire?"

"How could I forget it?"

Geneviève sighed a little. "It does seem hard if you are given only one attempt at a good life, doesn't it?"

Gillard picked up a menu. "I have to say I agree with you. Shall we choose our meal?" Once the waitress had left the table with their order, he looked at her seriously. "The world seems to be turning on its side these days, with Russia and America sabre-rattling and threatening us all with nuclear war. I sometimes fear for humanity."

For a little while the two of them shared their concerns for the world they now found themselves in - a world, they agreed, that felt increasingly alien. And then Gillard asked her: "Perhaps you can reassure me. Do you have any prophecies, any predictions for the years to come?"

"I am surprised you ask me, Henri, given my spectacular failures. You are asking the woman who predicted the triumph of Germany, its conquest of Russia, the collapse of the United States."

Gillard shook his head. "I am asking the woman who saw into the future and predicted the atom bomb falling on Japan, the awful tragedy of the Holocaust. I imagine looking into the future is like gazing into a pool of water - sometimes you see clearly what lies beneath the surface, sometimes currents distort the image."

Geneviève picked up a menu, but made no attempt to read it. "That is so generous of you, Henri. If only the Prosecutor who dealt with me after the war thought the same way. But I deserved what I got. I was a fool. My only excuse is that I was blinded by love." She stopped, wondering if it was unwise, or too self-indulgent, to continue. But Father Gillard was, after all, a priest - a man to whom one could, or even should, confess. "I have to tell you, Henri, as soon as I met Hermann I lost my gift, but I didn't have the courage to admit it. When I was younger, I had the most spectacular successes - I predicted the conquest of Ethiopia by Italy, the assassination attempt on Adolf Hitler, the division of Germany, and - as you say - I did indeed see a conflagration raining down on Japan, and other events that came to pass. But then Hermann arrived, and all I could think about was him. The past and the future vanished for me - I was no longer interested in them. I forgot everything I owed my parents, my family, my religion, my René. All I wanted was Hermann - his touch, his voice, his smile." She took in a deep breath and turned away from Gillard now, looking beyond him to the window, and out to the sea. "Instead of telling the truth - that I was no longer guided by my spirits - I lied. I made up those ridiculous verses in that madness of a book I called '1943 - Year of Hope'. I thought my lines would be so obscure, people would be intrigued by them and would find some meaning I had failed to grasp myself. But how could I tell the truth? That I wanted only Hermann? That would have been suicide."

She wanted to leave now. That was enough. She knew that stirring up the past was a bad idea. Now it was as if she had been lying with Hermann only days ago, his strong body against hers. Now it was as if his plane had crashed into the ground only yesterday, and she was caught again in the vortex of suffering. She could feel the tears coming. Gillard touched her arm. "We often only know how we should behave with the benefit of hindsight. Do not be too hard on yourself. You have done great good in the world. And you gained the love of two fine men. Both Hermann and René adored you, you know that."

She did know that, but it meant nothing to her in that moment. It seemed as if all her life had been wasted, had been built upon vanity and weakness. But she was saved from sinking further into despair by the arrival of their meal. She raised her glass. "To you, my dear Henri. May you soon leave the hospital, restored to good health!"

Gillard bowed his head with a smile, and then raised his glass, "To friendship!" For a few moments they ate their meal in silence, until Geneviève made a suggestion.

"Shall we go onto the sea after lunch? We could take a boat out to Gavrinis."

An hour or so later they were seated on a small boat along with half a dozen others and their guide. As they set out across the water they could see small islands in every direction. Three seagulls flew above the stern, as if to remind them that the open sea of the Atlantic was only a breath away. Through the megaphone the guide told them that there were forty-two islands in the gulf, some inhabited, most not. And there, to their left, they could see a semi-circle of stones on the edge of one of the smallest islands. "These are the visible remains of a stone circle that is half submerged. Remember this whole gulf was once a great plain inhabited by the people whose stone remains you can still see at Carnac, and all over this region." The boat began bouncing as it hit waves stirred up by the wind now blowing in from the sea. "In a moment you are about to experience the most magnificent of their creations. The tumulus of Gavrinis is the jewel in the crown of all Neolithic monuments, more splendid even than the famous site of New Grange in Ireland."

The boat was still rocking up and down as it came alongside the jetty. They climbed out, the guide holding out his hand to Geneviève, and then to Gillard. The ancient burial mound dominated the island, which consisted simply of a small area of meadow with a few trees that grew by the water's edge. The guide gathered his party around him by the entrance. "We think of these places as tombs of the dead. But some scholars believe that since they were built like great bellies of the Mother Goddess, they were also used as places of initiation, of rebirth - places to commune with the ancestors, to pray for their guidance and protection before being born again into the world. Perhaps this was the special destiny of just one member of the tribe, what we might call a shaman today, who would enter this dark tunnel to sit alone amongst the bones of the departed. Or perhaps it was the privilege of an elite, a priestly caste, whose role it was to peer beyond the veil of time and seek augury and make offerings. Or perhaps all the tribe came here to honour their ancestors and seek rebirth."

Geneviève and Gillard looked at each other and smiled in mutual appreciation of their guide's knowledge.

As they entered the tunnel, he threw a switch, and all at once the walls were illuminated, and they could see that every stone was carved with intricate swirls and spirals as if in imitation of flowing water, moving stars.

The passage led to a central chamber. Each stone was inscribed with zigzag lines like bolts of lightning, lozenges, shapes that looked like dragons' teeth, others like shields and axe-heads - and always the swirling fluid movements of a people who were guided by some mysterious force to decorate their temple in this way. One stone had been carved with what appeared to be two handles, as if it was a great door that led to the Otherworld and could be swung open. Or perhaps it was a place of birthing where women could stand, holding the handles tight to strain in the darkness.

The guide was talking, telling them of the latest findings of archaeology. Gillard closed his eyes. He wanted to sense the presence of the people who had created this place. He was one of them, a temple builder. He had been following the same impulse that they had followed - to make something of beauty that would house the dead, that would be a place to bless the new-born, that would be a portal between this world and the next. The people who created this tumulus were the second great wave of builders, he realized. Before that, they made their temples in caves. He thought of Lascaux - the figures of bison and horses rushing around him. He leant out to touch the walls of Gavrinis, to steady himself, and to feel the energy of the stones run through him. And he was back chipping stone with the quarry men in Brocéliande, back in his church watching the masons at work, the new windows being fitted. He felt a gentle strength returning to him. The difficulties he had suffered had taken their toll, but something was changing - he could feel it. He had been so focused on his goal, his gift to the world, that he had become hard like the stone that he had worked. But now he needed to soften. He needed to reach the gold lying in the darkness.

The guide led the party out. Geneviève and Gillard hung back and were the last to leave. They walked slowly, deliberately. They were being reborn, leaving the womb, entering the world again.

The sunlight was almost overwhelming when they emerged.

"Non, je ne regrette rien!" Edith Piaf is on the radio again. They start singing together, as they always do when this song is played, René by the sink, his hands in the water, Geneviève at the kitchen table, a cup of coffee in her hands. "Non, je ne regrette rien!" But then she stops. Puts the cup down. Tears well up in her eyes. Even though the radio is on full volume, René senses something is wrong and turns around. She is sobbing now - her face in her hands, mascara running down her fingers.

"Oh this is such nonsense!" she shouts, smacking the table with one hand. He walks over to her, holds her close, standing behind her, wrapping his arms around her. "Can we go out?" she eventually says. "I need to be high up. I cannot bear this unhappiness any longer. I want to talk to you, my darling. Tell you everything. But not here."

They drive to Tréhorenteuc and park just outside the village. They begin walking towards the Valley of No Return. Neither speaks. When they reach the Fairies' Mirror, Geneviève stops by the wall of the old forge. "The Valley of the Unfaithful," she says quietly, as if to herself.

René can feel his heart beating faster. He realizes he is frightened. "You said you wanted to be high up."

"Let's go up to Arthur's seat, but you must lead me, René," she says, tears starting to run down her cheeks again.

He takes her by the hand, and they climb up the path, past the gorse which is in flower now, brilliant yellow everywhere. They reach the high point, walking carefully across the granite slope until they come to Arthur's seat.

"Thank God there is no one here," she manages to say before turning to René. "I have to tell you something, my darling. It may break your heart. You may never want to see me again. But I have held this secret inside me for too long. I had hoped I would forget it, but it has become a poison inside me, and if I do not speak the truth now, I know it will destroy me." She breathes in deeply, almost gasping for air. "I betrayed you, my darling. I need to tell you this. It was a long time ago and I thought I could spare you the pain of this moment, but I cannot." She stops. How can she go on? "Hermann and I were lovers," she manages to say before stopping again. She holds her breath, knowing this is the end of everything, the cold moment of honesty that will cut into René like a knife.

He says nothing. He stands up and looks out across the forest. He seems unsteady on his feet and sits down again. "I think I probably knew," he finally says, his head in his hands. His voice sounds hollow. He looks up. "Did you love him?"

"I never stopped loving you, my darling. Never."

"But did you love him?"

"Probably. I don't know. Yes. It was such foolishness. It has taken me all this time to realize that the truth is more important than my desire not to hurt you. I am so sorry."

They sit for a long time in silence.

"Can you ever forgive me?" says Geneviève finally.

"Do you know when I was happiest?" René turns to her. "When we used to entertain our officer friends at the Manoir. It was our Camelot. You and I sitting there like the king and queen of our castle. But when Hermann came into our lives, I noticed that he looked at you in a certain way, as if he wanted you. I thought, 'Ah, but my darling will never betray me'." He breaks down now, sobbing like a child. But then he shakes himself and continues. "Later, I remembered the story of Camelot, of

268

Arthur's Queen Genevieve, of how she betrayed her husband, even though she loved him. From that moment my happiness was never the same - it was always tinged with fear."

The air feels unnaturally still.

"Look!" says Geneviève. René looks up. A buzzard has come to land on a tree just ahead of them. It opens its wings and drops from its branch, soaring straight towards them. As it gets closer, it veers to one side and then swoops and dives in front of them, repeating this manoeuvre several times before banking into the wind to catch a ride on a thermal, effortlessly spiralling upwards in ever-widening circles. They crane their necks as the bird becomes a speck of black against the bright sky. It climbs even higher until the speck itself vanishes.

"He's gone, René. He's not coming back."

The church looks so much smaller to Henri Gillard now that he is standing in front of it once again. It had grown in size in his mind as he lay in bed in the hospital, unable to sleep, wondering why he was in such darkness. But now he can see it for what it is, an ordinary-looking village church beside a small graveyard. And there is the phrase he painted above the door in the porch: 'The door is within'. He smiles to himself: 'How nice it is that one can be profound and humorous at the same time. How many people will be puzzled when they find themselves directly inside the church with no other door in sight? Perhaps they'll just think I'm a fool.'

He takes the key that his friend Abbé Rouxel has lent him for the day, turns the lock and slowly pushes open the door. A feeling of coming home, of regaining what is rightfully his - if only for this moment - of bathing in the smell, the muffled silence. He bows to the altar, gazes up at the eastern window, bows to the emerald grail. He then turns and walks down the aisle, the sound of his steps echoing in the silence. He soaks in the colours, the images - St Onenne's life being played out in glass, the Stations of the Cross being played out on canvas, here in the village, in the countryside around. And he walks up to the Twelfth station, to stand facing the image of Christ on the cross.

His eyes rest first on the feet of Jesus. He makes the sign of the cross and stares at the nails. He winces as he imagines the suffering. His eyes run up the legs, the knees, and then up the thigh that stands exposed, and involuntarily he imagines his hand running, with such a lightness of touch, such tenderness, up the leg, up the thigh to the stomach, to touch the heart, to give all his love, all his care, to this man who is dying, who is leaving this world. And then he dares to raise his gaze still higher and he looks upon the face of Christ, and he begins to weep. He sees Hermann looking back at him, looking straight into his heart. It feels as if his chest will burst open. He sits at a pew and closes his eyes.

He is feeling unwell, but at the same time better than he has ever felt before. The crying stops. He feels lighter, freer. He opens his eyes, looks up at the picture, and sees at once the sun radiating from Christ's body in the painting.

He can hear Hermann's voice now. "It's like the sun rising when you die. You think you are going to fall into darkness, but you fall into the light. Everything is stripped back, stripped away, through love and forgiving. And then, when the evening comes and the sun sets in the western sky, you can begin your journey through the sea of stars."

Gillard knows what he needs to do. He has to get to the sacristy. He walks slowly. He is unsteady on his feet now. He opens the door, and there is the sun and the sea of stars - the evening light pouring through the circular stained glass window depicting the zodiac, that he designed and installed in the church all those years ago.

"Sit down in the colour, in the light," he hears Hermann saying. And so he closes the door, moves a chair into the pool of colour, and sits there.

He looks up at the window, the light shining through each of the signs, and he notices that the circle of the zodiac is starting to slowly revolve. As the Great Wheel turns, so it becomes bigger. He seems to be floating towards it. He is outside now, lying under the stars, the night sky turning, the scent of heather on the wind. There is the tail of Pisces, and he is moving towards it. And he is in the water with the fish.

Time to go back now, back to the start of everything, swimming upstream into the Great Mother of Time.

And as he falls from his chair in the sacristy, the ground is not hard for him. The stone floor gives way, the earth beneath it gives way, and in its softness it welcomes him in, until he finds himself lying next to a young woman whose existence he had always doubted, whose warmth he can feel now in his soul. And he knows that he has found the grail - and the goose-girl, the princess, the one they call Onenne.

THE PROPHECIES

CHAPTER TWENTY-FIVE

Aachen, August 1963

On the same afternoon that Gillard and Geneviève were visiting Gavrinis, Hermann's sister Milly, 800 kilometres to the east in Germany, sat back against the pillows on her bed and opened once again the notebook Peter Koch had given her parents after the war.

They had glued their favourite photograph of Hermann to the inside cover. It was Milly's favourite too - Hermann standing beside his glider in 1933, looking so proud, so happy. She kept the notebook in a drawer beside the bed. Having it close helped her feel she had never really lost him. She would often just dip into it, opening it at random to read the thoughts and quotations he had jotted down in between accounts of his dreams, and notes to himself:

SUFFERING

It seems natural to want to depict suffering.
But is it in order to place it outside ourselves,
or is it to remind us of our own interior sorrow?

ACHING

How is it that an ache can place itself so exquisitely
on the boundary between pleasure and pain?
If I ache for you, you will smile.

Three nights now - always the same. The dark stone walls of Wewelsburg towering above me as I try to escape from the castle. The sound of dogs barking, torch beams darting to and fro. I turn back and see a door in the castle wall - ajar just a little, inviting salvation. I rush in, bolt the door and start running down the corridor, heart beating.

As I run I have the peculiar sensation that as I try to escape from all that I loathe, I am in fact rushing towards it. And a strange reciprocity establishes itself: the more I panic, the more I surrender into the certainty that my fate is sealed. Left or right here? Both corridors seem equally sinister but one could lead to my release, the other to an even deeper hell. I choose the right turn and fly along this tunnel until I come to a door that is again ajar, as if some guardian angel has prepared the way before me.

Pushing the door open, I see at once that my fate is indeed sealed. I am in the crypt of the castle. Flaming torches around the walls illuminate the circular chamber. The golden swastika in the centre of the vaulted ceiling shines like a pale sun.

And then there are shouting voices and the barking of dogs. The guards burst into the chamber from every direction. Rough hands pull at my arms, and I am forced into a chair. There is fumbling at my feet. I make no attempt to resist - it is clearly useless. My ankles are tied to the chair. My wrists are tied to its arms. A damp rope gags my mouth and pulls my head back as the rope is tied behind the chair.

Things move slowly now. Two Jehovah's Witnesses wearing those ridiculous pyjama uniforms bring planks of wood into the chamber and start to hammer together a cross. "But you don't believe in the crucifixion!" I try to scream at them, but whatever voice I have is stifled by the rope.

I am untied from the chair and ordered to undress. I do this slowly but no one seems concerned. They wait patiently until I stand naked. "Put a loincloth on him," says a voice from the back of the room and it is the Abbé Gillard who is saying this. A woman steps forward and ties a rag around my waist. She doesn't look like Geneviève, but it must be her. She and Gillard adjust it to their satisfaction, and they tell me to lie down on the cross. Gillard smiles at me and says "Don't worry - no nails!"

He and the woman tie my wrists and ankles to the cross and they do this with love - I can feel that. Four or five guards step forward and with a struggle lift the cross up and place it in a socket in the centre of the crypt. They hammer in wooden wedges until it can stand on its own, and I discover that they have built a small platform for my feet.

The woman and Gillard are carrying things into the room now: an easel, a stool, a small wooden case of paints and a small table. They slowly set up this equipment a few metres away from me. Gillard dons a smock and beret, smiles and winks at me, and sits down with a flourish at the easel.

He begins painting and for a while I am pleased. Happy even. I feel a sort of Christ-like glow. There is a rightness to this, and even as the rope starts to bite a little into my wrists and ankles I feel my body enjoying this, as if it wants to say: "Yes, there is life in death. Spring will come again even out of this darkness."

But then I hear people in the corridors shouting, then screaming. The castle is on fire. Everyone rushes out of the crypt. Gillard knocks over the easel in his haste to leave. Not even a backward glance.

I am left alone, waking as the flames approach me.

And when I turned to gaze at the grail chapel in the forest of Brocéliande, it was as if I was looking instead into a dark mirror and could see only the walls and towers of that castle in Germany

I asked Krause how they had managed to create the grail chapel when all that lay beneath the Obergruppenführersaal was a cistern built into solid rock. It would be a nightmare to dig into that.

He said that the workers are 'well acquainted with nightmares', that they had disposed of the criminals who had filled the camp - they were apparently useless labourers, and after two of them escaped, the rest were sent back to Sachsenhausen. Instead they'd brought in Jehovah's Witnesses. He said: "Their religion prohibits them from trying to escape and you can work them damn hard - far harder than Jews or gypsies. We have a few of those here but they die like flies, which is of course a good thing, but of no use if you want a job done. No - give me Jehovah's Witnesses any time."

There was a page from a popular history magazine inserted here in the notebook. Along the top was scribbled 'What insanity!' Milly recognised her father's handwriting.

All the work that was carried out on the castle was in vain. On Good Friday, March 30th 1945, SS Gruppenfuhrer Siegfried Taubert, Castle Captain of Wewelsburg, fled his post. Most of his men had deserted already, the prisoners long since transferred to Buchenwald and Niederhagen. Before leaving, he told the remaining soldiers that the Americans were on their way and suggested that they too flee.

The next morning three SS trucks drove into the courtyard. Captain Heinz Macher and his fifteen men searched the castle for any signs of life. They had received orders from Heinrich Himmler to destroy the entire building. By this time, only one loyal soldier remained, SS officer Gottlieb Bernhardt. Macher told him to report immediately to the nearby concentration camp at Niederhagen. He handed Bernhardt a list of prisoners that he should execute there. They were all Jehovah's Witnesses who knew the location of art treasures hidden in the region. Macher then shouted to his men to begin laying mines in the south-east tower. As they did this, he went into the north tower. In the basement, he found an empty circular chamber, lit by high window lights. It was the grail crypt of the SS. There was nothing in the room apart from a chest with its lid open. It was filled with the death's head rings of fallen SS officers. He ran upstairs and into the Obergruppenführersaal. There stood an enormous oak table with twelve chairs around it. On the floor above, he found Himmler's private apartment, the bed made, a drinks cabinet with every bottle empty. There were other rooms too, with bookcases, desks and armchairs, each room decorated in a different style. He ran down the stairs and was met by one of his men, who told him they only had enough explosives for one tower.

There was no point in getting angry. Nothing worked anymore. The Americans would be here at any moment. They took jerry-cans from the trucks and ran from room to room in the other two towers, tearing books from their shelves, throwing petrol on them and on the furniture. Macher then told two men to go back into the towers soaked in fuel. He ordered them to throw grenades into the rooms, and then run out through the main gate, while they drove the trucks out of the courtyard.

Within minutes the men were running towards them. They jumped into the trucks, and as the engines were running, Macher gave the order for the explosives to be detonated. As they drove away, the southeast tower collapsed in a pile of rubble as flames spread rapidly through the rest of the castle.

SS officer Gottlieb Bernhardt had already left. He was on his way to Niederhagen. He found the camp commander, and told him the Americans were on their way. The commander and his men needed no persuasion, and were soon gone. Bernhardt released the prisoners and fled himself.

When the US Third Infantry Division marched into Wewelsburg the following day they found the castle completely gutted by fire. Nothing remained, except the death's head rings, which soldiers took as souvenirs. On that same day, when Macher reported the success of the mission to Heinrich Himmler, he was promoted to SS Sturmbannführer. Three years' later Bernhardt became a Jehovah's Witness.

MESS

*M is for mess and muddle and misunderstood - for murder
and mayhem as well as mother and the milk of kindness.
M is the matrix which holds us all, the great Mother of
Light and Darkness who rocks us in her arms, crushing us
like Kali when our time has come, moulding us like a potter
at her wheel when our bodies are formed,
holding us to her breast as we grow in her arms.*

COSMIEL'S GIFT

*The Ecstatic Journey beyond the sea of stars,
beyond even the Seventh Heaven*

I dreamt the other night that I died. My plane crashed
as I was flying over the Manoir. There was a jolt, the
shock of the plane hitting the ground, and all at once I
was with Geneviève at the window and I could feel her
body close to mine, and I looked out across the fields
and saw the plane coming out of a clear sky. I thought,
"It hasn't crashed. How strange." I was so happy to be
with her, and we could have been standing there for
eternity - our hearts wide open to the heavens.

Then I saw the plane plunging to earth and I heard
the explosion and saw the flames, and I even saw
myself sitting in the cockpit. I felt no shock myself, but
I felt it hit Geneviève like a wave. And I reached out
towards her to hold her close, but found I couldn't feel

her body any more - she was no longer solid. My arm just slipped through her as if she wasn't really there. She started sobbing and I wanted to console her and say 'It's alright, I'm here. It's alright, I'm alive! Can't you see me?' But I knew what was happening. I was dying or perhaps I was already dead. I found myself being pulled upwards. I reached out, but Geneviève, the Manoir, the wreckage of the plane, all dropped away from me. All that I could see, all that was on Earth, became toys, miniature copies of real things that kept getting smaller and smaller, until I could no longer see them.

And then I could see nothing. I was sinking into my mother's arms as a child, a warm bath, the embrace of night. Soon there were dreams - dreams within my dream. Sometimes beautiful, sometimes dark and terrifying

In the dark times I would feel as if I was drugged - paralyzed, unable to move, unable to run away. I saw all the hatred and horror of war paraded before me - wounded soldiers crying out in pain, faces of countless men, women, children, being killed in the prison camps. I would shake with sorrow, my heart unable to bear the enormity of the suffering until I sensed a presence beside me. At first I thought it was my mother or father and they would reassure me, but then the presence would seem to be neither of them, but something more, something that could take on different masks whenever it wished, and it would soothe me with singing. And then it was that I discovered the identity of this being who could wear so many masks: it was my Guardian Angel, whose name, he told me, was Cosmiel. He said it was foolish to think of him as male or female, and that I shouldn't even bother too much about his or her name, because what was more important was the gift he was about to give me. "In my world we can become anything we wish," he said, "and I am wishing now that I am a river." And he smiled at me with such love, and stretched out and held my head in his hands, and I began to feel as if I was floating on the river he had become, and it was broad and wide, and the water that flowed along this river was made of love. And as I floated along, I heard Cosmiel speaking to me: "This is the river of the Holy Grail, the well-spring of life. This is the Ganges, the Brahmaputra, the river Boyne, the Jordan, the sacred Nile."

I looked at the river bank, and I could see children playing in the reeds. They were laughing as they splashed about in the water. Some of them had found a basket, and an older boy carried it up on to the bank. I drifted over and climbed out, and together with the children, we watched as the boy took out a knife and carefully cut through the black leather cover that sealed the basket. And then all at once I was lying in that basket, and his knife had cut away all the sadness, all the pain of my past, and I was a naked baby lying fresh and new, the sunlight playing on my eyes. And then I woke up.

Cosmiel felt so real to me, I tried at once to communicate with him. I lay in bed and imagined he was sitting beside me. I confessed to him all that I had wanted to confess to Father Gillard, but couldn't, and once I had told him everything, every foolish mistake, every betrayal and stupidity I had committed, I could feel that something was being freed inside me. It was as if a weight, or rather many weights attached to tangled cords that had wrapped themselves around me, were slipping away.

Cosmiel must have known this was happening because he said, "It's like that here, you know, in the world beyond death. Things just fall away from you - you can't tell when. The nightmares stop, being gripped by fear and regret stops, and you find it's all been stripped back, stripped away, through love and forgetting and forgiving, and reliving over and over, and that's when you can begin your voyage through the sea of stars."

I started to fall asleep again, but my memory of what happened whilst I slept was crystal clear when I awoke. Cosmiel said to me, "Let me show you the journey you will take when you leave this world. This will make it easier for you when your time comes. I do this in the spirit of the Austrian monk Abraham a Sancta Clara who wrote: 'If you die before you die, then when you die, you will not die.' "

To do this, Cosmiel said we should go to St Onenne's well. And all at once I was in Tréhorenteuc, following my Guardian Angel as he moved silently down that familiar road, past Harel's, along that lane between the rectory and the Mairie.

When we got to the well, its surface was covered in hawthorn blossom. "Best to go quickly," said

Cosmiel, who dived into the pool and disappeared beneath the flowers. After only a second of hesitation I followed.

We were both travelling through what at first I thought was water. It was dark, and to move forward I had to swim. I was a fish, a baby born in the sea, a dolphin on the wave, and just ahead of me swam Cosmiel. As I followed him, I started to see gleaming lights, phosphorescent fish perhaps, underwater fireflies, but as we swam further I realized this was not water we were swimming through, but Space Herself in all her dark majesty.

After some time, as we slowly traversed the ocean of Space, the moon came into view - a vast white sphere glowing with such brightness I could hardly look ahead. No longer were we swimming in darkness, we were swimming in light, in the milk of Isis. And gradually the Moon grew larger and larger until I realized we were going to land on its surface.

As we came closer, I saw that we were coming to rest beside two silver pomegranate trees in the gardens of a great palace, carved in white marble and moonstone. Cosmiel beckoned me to follow him up a flight of stairs that led towards the entrance. Beside its doors stood a tall naked man, who said at once, "Do not be surprised. This is the place of divestment - the first sphere of cleansing."

And I looked at my body and I saw that I still had clothing on - trousers, shoes, a shirt. He said, "Leave all of these here by the door. As you remove each one you will feel yourself becoming lighter, freer. Then walk forward. Walk into the palace-temple."

And it was there that I underwent my first initiation. I was challenged by an angel swathed in grey mist whose eyes glowed with a preternatural light. He told me to cover myself for shame, and urged me to dress again, to keep my clothes, because they were now all I possessed in the world. I laughed at him, and he finally laughed too and allowed me into the inner sanctum. There another angel stood, with a calm and radiant countenance, and she told me that the sphere of the moon is the realm of the etheric, the energy field that enlivens our physical being. With gestures of her hand around my body, which left me mesmerised with their grace, she took all that I had learnt and experienced in my energy body, and poured the resulting distillation into a silver cup, which she then offered to my lips.

As I drank the liquid, my etheric body fell from me as the last clothing falls from the beloved when she enters the bed chamber.

Cosmiel took me by the hand and led me from the temple, until we were standing beside the pomegranate trees in the garden. "Walk between the trees slowly with me," he said, and as we did this, it was as if our feet had wings and we were lifted up into the air, and we journeyed higher and higher through space as we made our way to the Second Heaven, which was on the planet Mercury.

Already I was changed. Without my etheric body, I flew with Cosmiel as fast as thought itself. And when he and I came to stand at the entrance to the temple-palace of Mercury, we were met by a man with the head of a bird, who ushered us into the outer chamber, where I was challenged at the point of a sword by the dark angel of Mercury. "Hold fast to your mind, old friend," said the angel, "or you might lose it." And for a moment the fear of losing all my memories, all my cherished thoughts and visions, terrified me, until I saw a light in his eye, and I could laugh with scorn at his attempt to frighten me. He laughed too, and lowering his sword beckoned me forward.

And it was here, in my second initiation, that I was stripped of my thinking-self. All that I had thought, all those opinions I had formed, those theories about life and about how the world worked, I cast aside as easily as one would cast aside a pair of old spectacles no longer needed. All that I had learned, all that I had ever conceived, was distilled and handed to me as an elixir in a phial of crystal by an angel standing before me. I drank the elixir, and Cosmiel took me by the hand and we journeyed through space to the Third Heaven, which was on the planet Venus.

Freed of two sheaths that had covered my inner being, our travel to this planet was but a moment. As Cosmiel and I landed before the gates of the temple of Venus, we were met by a tall naked woman who handed me a single rose. She showed me into a circular room with a domed roof and invited me to lie on a couch that stood in the centre. As I lay there, she placed her palm on my forehead, and it was as if every dream, everything I had ever imagined or desired, was shown to me in succession in glorious and radiant colour. She lifted her palm from my forehead, I opened my eyes, and I watched as, with just a movement of her hand, all these images were reduced to but one translucent drop of perfume, which she touched to my brow.

After resting for moments which seemed to last an eternity, Cosmiel took me by the hand and we journeyed through space to the Fourth Heaven, which was on the Sun itself.

We walked towards its temple with joy in our hearts. A child was waiting for us, seated naked on a white horse, pointing to the entrance to the temple, made from sheets of burnished gold. But I will write no more of what happened there, for each of us is challenged in the depths of our heart in a different way, known only to our soul and our Guardian Angel. And in like manner, each of us receives in our own way the ecstasies of love and the illumination of this sphere.

From the Sun we travelled, Cosmiel and I, to Mars and Jupiter and Saturn, and in each sphere I was challenged and I was freed. I was reduced, and in reduction I was enlarged in love and in clarity of perception, until we travelled beyond the Seventh Heaven and entered the worlds of the zodiac and the Primum Mobile, the Place of Beginnings.

And it was in this place beyond Time, beyond even the confines of Space, that I came to know that at some stage after my death I would make the return journey, taking on the tasks and virtues of the angels of each sphere, gradually clothing my soul with the materials needed to think and feel on Earth again, so that when my mother gives birth to me, I will have a physical body drawn from the elements of this planet, an energy body of the Moon, a thinking self guided by Mercury, an imagination with the gifts of Venus, a heart that can warm like the Sun.

Since taking this ecstatic journey with Cosmiel, I no longer fear death. Instead I know of the wonders that lie in store for me, once freed of the physical body. Death, I now know, is a process of shedding, of letting go of attachments, of longings, of defences, of garments of thought and feeling that cover the pure radiance of the soul.

When it is time for me to be born again, I will take on the coverings I need to enable me to function in this world. Until that moment comes, to plunge once more into the realm of the Earth, with her joys and her sorrows, my soul will live in freedom in a world of bliss and joy.

A hand-written note from Hermann's father was written in the margin: 'This is Merkabah Mysticism. He must have read Kircher's 'Ecstatic Journey'.'

MYSTERY

How can I find the Mystery in the light where everything
can be seen? Only the unknown can give birth,
and the unknown lives in the darkness,
and the silence.
Give me more,
you might say.

But I can only give it to you
out of the darkness of my being.

Then there were photographs taken by Peter Koch of the villagers posing for the Stations of the Cross, of Gillard's church, of the Fontaine de Barenton and Arthur's seat. And a quote from Seneca with a circle drawn around it for emphasis: *The willing, Destiny guides them. The unwilling, Destiny drags them.*

Beneath this was a sketch of the ground plan of Gillard's church and a quotation beneath it:

Where those who pass see only an elegant chapel, I have placed the memory of a clear day in my life. O sweet metamorphosis! No-one knows this delicate temple is the mathematical image of a girl of Corinth...
Within it specific proportions are faithfully reproduced.

Paul Valéry, Eupalinos

There were notes comparing Gillard and Geneviève and their interests, and then, saddest of all, thought Milly, were the last words he had written before more than half a book of empty pages followed. It was a quotation from one of Hermann's favourite authors, Rainer Maria Rilke:

The purpose of life is to be defeated
by greater and greater things.

CHAPTER TWENTY-SIX

When the Comte told me about Geneviève's lover, he also told me how he died, and whenever I stayed at the Manoir du Tertre, and stood at Geneviève's bedroom window looking out across the fields towards the forest in the distance, I couldn't help seeing his plane hurtling towards the ground, a heart of white vapour slowly dissolving in the sky above.

I could find no proof that the story was true, but despite this, it continued to haunt me. I walked around Point-Clos, the trees planted by Commandant Ernst still there, the concrete remains of the buildings and swimming pools built by the Germans still visible in the undergrowth, all trace of the runways gone.

For a long time I felt I shouldn't write about a relationship that may never have existed, until one day I drove from the Manoir into the forest and sat in a clearing, waiting for inspiration. The war had ended over sixty years ago, but it felt as if those dark days were unbearably close, still lying like the gaping concrete foundations at Point-Clos, just beneath the surface.

As I sat in the forest wondering whether I should forget the Comte's story and return to England, a bright shaft of sunlight broke through a heavy bank of clouds, and the forest seemed to say: "No, go on! There are stars glittering in this dark firmament. There are secrets here to be revealed."

And so, leaving the clearing, I decided to drive through the countryside, taking whatever turning my intuition, or simply my whim, dictated, and I found myself driving out of one section of the forest, towards heathland that rose above it in a kind of plateau, until after a while I could see the trees again shimmering below in the distance. And there to my right was a sudden turning down a dirt track that I overshot, but which I knew I should take.

I turned the car around and drove down the track. After half a mile it came to an end at a gate into a field. I walked up to the gate and leant against it, and at that moment I realized I was not alone. Sitting on a fence just a few metres away was an enormous bird - a buzzard. It looked at me quite calmly, and then, instead of resenting the intrusion and flying away, it began to treat me to a private aerobatic display, swooping within an arm's length of me before turning and soaring upwards, its graceful body and wings climbing higher and higher into the sky, then wheeling in a great arc ahead of me before plunging down to skim the ground.

The bird returned to its place on the fence and looked directly at me, and it was then that I knew I should write about the story the Comte had told me that summer, in his château in Brocéliande.

HISTORICAL NOTES

The Prophecies is a work of fiction, based upon the real lives of Abbé Henri Gillard, and René and Geneviève Zaepffel. A good deal of the facts cited in the book are true, but not all.

The Nazis did establish a division of the SS called the Ahnenerbe, and its mission was exactly as described - to find the historical justification for the idea of Aryan supremacy. It also pursued its occult agenda, with the true story of Otto Rahn's activities within it providing the inspiration for the fictional film character Indiana Jones. A comprehensive account of the Ahnenerbe's work can be found in Heather Pringle's *The Master Plan: Himmler's Scholars and the Holocaust*, and information about its occult background can be found in Nicholas Goodrick-Clarke's *The Occult Roots of Nazism: Secret Aryan Cults and Their Influence on Nazi Ideology*.

Similarly, the Wewelsburg project, lunatic though it sounds, was indeed begun, with much of the building work undertaken by Jehovah's Witnesses. The account of the project comes from the written reports of its architect Hermann Bartels. Work on the castle took place between 1933 and 1943, with Niederhagen concentration camp being established nearby to provide slave labour. In total, almost 4,000 prisoners were held in the camp, including political prisoners, Romanies, homosexuals, and Jews, as well as Jehovah's Witnesses. Almost a third of the inmates did not survive, dying of hunger, cold, disease and the consequences of ill-treatment. In 1942, a crematorium was built at the camp, with the ashes scattered or used as fertiliser in the camp nursery. In the story, Himmler comments on how delicious the lettuce grown in the nursery tastes.

SS weddings did occur at the castle, but I was unable to trace names of brides and grooms, and so I imagined the Castle Captain von Knobelsdorff being married there, and while I invented the marriage ceremony, preferring this to the dull wording of the actual rite, the details within it are historically accurate. The castle itself was set on fire and the southeast tower destroyed by explosives under orders from Himmler in the final days of the war. The last guard, Gottlieb Bernhardt, disobeyed orders and refused to execute prisoners, becoming a Jehovah's Witness himself in 1947. His account can be found in *The Watchtower* online library, *Awake! 2010*.

Whatever contents of the castle remained were looted by villagers and the American troops who arrived a few days later. The 11,500 death's head rings of fallen SS officers that were reportedly stored in the crypt disappeared, as did the safe Himmler had installed. Parts of the castle were restored and reopened as a museum in 1950. The north tower, with the grail crypt and Obergruppenführersaal, was restored in the 1970s, and in 1982 the entire castle was opened as a war monument with several survivors of the castle prison camp present. The monument now houses a permanent exhibition, 'Ideology and Terror of the SS', which presents the history of SS activities in Wewelsburg.

I do not know whether Geneviève used the Lenormand or Tarot cards, but the account of her appearance on stage in Paris is taken, with verbatim excerpts, from Geneviève's book *1943, Année d'Espoir*. The police file that Hermann reads in the Ahnenerbe headquarters can be found online and the excerpt I used has only been edited in minor ways.

Geneviève recounts, in one of her books, a conversation about reincarnation with a friend who is a priest and the old colonel who lodged for some time at the Manoir. I recreated this scene, and used it to tell the legend of St Onenne, as if Geneviève had dreamt it. Although she believed in reincarnation and experienced out-of-body states when ill as a child, she did not - as far as I know - claim that she had been Onenne, although she did express a great affinity with her.

The information on Abbé Gillard has been obtained from his biography and his work, listed in the Bibliography, discussions with historian Jacky Ealet and friends, a study of Gillard's medical records at the St.Avé hospital, Jacky Ealet's book *Tréhorenteuc en Brocéliande,* and from the book *Brocéliande et l'Enigme du Graal,* by Gillard's long-time friend and student Jean Markale.

Gillard did start a cinema in the rectory, visited a nearby quarry often, and held several village fêtes. The bronze statue of a naked goddess that Gillard shows to Hermann was in reality unearthed by another priest, Father Brouyssel, who died in Tréhorenteuc in 1875. It is said that he found it in the field known as the 'Château de St Onenne' - near to the well, and the site of a 3rd century Gallo-Roman villa. In the *Journal de l'Association Bretonne* they note that it must have been an image of Venus. Its whereabouts are unknown.

As regards the depiction of Hermann, research confirmed that it was certainly possible that a Luftwaffe officer could be skeptical of Nazi ideology and not anti-semitic. Information about life as a Luftwaffe pilot was derived from the biography of the most famous German fighter pilot of the Second World War, Adolf Galland. The information given about the Lebensreform (Life Reform) movement, and the activities in Ascona can be found in Martin Green's *Mountain of Truth: The Counterculture Begins, Ascona.* This aspect of cultural history is hardly acknowledged in Germany today, and yet so much of the counterculture, and even the mainstream, has been informed by the exciting and positive ideas generated by Lebensreform thinkers. Their connection with the hippy era and its ideals can be found in Gordon Kennedy's *Children of the Sun: A Pictorial Anthology*

From Germany to California 1883-1949. Information about the associated nudist movement and the resort of Freilichtpark can be found in Cec Cinder's *The Nudist Idea*, and John Alexander Williams' *Turning to Nature in Germany: Hiking, Nudism and Conservation 1900-1940.*

Naked Germany: Health, Race and Nation by Chad Ross provided information on circumcision in Germany for non-Jews for the detail in Chapter Twenty, in which Hermann's circumcision is noted by fellow officers. Those who were circumcised were often afraid they would be mistaken for Jews, and pulling suspects' trousers down in occupied territory was used as a way of identifying who might be Jewish. But not all were concerned: the circumcised SS officer Major Hans Surén posed openly for photographs in nudist magazines.

The information given about Geneviève's prophecies is based entirely on fact. The anti-semitic statements in her 1943 book *Espoir*, were written by René in his commentaries on her predictions, and these statements echo the widespread anti-semitism that existed in France at the time. Almost 76,000 Jews were sent to concentration camps in France or Germany during the occupation, with the complicity and full cooperation of the French police and the Vichy government. Only 2,500 survived. Four films offer a powerful education in this subject: the documentaries *The Sorrow and the Pity*, made in 1969, but banned from French television for 12 years, and *Collaborations*, by Gabriel Le Bomin, released in 2013, and the two fictionalised dramas, both released in 2010: *The Round Up* and *Sarah's Key*.

Geneviève was imprisoned three times as a collaborator, once before the war and twice after the war, and was given a sentence of 'National Indignity', which meant that although freed, she was deprived of her ability to vote or hold public office for ten years. She spent the years after the war giving individual consultations, and ran her home as a guest house, with a restaurant that was open to the public. She published a number of books, and two autobiographical works which recount the story of her first two imprisonments. An interview with her in 'Bretagne Magazine' No.23 in October 1967 shows her continuing to give psychic readings, including one for her interviewer, in which she tells him that she sees him 'in flames', and suggests he makes sure his office is insured against fire risks. It is not a sympathetic account, although the caption beneath a photograph of the Manoir reads: 'A delicious confusion between dreams and reality.'

Her last books cite her predictions, many of them uncannily accurate: the fate of Mussolini, the failed assassination attempt on Hitler, India's independence from Britain in 1947. But they fail to mention her many predictions that never came true. Her books have long been out of print, and her work is now largely forgotten. Today it makes almost impossible reading, filled as it is with saccharine religiosity, threats of damnation worthy of a Southern Baptist preacher, delusions of grandeur, and rehashed occultism. Despite this, even in her later years she had her advocates. A sympathetic account of her last years with René at the Manoir can be found in

Pierre Cognez's *Les Dernières Prophéties de Geneviève Zaepffel.* She died, at the age of 79 in 1971. René died at the age of 92 in 1983.

The relationship between Geneviève and the fictional character Hermann is entirely imagined, as is Antoine and his personal story recounted on pp. 20 & 21. The relationship between Geneviève and Henri Gillard is also imagined, since I was only able to trace one anecdote that linked Geneviève and Henri Gillard's lives: apparently she left baskets of food for him by the rectory door.

As I began work on the book, I learned that Henri Gillard suffered a breakdown in the 1960s. I managed to obtain his psychiatric records and visited the hospital where he stayed for three courses of treatment. I could find no evidence that he and Geneviève ever met after the war, but I imagined what might have happened if she had visited him. In my mind's eye I saw them sitting by a lake, which I discovered and photographed when walking in the hospital grounds several months after writing the account. Gillard's journal entry, written in hospital, is invented, as are all the interactions between the characters in Chapter Twenty-Four.

The information given about Gillard's church is based entirely on fact, obtained from Gillard's writings, his biography, and in Élisabeth Cappelli and Alain Gérardin's *L'Église du Graal.* More material on the church can be found on my website: philipcarr-gomm.com

Otto Rahn's 'Crusade Against the Grail' was published in French in 1934, and it is likely that Gillard, being so interested in the grail, had read this work. Gillard started renovating his church in 1942, and achieved his dream of completing it directly after the war. In 1943 St Onenne's tomb, which had already been moved twice within the church - in 1914 and 1927 - was completely removed, but its existence was acknowledged in a plaque on the altar. Of the saint's remains, Abbé Le Claire, in the *Journal de l'Association Bretonne*, in 1927, writes: 'Her body, placed in a lead casket, was buried in the church of Tréhorenteuc... It is not known what happened to the casket. However, recently, in levelling and renovating the stone floor slabs in the church, in the area of her tomb, a head was found which is believed to be that of St Onenne.' According to Jean Markale, the tomb was 'stunningly ugly', with a statue of the saint lying upon it, showing a swollen stomach, which made no sense since she was revered as a virgin. Gillard removed it for aesthetic reasons and to free the church of an 'object of superstition'. Like Markale, he did not believe in the historical existence of Onenne.

In an uncanny echo of the way in which Himmler's grail crypt had been worked upon by prisoners of war, in 1946 Gillard obtained permission to take two German prisoners from a camp near Rennes, and they lived with him in the rectory for six months. One was a carpenter, Peter Wisdorff, the other a painter, Karl Rezabeck, and together they produced the Arthurian paintings, the Stations of the Cross, and an arched wooden ceiling. A new eastern window was installed that depicted the grail mystery, a zodiac window was created for the sacristy, and mosaics of a white hind and of the beginning and end of the zodiac were placed on the walls of the nave in the 1950s. Years later Karl Rezabeck spoke fondly of the long walks he had with Gillard in the countryside, listening to his stories of local folklore and the Arthurian and grail legends. It was knowing of these walks that allowed me to imagine Gillard's walks with Hermann so easily.

The scene of the villagers posing for photographs is imagined, although many of the faces in the actual paintings of the Stations are of locals. Karl Rezabeck painted himself as a centurion, the local teacher did pose as Morgane, and Gillard himself modelled for Christ. This reminded me of the story of the paintings in Berwick church, not far from my home in Sussex, where during the war the Bloomsbury artists, Duncan Grant, Vanessa Bell and Quentin Bell painted scenes from the life of Christ, set in the local landscape, using friends who modelled for photographs. In Gillard's Stations of the Cross, the minimalist loincloth that exposes one full side of Christ's body was probably inspired by an ivory crucifix in Paimpont Abbey, but such minimalism is found rarely in paintings, most notably in the 1880 canvas 'Crucifixion' by Thomas Eakins, who tied a young man wearing only a loincloth to a cross to pose as Christ, not only on the roof of his house in Philadelphia, but also on a secluded island in the Delaware river.

Gillard was clearly inspired by the story of Christ as well as by the stories of the grail and King Arthur. Single-handedly he brought life to the village: his renovation of the church to make these stories more widely known, the rectory cinema, the youth hostel he started after the war, his publicity on the radio, and later the television, made him a local hero. Tréhorenteuc had been a village so poor it had functioned with a barter economy. Soon after the war it was a place of pilgrimage, and quickly became a centre of tourism. In 1963, after appearing on a television programme about his work, Gillard received a poison pen letter accusing him of bringing the Church into disrepute, and criticising him for removing the tomb of St Onenne. In response, he locked his church and spent two months in Paris looking for another job. On his return he received a letter from his bishop insisting on his retirement. He was given one month's notice to quit the rectory he had renovated with his own money and lived in for twenty years, and was obliged to turn to the State for a pension, and live in a church home for the elderly. It was then that he suffered a breakdown and was hospitalised three times over the next few years for severe depression and anxiety.

Henri Gillard was the last rector of Tréhorenteuc - after his dismissal by Bishop Le Bellec in 1963, no-one was appointed to replace him. After the Second Vatican Council, which finished in 1965, his ideas were no longer considered so heretical, and he was allowed to act as a guide in his old church at Trého. In his last years, he spent much time with his friend Abbé Rouxel, the rector of Néant-sur-Yvel, and designed a mosaic of the grail for the church in that village. He died on the 18th July 1979 in a nursing home in St. Anne d'Auray, and his body is buried near to the altar in Tréhorenteuc. In 2014 the altar was moved from the position it had occupied since 1965, to show again his floor mosaic of the Holy Grail.

When Christ said "It is finished" on the cross, when Hermann said "It is finished" as he collapsed into Geneviève's arms with his 'petite mort', when Charles de Gaulle gave his speech at the liberation of Paris and said "It is finished", they all knew that it wasn't. The story of Christ had only just begun, Hermann had yet to fulfill his destiny, and in the two weeks after de Gaulle's speech, an estimated 10,000 Frenchmen were killed by their own people, and over 20,000 women had their heads shaved and were publically denounced for 'horizontal' and other kinds of collaboration. Stories shift and change, are forgotten. But they give birth to other stories, or reappear unexpectedly out of the darkness of time. They never seem to finish.

ACKNOWLEDGEMENTS

I first experienced the mysterious atmosphere of Brocéliande, and the even more mysterious atmosphere of the Manoir du Tertre, when I was invited to give a talk at a Celtic festival, organised by the harpist Myrdhin in 2005. Huntington Castle, home of the Fellowship of Isis in Ireland, and the landscape around it, was the only other place which evoked the same feelings in me - as if I was living on a threshold between worlds. Sitting by the great fire in the Manoir, beside that wonderful old staircase in the evenings, I had no idea that some years later I would be writing about it in *The Prophecies*. And so I have Myrdhin to thank for introducing me to this evocative place, and Kate Parkin, my publisher at John Murray who, at the launch party for *The Book of English Magic* in 2010, suggested I try writing fiction. Her encouragement in the years that followed was invaluable.

I initially thought I would develop a story featuring one of the exotic characters who appear in *The Book of English Magic*, but the following summer, while I was in

Brittany, staying at the Manoir du Tertre, I drove into the forest and sat in a clearing in the sunshine, and it was there that I received a message from my unconscious, the world of Spirit, who knows? It told me that the story I should write was under my nose, here in the forest. I had heard that Geneviève had been called 'The Druidess of Broceliande', and as a student of Druidry I should have followed this up, but I hadn't - partly because there were no books about her or her predictions easily available. But now I decided to research her life, and the life of Henri Gillard, to see if a story emerged.

I soon discovered the dark side of Geneviève, reading her police file online, and obtaining copies of her books, thanks to Klaod Roparz who allowed me to photocopy his collection, and who has kindly given permission for me to use his evocative photo-montage of Geneviève. And so I was drawn - very much against my inclination, which has always been towards writing about uplifting, positive topics - to research the subjects of anti-semitism in France and the Nazi occupation of Brittany. During this time, despite learning a great deal about the lives of both Geneviève and Gillard, an actual story eluded me until a year or so later. I was staying at the Manoir again, which was now under the new ownership of someone I felt a great liking for - Amar Driff, (who in no way resembles the Antoine of Chapters Two and Three). Amar, on leaving Paris had found himself irresistibly drawn by the strange magnetism of the forest to purchase the Manoir, and when he learnt of my project, he drove me at once to the château, as I describe in Chapter Three, where the Comte told me about Geneviève's lover, and about how he died. I am deeply thankful to Amar and the Comte, whose name I have changed to protect his privacy, since it was these few remarks he made that provided the basis for the story I developed.

I am also grateful to the authors Olivier Pepère (Ozégan) from St.Malo, and Jean-Claude and Elisabeth Cappelli, who live in Folle-Pensée, who helped me with precious information about the area and Gillard's church, and it was the Cappellis who took me and my wife Stephanie on a visit to what remains of the air base and Commandant Ernst's arboretum at Point-Clos. My thanks are also due to local historian Jacky Ealet, in Tréhorenteuc, who patiently answered all my questions and provided me with press cuttings, and to Myrdhin again for arranging this, and for telling me about his meeting with the old abbé.

Gillard believed the grail symbolises hope, and for some time the book was going to be called *The Game of Hope* - after a German fortune-telling game of the same name. I prepared various letters between protagonists, police reports, memos from Hermann to Krause and so on, and wanted them to be published loose-leaf in a box. The reader could then shuffle the papers, and each person would take a different route through the material. This has been tried before - by Marc Saporta in his *Composition No.1* in 1962, and by B.S.Johnson in his *The Unfortunates* in 1969.

Although *The Game of Hope* worked for me, it required too much investment for someone who was unfamiliar with the story. In despair I almost gave up, but Stephanie encouraged me to keep going and applied her considerable common sense and editorial skills to the project, as she has done so brilliantly throughout my writing career. Suzanne Levine encouraged me to persevere too, at another moment when I was sick with thinking and writing about the Nazis, and wanted to abandon the whole project. Then, with the skilled and invaluable mentorship of the novelist Susannah Waters, I found a new structure for the book. Its working title became *Cosmiel's Gift*, after the account of Hermann's journey in the After-life, which was inspired by reading Jonathan Black's *The Sacred History*. I am also grateful to the book's author, whose real name is Mark Booth, for offering me such helpful advice when I was struggling to finish the book.

As I researched the world of Lebensreform, of the SS-Ahnenerbe and of Germany in general, I was thankful for the specialised knowledge of Dr Sebastian Hesse-Kastein. I am grateful also for the help of three psychiatrists, as I researched the mental state of Abbé Gillard: Dr.Michel Caire, Dr.Parolin, and Dr.Haraldur Erlendsson (who elucidated for me many of the uncanny geomantic connections that seem to exist between the two grail sites).

Eight friends were kind enough to read a draft version that had still not found its title: Dany Seignabou, who also helped me greatly in tracking down Abbé Gillard's death certificate and translating difficult texts for me, encouraging me at every turn, Maria Ede-Weaving, Annie Gayford, Paul Bompard, Tarquin Gotch, Peter Owen-Jones, Jay Ramsay and L.R.Fredericks, whose detailed craft notes proved invaluable. I am extremely grateful to all of them for their helpful comments, and those of my cousin and art historian Sarah Carr-Gomm, who advised me on the obscure matter of the amount of cloth shown in depictions of Christ on the cross.

I began the actual writing of this book in the retreat house at the monastery of the Celtic Orthodox Church in St.Dolay, Brittany. I had providentially come upon the brothers and sisters of this unique and extraordinary community as I started to research the book, and over the following five years came to know them all and respect them deeply. Metropolitan Maël welcomed me as a long-lost friend when I began this journey, and I often felt his love and warmth as I struggled in the dark places that this book endeavours to describe. I finished writing at the monastery too. Metropolitan Maël had died, but now Metropolitan Marc kindly provided a quiet place in which I could work, a wooden retreat hut in the forest, where St Tugdual wrote that he had sensed amongst the trees the 'very real presence of the Nameless One.'

LIST OF ILLUSTRATIONS

Cover design by Christian Fuenfhausen

p6. The bouquinistes of the Seine, 1906

p7. Title page *Dictionnaire du Bonheur* by Geneviève Zaepffel, 1942. Courtesy Klaod Roparz

p13 The Manoir du Tertre. Photo: Philip Carr-Gomm

p15. The Manoir du Tertre interior

p16. Portrait of Geneviève Zaepffel. Photo: Philip Carr-Gomm

p18. Geneviève Zaepffel's bedroom - La Chambre des Druides. Photo: Philip Carr-Gomm

p18. The Manoir du Tertre interior. Photo: Philip Carr-Gomm

p24. René & Geneviève Zaepffel

p25. Geneviève Zaepffel montage. Klaod Roparz

p28. Wandervögel

p39. Hermann Hesse

p41. Entrance to the Sanatorium Monte Verita, Ascona, 1907

p41. Rudolf Laban and his dance troupe at Ascona. 1914 Photo: Johann Adam Meisenbach

p53. Ahnenerbe Headquarters, 19 Pücklerstrasse, Berlin

p59. Geneviève Zaepffel. Montage: Klaod Roparz

p68. Rickshaw-taxi, Avenue de l'Opéra, Paris, 1942 Photo: Robert Doisneau

p73. 'Le Juif en France' exhibition Paris, 1941. Photo: Roger Berson

BIBLIOGRAPHY

Baker, David, *Adolf Galland: The Authorised Biography*, Windrow & Greene, 1996

Cinder, Cec, *The Nudist Idea*, The Ultraviolet Press, 1998

Cappelli, Élisabeth Cappelli & Gérardin, Alain, *L'Église du Graal*, Les Oiseaux du Papier, 2012

Cara, Serge, *Introduction à la Philosophie Cosmique*, Cercle du livre, 1953

Cognez, Pierre, *Les Dernières Prophéties de Geneviève Zaepffel*, La Compagnie Littéraire, Paris, 2006

Ealet, Jacky, *Tréhorenteuc en Brocéliande*, Les Oiseaux du Papier, 2008

Ghyka, Matila, *The Geometry of Art and Life*, Dover 1977
    - *Le Nombre d'Or: Rites et Rythmes Pythagoriciens dans le Dévelopment de la Civilsation Occidental*, Gallimard, 1959

Gillard, Henri, *Le Recteur de Tréhorenteuc: Oeuvres Complètes*, Église de Tréhorenteuc, 1990

Goodrick-Clarke, Nicholas, *The Occult Roots of Nazism: Secret Aryan Cults and Their Influence on Nazi Ideology*, New York University Press, 1992

Graddon, Nigel, *Otto Rahn and the Quest for the Holy Grail: The Amazing Life of the Real 'Indiana Jones'*, Adventures Unlimited, 2008

Green, Martin, *Mountain of Truth: The Counterculture Begins, Ascona 1900-1920*, University Press of New England, 1986

Kennedy, Gordon, *Children of the Sun: A Pictorial Anthology From Germany to California 1883-1949*, Nivaria Press, 1998

Markale, Jean, *Brocéliande et l'Enigme du Graal*, Pygmalion 1989

Pringle, Heather, *The Master Plan: Himmler's Scholars and the Holocaust*, Harper Perennial, 2006

Rahn, Otto, *Crusade Against the Grail: The Struggle Between the Cathars, the Templars, and the Church of Rome*, Inner Traditions, 2006

- *Lucifer's Court: A Heretic's Journey in Search of the Light Bringers*, Inner Traditions, 2008

Rosbottom, Ronald, *When Paris Went Dark: The City of Light Under German Occupation, 1940-44*, John Murray, 2014

Ross, Chad, *Naked Germany: Health, Race and the Nation*, Berg 2005

Various contributors, *L'Abbé Henri Gillard*, Église de Tréhorenteuc, 1990

Williams, John Alexander, *Turning to Nature in Germany: Hiking, Nudism and Conservation 1900-1940*, Stanford University Press, 2007

Zaepffel, Geneviève, *Ce que les hommes ne comprennent pas*, Paris, 1930

- *Le Livre de mes Prophéties (1938, Année Décisive)* Baudinière 1938

- *Mon Combat Psychique (1939, L'an Rénovateur)*, Baudinière 1938

- *Prophéties 1941* (L'Arrêt du Destin) Paris : Éd. du Centre spiritualiste, 1941

- *Livre Documentaire et Prophetique (1942, La Sentence des Dieux)* Éditions du Centre spiritualiste 1942

- *Le Dictionnaire du Bonheur*, Éditions spiritualistes 1942

- *1943, Année d'Espoir*, Éditions du Centre spiritualiste 1943

- *1944, Le Miracle des Armes*, Éditions du Centre spiritualiste 1944

- *7,000 Captifs Sans Haine et Prophéties Mondiales*, Éditions spiritualistes, 1948

- *Mes prophéties 1944-1950 : Le Miracle des Âmes*, Paris, Éditions du Centre Spiritualiste, v. 1950.

- *Comment Je Vois l'Avenir du Monde*, Éditions spiritualistes 1954

- *Arrangez-vous La-haut! Prophéties jusqu'à l'an 2000*, Paimpont 1967

Information on Geneviève Zaepffel can be found online at: broceliande.brecilien.org/Zaepffel-Genevieve
Her police file can be read at: octonovo.org

THE AUTHOR

Philip Carr-Gomm trained in adult psychotherapy at the Institute of Psychosynthesis in London, in play therapy for children with Dr Rachel Pinney, and in Montessori education with the London Montessori Centre. He founded the Lewes Montessori School and leads the Order of Bards, Ovates & Druids, which publishes a distance-learning course in Druidry. He lives in Lewes, East Sussex, and gives talks and leads retreats and workshops. See his blog and website for more information on the topics in this book: philipcarr-gomm.com

71330590R00187

Made in the USA
Middletown, DE
22 April 2018